WALKING WAKAN

a novel

by: B B H a n s e n

2012

*publisher's inquiries, please email: bbhansenauthor@outlook.com

ACKNOWLEDGEMENTS

This book is dedicated to my dear sons who have given me a life full of inspiration. Thank you for being the very best companions on many great forest treks and traveling adventures.

Heartfelt thanks to the friends who have given me enthusiastic support for this story. You read the rough manuscript, disapproved and approved, edited and commented, helping to make the story so much richer and fuller.

To the tribes of native peoples everywhere—a wish for rich blessings and all that is wakan to preserve your native languages, customs and lands.

Mitakuye Oyasin!

CHAPTER ONE

When I was only a wee white girl of eleven years old, my family relocated from the bustling town of Minneapolis, Minnesota to the wild western mining town of Hot Springs in South Dakota. There, I had the good fortune of getting to know a family from the great Lakota Nation. In addition to their unwavering friendship, they taught me many things--far more useful and meaningful things than I ever learned in school or from any other life experiences.

The late 1970's was a tenuous time in America's history. Oftentimes, it was a struggle for all cultures to find their place in the mix of it together. Most of the Sioux, as the white men had named them, lived on reservations across the Midwest. Some had also purchased modestly priced properties near our family's homestead which were within hiking distance for a curious young girl like me, Laura Helena Hansen.

After learning about the history of these people and about their arduous existence, it seemed strange to me that they paid for what had once been their land, but they lived within the boundaries of our world too. Mostly.

There was one particular mother and her son who eventually indulged my endless youthful queries about their ways. They left an indelible impression on my view of the world and on my overall approach to life. For example, they taught me how to locate the illness inside of a person using an eagle feather and how to pray gratefully and reverently. I learned the ritual of the Inipi sweating ceremony to purify my mind and body of the toxins that lock humans into limiting habits. When I visited their reservation, I learned to dance with unbridled joy, more than just with the technique I had mastered in ballet class.

Over a period of many years, I learned to walk decisively with my own footsteps instead of in the way that someone told me I should. Where my life began, where it has been and where it's headed now didn't happen merely by chance. The experiences I had in the vast green prairies and gold-filled mountains of my youth (the good and the bad) will follow me forever.

My adult life began in New York City, geographically and culturally distanced from the Great Plains. I can't say that I've adapted completely to city life. My days are still precisely guided by distinct voices in dreams, a slight shift in the wind that carries new smells or a simple visit from a bird on a windowsill. That strong voice in my heart and in my gut always tells the truth, even when humanity lies, and I listen to it. Perhaps it is the Lakota living in my heart, even though I haven't an ounce of Indian blood by birth, which defines my strength and has clarified my purpose.

I'm a clothing designer under my own label, 'LHH' and it's an occupation that I truly love. I spend countless hours drawing, mulling over concepts and writing down ideas in order to develop my creations from the comfort of my rented apartment that overlooks the city. My latest line is called 'Little Star', in honor of the woman who gave me that nickname. Indigenous influences run untethered throughout the entire collection. One prominent New York fashion writer recently dubbed it 'a vividly proud and uncommon display of American talent at its finest', but they aren't a nod to Americana at all. These distinctive pieces wouldn't exist had I not been taught a cherished skill which I'll continue to practice until I'm too old to see or until my fingers are too stiff to work--the centuries-old traditional Lakota beading.

When my models take to the catwalk, with stoic pale faces and avant garde hairstyles teased up

4

into fancy bird's nests, I watch them pass. There are rows of potential fashion buyers, sitting hopefully and critically in their seats, studying every nuance of my work. They notice immediately the painstaking attention to the structure of the garments, seeing within the details that I cared deeply about this collection. These one-of-a-kind garments have been assembled with durable and reliable earthly materials. With clashing colors, tight circular patterns and fringes of delicate beadwork, my clothing consistently reflects the timeless strength of nature while elevating the unrivaled beauty of true womanhood.

As the ambient lights bounce off of each piece, carried expertly on the bodies of the models, I imagine the layered patterns and the hand-selected fabrics dancing to the beat of Lakota drums. The careful color choices hold reasoning and meanings too personal and complex to explain to an ordinary person; so I wouldn't even begin to try. These colors are true and powerful--the turquoise blue of a serene summer sky, the deepness of red from a fresh wound, the blend of pink and purple that speaks of cold mountain sunsets or the soft ochre shades of prairie grasses and wheat. Even the textures of the fabrics, if one looks deeply enough, will speak of unbearably frigid winters, the harvesting of plants for food and fibers and the resilience of spiritual beings who reside within the Earth's hidden worlds.

Even my lingerie line incorporates the tediousness of my traditional beadwork training. Our design team's gamble of producing comfortable romantic underclothes paid off and the sales at LHH Ltd. have increased tenfold. Our vintage western corsets and adorned bloomers were a shock to the rest of the lingerie designers who communally opened their shows again this year with a decidedly contemporary French feel.

It can be a struggle for my staff to keep up production for everything that we have sold. Myself, I don't mind working the extra hours. Besides having a career satisfaction that few people I've known really do; creating beautiful things for ordinary people is the core of who I have become.

Often in the midst of all of the urbane motion where I live now, I pause to consider a sudden shift in the direction of the wind, the foretelling movement of insects on a littered sidewalk or other signs from the Great Spirits who might be trying to tell me something.

CHAPTER TWO

My parents inherited a ranch in Hot Springs, South Dakota consisting of nearly three hundred acres and a few hired hands with various skill sets to fill in the gaps where their former, more urban lives, had left them unprepared. My great-grandmother, Laura Helena (after whom I was named), had settled on this same property in the late 1800's, but her only daughter, Kate, had chosen to launch her adult life far away, in Minnesota. The old family homestead laid dormant, unvisited for nearly a century except through the pages of the old photo albums that accompanied my Grandmother Kate with every visit to our Minneapolis home. Through these cherished personal records of history, she illustrated many incredulous stories about a tumultuous time and place that might have otherwise been forgotten.

I remember the Winter of 1972 when she visited us, as she had every year since I was born. My entire family had been together earlier that afternoon, to see my ballet recital. The show went perfectly and I knew that mother was proud of the technical advancements I had made since the previous year. She had high hopes that I would become a professional ballerina when I was grown, and I had promised her that I would try. For now, I had changed out of the rose-tinted satin shoes and billowy dress into my soft suede pants and blue mohair sweater. This was the time I always looked forward to the most.

Grandmother Kate and I stretched out on the living room carpet, side by side, and began once again, to turn the pages of her mother's old leather-bound scrapbooks. We spent the waning hours of that afternoon, engrossed fully in faded photographs of Sioux Indians and western saloons. She had told me many tales, during prior visits, about my great-grandmother, Laura Helena's, long trip westward along with snippets of happenings along the rugged trail between Chicago and Hot Springs. On this particular visit, she had promised to tell the final chapter of the saga. As usual, she narrated these mementos with lively, detailed accounts of her mother's life. Her proud voice and words come to me clearly still: "During this time, a young married woman should've been throwing proper dinner parties or homemaking in the bustling city of Chicago, but your great-grandmother Laura Helena was attending a protest in the Hot Springs city square, rallying against the government's broken treaties with the Indians. Defying even further the standards of those days, she took in a young Indian woman who had run away from a Catholic Mission school. That woman ran away after being beaten for speaking her native tongue instead of English. Your great-grandmother wrote secretly in her diary about the misfortune in that woman's life—that the woman had been shortly thereafter, captured on the trail by men who sold her for two hundred dollars to the operator of a red-light district in Butte, Montana."

My father, seated near us in his reclining chair, cut in on our conversation. "Come on now Kate, really! The girl's only eleven—should she hear stories about red-light districts?" I didn't know what a red-light district was, but my father shot a fretful look at mother for help. She pretended not to notice.

Kate continued reading her mother's written notes, as if there'd been no interruption: "*Some years later, a big dirty gold miner posing as a paying customer helped that poor woman escape out a second-story window and delivered her into Hot Springs for a chance at a new life.*"

"And, they all lived happily ever after," my father groaned in the background.

8

"This Indian woman here," my grandmother said, pointing to one particular photo, "became Laura Helena's household helper since that was the only employment she was offered. Instead of treating her harshly or almost as a slave as many wealthy settlers did their hired help, those two formed a valuable kinship. They taught each other's language, not only to themselves, but also to the schoolchildren. They leaned on each other emotionally when times were hard while completing the day-to-day tasks which always had to be done. When this woman asked her employer to give her a proper American name, Laura Helena chose the name 'Lorena', which the woman used proudly for the rest of her life."

The fact that the Indian woman's new name sounded like a combination of both of Laura Helena's names, was not lost on me. Of course, I also wondered if all of this was true. Before I could think it over, Grandma Kate turned the pages again and continued: "Many of the women in the settlement talked quietly amongst themselves about the dangers of settlers taking an Indian into one's home, but no one dared say it to my dear mother directly. According to all accounts back then, Laura-Helena would turn those powerful blue eyes into a stubborn glance that could be quite intimidating to opposition. I knew her my entire life and never opposed her. Never needed to because she was simply wonderful."

I glanced sideways, noticing that the wonderful blue eyes that she spoke of also belonged to her, my mother and me. I had never thought of them as powerful. In fact, I knew that I was fairly timid.

Grandma Kate tapped her finger twice on the next faded image of the old Hot Springs main street. "Laura-Helena reached a pinnacle of respect in this town. Her husband's stature financially, as he became more involved in real estate, was growing during this time. He had taken their original homestead from forty acres to two hundred within a five year period. Politically, they were ingrained in the establishment of government there and were as proficient as any family in their involvements. It was through your great-grandparents' efforts together that the new church had been able to raise enough money to build a proper building."

My father looked up from the newspaper he was reading. "At last, you mention her husband, Kate. I was beginning to think that dear old Laura Helena had single-handedly settled that homestead in the Wild West, all by herself."

Kate sat up straight and turned to face him. "Well, it almost was like that. The men of course had their role in managing the heavy work. Wasn't easy by any means, but for sure, the women had a heavy, heavy burden. Just cooking and taking care of the children along the pioneer trails, even before they arrived must have been hard, Monroe."

"So, what was it those women had that any other woman today doesn't? Who's to say this group weren't the same as any other?" my father returned.

"They had unfettered optimism for one," Grandma Kate answered, tilting her chin up as she spoke.

"I'll bet that darn optimism took them a long way with wolves chomping at their butts and Indians riding down off the plains to attack them. I've seen my share of conflicts in the military and one thing's certain; it wasn't optimism that kept most men alive. It was precise training and plain ole' survival skills."

"Oh, Monroe! I'm only telling the stories as they came to me. Must've been part of that too, but I still say 'twas a healthy dose of determination and big optimistic dreaming overall that kept them there."

"It couldn't be easy creating an entirely new town from nothing," he conceded. "Arriving, planting your stakes in the ground and saying 'here's where we make a town'. The logistics alone would be a bear."

"People didn't think logistics then. They said this is what we're gonna do. Then, they'd figure out how afterwards. My mother's group of women set up their own standards for teaching, recruiting new teachers from back East, even as the school itself was being built."

"Those teachers were possible brides for the men too, I guess?" he asked.

"Probably were," Kate said. "After that, they started planning a local library to be supplied entirely by citizen-donated books. That's how, unplanned, one step at a time, homesteaders built new towns."

Father always talked at great lengths about things like logistics, systems, readiness, units and such. He was skilled at planning—that was his military background in full swing. However; the doing part could leave his plans unfinished or with someone else stepping in. Often, that someone was mother, who never complained about finishing things that he had started or hiring a person who could.

Grandma Kate began picking the albums up off the floor. I gathered the loose photos and letters that we had spread all about us, and followed her towards the dining room where mother was cooking dinner. As we walked, I shuffled the photos in my hand for one last look. In one, my great grandmother stood with the Indian woman named Lorena again. They were outside in the morning sun, smiling wide and dressed only in their bloomers. I showed the photo to Grandma Kate. "Can't you tell me about one more picture before we put these away?" I asked.

"Of course," she said as we settled down on two chairs, side-by-side: "Laura-Helena's mornings usually began with the baking of bread by the light of a lantern before sunrise. Even as the sun was rising, she and Lorena would walk out past the horse stables to say their daily prayers in the Indian style together. They would be dressed only in their cotton bloomers—hands raised reverently toward the sun, feeling the warmth pour over their bare skin as the sun rose. This morning ritual stayed with your great-grandmother her entire life. When I was a child, we did the same, but when I married that was the end of that. My husband was much more civilized."

"How could any sane person pray half-naked that way?" my mother commented. "Too dramatic." She rarely offered anything to our conversations, during these visits.

Kate closed the book and stood up. "Agreed. Traditional prayer by kneeling is best and, of course, fully dressed. Did you know, they sewed those bloomers and the whole family's clothes back then, by hand? I had mother's old Singer machine stored at the Hot Springs homestead, but I finally gave it away because I never learned to sew myself."

"Neither did I," said my mother.

I guessed that I probably wouldn't learn to sew either. "What'd they do for the rest of the day?" I asked.

Grandma Kate was eager to continue. "After prayers, there were laundry and animal chores. Then, Laura-Helena and Lorena would take the surrey buggy into town for visits. Some days they visited shopkeepers for necessities or to catch up on local happenings. In the tiny town of Hot Springs back then, everyone knew everyone else's business. Other days they'd call on those who were sick to see what they could do to help. Lorena became known for

12

her ability to heal using herbal remedies and such which were previously unknown to the townspeople. Laura-Helena never let out the secret of Lorena's past life at the bordello though because the townspeople would've made an outcast of her."

My mother had been listening more than I thought. "It's terrible how a society will punish a woman for what a man has done to her, instead of the other way around," she offered.

"I agree," Kate said.

These story-sessions continued almost every night for the long summer months. Even when my parents were in the same room, most of the conversations only took place between my grandmother and I. Charles bowed out of the mix by retreating to his room, like clockwork, as soon as dinner was finished. My brother, who was two years older than me, spent only enough time with Grandmother Kate to show that he had been taught manners. I couldn't tell if I was my grandmother's favorite or if she simply could relate to a girl better than a boy. I chose to believe that I was her favorite.

Now and then, when she and I looked through the saved boxes, a letter or some oddity would fall out of one of the books and we would examine it together. These keepsakes would always tie deeper into the overall story. We forged a shared interest through this history and, even at that young age, I could feel a bridge bonding me to a long-dead great-grandmother whom I hoped to meet in heaven someday. Although, I was questioning if there really was such a thing.

My mother never showed much interest in her family's distant past. She had been raised with the comforts of an ordinary Minnesota city woman, enjoying a full social life, expensive shopping habits and domestic conveniences. Lively and focused, she lived very much in the present. I sensed towards the end of that particular visit that everyone in our household, except for me, had grown tired of Grandma Kate's wild anecdotes about her mother's life out West. She had spent the entire visit immersed in the past, blatantly interacting with me more than the other family members. I remember on one night my mother declaring finally as a hint, "I'm not going to live my life through the ghosts of my ancestors. They lived their life how they wanted and I'm going to do the same." It was her way of saying she'd had enough. Then, she added, "Besides, I'm afraid of ghosts."

Putting his arms around her, my father offered his opinion. "It's not ghosts you have to worry about in life. It's living people you'd better look out for." With that, he walked over to open the coat closet and said, "I'm gonna' leave you ladies alone and head down to the local watering hole for a bit."

Grandmother Kate had thrown me one of her unimpressed looks after that. I pressed my cheek lovingly onto hers in a hug so that I could smell the slight perfume of her face powder. As father put on his coat and hat, she said to him, "Monroe Hansen, since you've retired, you've far too much time on your hands. Instead of philosophizing and watering, maybe you could finish my granddaughter's treehouse you started building four months ago. The poor girl is stranded in this house every day. It's not healthy. She needs to be outside finding adventure."

Mother cringed and put her finger silently to her lips to shush her.

"It's going to have to wait until spring now, I'm afraid," my father replied. "It's around twenty degrees out there today. Not exactly treehouse building weather for me. Besides, she finds plenty of adventures between the pages of those books you bring every year, Kate. So glad you came. We wouldn't know what to do with the child otherwise."

That was the day I came to realize that my grandmother felt my father wasn't the right man for my mother. Clearly, she tolerated him to be near our family. He usually spoke to her in a civilized way, but I'd also heard him being rude when he'd had enough of her suggestions.

After he walked out the door, my mother had a talk with her mother in the kitchen. "He hasn't been the same since he left the Navy," I heard her say.

"Told you when you married him you should've kept him in the Navy indefinitely. He's never gonna function right without someone giving him orders. He's a military man through and through."

"Lately, he's easily irritated with me and the kids. I'm wondering if he feels well. Maybe he needs to see a doctor." Hearing my mother worry made me worried too.

"Cut the crap," Grandma Kate said sharply. "That man's perfectly healthy. He's lazy and he never had to be around his family full time. I'm sorry to say it because I know you love him, but stand up for yourself. Demand that he do something worthwhile. He can't just sit around the house day in, day out. He'll drive you nuts."

"You can stop there," mother said, folding the kitchen towels hurriedly and shoving them into the drawer.

Then, I saw my grandmother walk over and embrace her daughter. I think mother was crying, but she turned her head so that I couldn't see.

"I'm sorry," Kate said. "I never did know when to shut up."

They both laughed aloud and I did too.

My dear grandmother passed away unexpectedly that following summer and my mother decided to move all of us onto the old Hot Springs family homestead that she inherited. For as long as I could remember, my father had always made the important decisions for our family, but here he was acceding to mother's wishes. This turnaround in his actions was as shocking to me as what we were about to do. Reading about rural life, prairies, mountains, Indians and bears in books and seeing photographs was one thing--actually going there was quite another! My heart was filled with the sadness of losing my beloved Grandmother Kate, knowing that I would never get to laugh and learn from her another winter season. Heavier than that now, was the anxiety which was building day-by-day. The more I heard my parents telling our neighbors and friends about where we would be living, the more I pleaded to the heavens, "No. No. No."

There were long months of planning, arranging the sale of our house and saying extended goodbyes to our neighbors and friends before setting out for Hot Springs, South Dakota. At twelve years old, I tried to imagine how Kate must've felt moving out West all those years ago, at a time when the First World War was beginning and tensions were high. She was a new bride at the age of seventeen--just five years older than me--leaving a comfortable home in Chicago, taking with her nothing but a formal education and a horse-drawn wagon packed full of only the most vital belongings. Amid a multitude of unforeseen hardships, she had forged a home, made new friends, and created moments of complete magic. So much was unknown then. Without a doubt, my great-grandmother's journey had thrown many impossible challenges her way. Even though our family was now moving there over a hundred years later, I couldn't feel anything but scared.

My older brother Charles sensed my fear and had a great time sneaking up behind me, shooting me with a rubber bow and arrow set or grabbing my ponytail while yelping like a wild Indian, "I'm gonna' scalp ya!" He had me so on edge that, with even the mere thought of such an attack, I would cry and run to my room. My father seemed amused at all this upset in the house and never reprimanded Charles against teasing me.

"You've gotta' stop being such a pussycat and a crybaby all the time," Charles said one day. "What would you do if you ever had to defend yourself? Roll up in a ball and cry?"

"I'm a girl," I shouted. "Girls don't have to defend themselves." That's how I had been raised so far.

"Puss, puss, puss!" he chanted in a high-pitched voice.

I regarded my thin legs, then tried haplessly to make the muscle in my forearms stand up. Five years of ballet lessons had given me agility and grace, but very little in the way of self-defense.

As if he wanted to empower me, Charles quickly produced a double set of wooden swords and shields. "Let's swordfight," he urged.

There was no way out. I took the weapons and battled like a maniac, knowing full well that I was no match for my older brother. Time after time, we would re-enact these same battles in which Charles always came up the winner. He would get so caught up in the adrenaline that sometimes he actually struck me with the wooden sword. More than once I carried bruises on my arms or legs, but I kept trying

17

nonetheless. Each time we would swordfight, I felt more and more helpless. The dreaded truth drained me of any strength I might have gained--that these child's toys were no defense against the real dangers we might soon be facing.

As our moving date neared, mother and I took several last trips to the Minneapolis shopping mall at my insistence. I was sure the stores in Hot Springs sold ugly shoes and plain clothes. Mother promised to find a ballet studio there so that I could continue my lessons, even if we had to drive to a larger city. The thought of meeting new ballerinas my age gave me a sliver of hope while the thought of long dowdy dresses or dressing like a farm boy didn't appeal to me at all. If I had to leave civilization as I had known it, I wanted to at least keep up my own girlish style of lace and dresses and fancy shoes. Forcing a courageous face, I braced myself for the possibility that horrible things could happen.

CHAPTER THREE

The moving truck departed, loaded with everything we owned, and our family car was packed. As over six hundred miles of highway led us towards our new home, we did what we supposed every family did on trips such as these. Charles and I played 'find-each-state-on-auto-tags' while mother sang old folk songs to us.

After crossing over the South Dakota state line, we stopped at a rustic roadside eatery to take a break. After eating a hearty meal, we visited the gift shop which sold tourist souvenirs, fishing supplies and other things that travelers needed. Father said that Charles and I could choose one souvenir each. It seemed odd to need a souvenir since we were moving to the state, but I chose a beaded Indian necklace with a symbol on it. Charles chose a pocket-sized drawstring bag of shiny gold rocks. As my father was paying for the merchandise, the man at the check-out counter advised us on our purchases.

"I see you chose the Sioux Indian beadwork," he said, pointing to me. "That's a nice medallion. That bird on it is the thunderbird. It was supposedly very powerful."

I already had it around my neck, so I turned the medallion to face me and studied the squarish bird emblem on its front. It didn't look powerful to me but I liked the colors. "Okay," I said timidly. "Thank you." I turned it over to the leather side and a tiny white sticker said, 'Made in Japan'. *I can pretend,* I thought. With one swipe, I picked the sticker off.

Then, the man looked to Charles. "Those rocks are called Fools Gold or iron pyrite. They're not real gold, but it's enough shine to incite the fever to find the real stuff."

"There's real gold left in the mountains?" Charles wanted to know.

"A little," the man answered. "Try panning in the streams. You'll probably find some flakes."

Enthusiastically, we all returned to the car for the last leg of our journey. As we traveled the last fifty miles of highway, I read from great-grandmother Laura Helena's books. Mother had passed the entire collection of scrapbooks, photos and journals on to me in Laura Helena's original steamer trunk, knowing as mothers do, how to find the thing that quiets their own child's nervousness. It would be up to me to carry on what Grandma Kate had started and keep the story telling alive.

"Listen to this," I said excitedly from the backseat, as I held open a newly discovered journal. "Everybody try to imagine this day that Laura Helena was writing about--because in a few hours, it's the place where we're gonna' be living."

This move held a certain moment of truth, a reality that was changing our lives forever. I could feel the anticipation in the car as I read:

"Towering sunflowers and prairie grasses waved to me from the vast open fields as we passed on our

way to plead for sparing the convicted man one last time before the hanging."

I saw my mother grimace at the thought. "There was a man being hanged!" I shouted out, seeing that I even had my brother's complete attention. "Then, she's writing more here:"

"Nothing we said on his behalf could help. I feel weary inside for that man, and the scent of my husband sitting next to me, his sweat seems more than usual in the hot air. So tired. Possibly it is the heaviness of recent events which make me feel that way.

Many difficulties await us still, despite a growing tendency toward contentment. Days go by fluid and quiet, but one can't let their guard down in this unsettled place. We have forsaken our lovely home in Chicago for this. Even if we didn't think it's been the right decision, there's no turning back now. As we bounded down the road, I raised my parasol to block the sun, looking dreamily up into it admiring the lacy fringe about its edges. It's one of my last treasured possessions from Chicago, one not lost along the trail. I take it with me always.

Doesn't appear that anyone has traveled this exact route for there are no markings along the way. No tracks from wagons. Dandelions grow thick in patches. When we stopped for break I harvested some for Lorena to make jelly which she says will guard us against the season's pollen."

I stopped there and closed the journal.

"Read the rest," Charles pleaded. "Go on."

"That's it," I said. "Sometimes it's like that. Pieces of stuff without writings before or after to explain."

"We'll just have to imagine what must've happened to the poor guy they were hanging then," father said. "They don't hang guys anymore, if that's any consolation to you kids."

"How would you know?" Charles asked quickly. "Because they never hanged anybody when you were in the Navy?"

Mother shot a look into the backseat and stared at Charles pensively. He never used to talk cynical like that toward our parents and now it seemed he doubted them all the time.

"Let it go," father said quietly to my mother. "The kids are anxious. It'll work itself out." We were nearing the final miles of our long drive and I was sure he didn't want to think about anything except getting to Hot Springs.

When we arrived at the old homestead, a slight wash of purple from the setting sun was reflected on the white masonry walls on the outside of the house. I recognized the house instantly from all those years of Grandmother Kate's storytelling. The box elder trees lining the outer perimeter of the property, I knew, had been planted by my great grandfather. The view felt familiar even though I'd never been there. As we drove nearer to the house, I noticed unruly clusters of wild roses, in full bloom. Two stately cottonwood trees stood at either side of the footpath leading up to the house like timeless guardians. Mother had hired a local lawn service to do trimming and cutting before our arrival, so at least the grounds around the house had been recently tended. Still, it was nothing like our well-kept lawn in Minneapolis.

Charles and I bounded out of the car, stretching for a moment, then standing straight like two of the curious prairie dogs we had watched on the roadside earlier in the day. They had been gazing off into the distance in all directions just as we were doing now. In the high elevation, the summer air grew colder by the minute. Enormous evergreen trees by the hundreds outlined the edges of the property and I imagined wolves and bears living there. Surely, the thick waist-high sage grass could have hidden a mountain lion, too.

Inside the house, while we still had the opportunity for daylight, mother moved from room to room opening the curtains, while our father located the light switches. The dwindling sun flooded the rooms making them seem larger than they actually were.

"Why's it so small?" I asked no one in particular.

"I thought this house looked bigger in the photos from Grandma. This place is tiny," Charles suggested incredulously.

My father had been silent, taking it all in. After a moment, he said, "You know, kids, we're going to renovate this old house...build on the back and one side. Much larger than the original house. You'll see—it'll be great."

"Crap," Charles said when we were out of earshot of our parents, "Another one of Dad's 'going-to-be-great' projects."

Down a short narrow hallway, opposite of our parent's bedroom, there were two extra bedrooms to choose from and I picked mine first. Charles let me have that one without complaint. He had always been the kind of boy who was content with only a pillow and a blanket. Whatever else came with a room didn't matter much to him.

After unloading most of our belongings from the car, mother put away boxes and several bags of groceries we had picked up en route, stocking the refrigerator and cupboards with enough food to feed a small army. "We're going to live in this house, as it is, for now," she announced optimistically. "There'll be a lot to do in the morning. I want everyone to rest up. We're getting up early." I had noticed that she was taking charge here a great deal more than she ever did back home. It was a change I admired.

During that first night, I laid awake for a long time in my bed, listening to unfamiliar sounds outside. I thought I heard a wolf howling in the distance. Then, Charles came from his room across the hallway, into my room. He was holding a flashlight. He said he had also heard the noises outside and that it was hunting cries of hungry coyotes. I asked him to stay and sleep on the carpet beside my bed and, after sprinting back to his room to retrieve a pillow and blanket, he did.

When the first light of dawn appeared, I woke Charles and sent him back to his own room so that I could begin setting up mine. I placed the steamer trunk of Laura Helena's possessions next to my bed in case I ever wanted to retrieve something to read in the evenings. There was a steadying comfort in possessing these items now--in the very place where my great-grandmother's stories took place. Within these timeless images and personal writings there were unmistakable points of reference I planned to use to help me get to know our new home better.

Father wasted no time hiring a crew of five workmen to begin updating the house and to eventually build on a series of larger rooms. We were awakened the next morning, as the sun was coming up, to the unmistakable whizzing of an electric saw cutting wood right outside our front door. I pulled back the worn cotton curtains on my bedroom window and peered out upon a patchwork field of wild yellow daisies and tall spindles of purple liatris, overgrown and dancing in the frenzied wind. Dressed in only blue jeans and my favorite yellow peasant shirt, I walked outside where a pair of workmen had started repairing the rotted exterior trim as well as a section of concrete at the front steps. My father was circulating himself between each project, shouting orders over the noise as the work progressed. After sharing breakfast with the men over a folding table outside, Charles and I tried to make ourselves useful helping inside the house.

That first week, we stayed immersed in tasks like unpacking boxes and wiping out kitchen cupboards to, as mother said, "keep some semblance of housekeeping going despite the mess." It was amusing to watch Charles lift and place furniture along with father, trying to be patient when it didn't fit or look right, and having to move a piece again.

We were tired at the end of each day, but we were working well together as a family.

As the house became more settled, Charles and I, a few leery steps at a time, released ourselves out of our assigned household chores to venture outdoors together. We ran unbridled through the tall golden grasses and vast open fields, hardly believing our new surroundings. After living in an urban neighborhood our entire lives thus far, with neighbors close enough to wave to each morning, we now owned an expansive property with no houses visible in any direction.

Past the open fields surrounding the house, we discovered a magical land which changed dramatically from flat verdant plains to lush rolling hills, then back again, within one hour's hiking distance. We were making a concerted effort to explore every inch of it, while our ultimate goal was to one day reach the distant dark-forested mountains, misted in grey clouds. We satisfied our newfound sense of adventure closer to the ranch house. The quick narrow streams which ran to unknown destinations were gushing with clear waters and plump rainbow trout wiggled below their surfaces. We delighted in the occasional sightings of speckled hawks or flying squirrels and the curious prairie dogs. Our parents had forbid us to venture any further by ourselves than the outer edges of the forest so that we wouldn't be out of their view from the house, but after conquering several one-hour hikes, the opportunity came for my big brother and I to explore deeper into the outer edges of the Black Hills.

While our parents had become preoccupied with the daily routine of settling in and taking trips into town for supplies, we had convinced ourselves that they never noticed us missing. Initially, we explored the steep hills that rose up abruptly out of the flat plains like fertile islands. Each time we would climb up one bluff, then down into a valley and up higher into another bluff until our legs grew tired. We'd rest a while, eating whatever snacks we had brought along and then retracing our steps back home. Gradually, we became fit enough to hike three and four miles one-way. With the ever-uncertain weather in the mountains, a warm sunny day often meant a cold windy afternoon on the way back home.

It was a surprise to us when the local newspaper featured an article about how the Hot Spring's newest residents, The Hansens. It announced to the community that my parents had made great strides in their ambitious plans to simultaneously open two businesses in town. The article told that the first was a general store which was to be housed in one of three dozen boxy sandstone buildings located on River Street, the main street in the original town that fronted the Fall River. When the writer for the newspaper came to the house, mother loaned him a portrait photo of Laura-Helena standing in front of the same building in the late 1800's. In the interview, she told how she had inherited the sandstone building from Laura-Helena's daughter Kate, as well as the old homestead. It had historically always been a food market, but she explained how our family would offer hardware, clothing, sporting goods and grocery necessities including fresh vegetables from our ranch. Several buildings away, on the other side of the street, they had leased a smaller space in which to open up a tourist shop, hoping to sell items that reflected the special qualities of Hot Springs. All of this caused a great deal of interest after the newspaper article was written. Several townspeople stopped by our building even though nothing had opened yet, just to watch the progress.

Charles and I were interested in our parents' plans in town, but we stayed back at the house with the workmen whenever we were allowed. The wondrous forests of giant evergreen trees were calling us into those hills, like thick green velvet arms waiting to embrace us. To me, they seemed more than alive. I couldn't explain, even to myself, what the fascination was with the trees in that forest. They were simply majestic. From the moment I first hiked there, the darker the forests became the more enchanted I felt inside. We had never known that there could be forests like these teeming with wildlife. Our idea of nature before this had consisted of a walk in a city park. Now, we had automatically adjusted our footsteps to a lighter pace and quieted our voices so that we might witness the closeness of a family of white tail deer or observe the vigilant eagles that shadowed the ground as they flew overhead. I feared encountering coyotes or maybe a bobcat, but my curiosity of the land compelled me to continue hiking.

When my parents first opened up the general store, Charles and I rode along with them into town, spending many long days helping wherever we might be needed. There was an efficiency apartment attached to the upstairs of the building, so often our family stayed there overnight on weekdays, instead of driving back to the ranch house. Since our lumber and hardware supplies were being purchased at wholesale prices through the business, the costs of the various projects were coming in cheaper than my father had budgeted. Mother seemed to have been unaware of this side of his abilities and seemed proud of his accomplishments.

Even while our family tried to approach our new home place with optimism, in the 1970's there was a well-known deep segregation between the people living on reservations and those living in western towns. One day, father announced that he heard that a group of real Indians had been spotted in town. There was a marked apprehension in his voice when he spoke.

Suddenly, I was terrified.

Father told exactly what he'd heard. "They were in and out of several shops, coming in as a group. Not buying anything. Just looking. The shopkeepers told me that they always run them out of their stores, straight away. Apparently, these Oglala as they're called, are thieves, fairly dirty in their way to dress and in their habits. Mr. Throckmorton has the biggest shop on River Street and he says he's had heated shouting matches with some of them, with obscenities all over the place."

"What're we going to do?" I asked nervously. "Will they come here? Don't the police watch them?"

"Have they done anything wrong?" mother asked.

"I'll shoot them in the ass with one of our guns!" Charles said, puffing his chest out.

"Don't worry," my father said to all of us collectively. "I'll keep my family safe. We'll see when we meet them how it goes for us."

"Wait and see sounds like a bad idea," I said, not wanting to go against my father's conclusion, but rather trying to prompt him to come up with another, more protective plan. My heart dreaded something which could or could not happen. In these modern times, although it was doubtful that these wild people were going to ride down off the mountains and into town on horseback wanting to kill us, I was sure there was trouble ahead. This dread stayed with me for a week then subsided when nothing happened.

After the store and the old-time cash registers were up and running with regular efficiency, our parents hired a full time sales clerk. It lightened their own workloads and freed Charles and I from our meager part-time contributions. We had two more months of summer left at that point and we wanted to make the most of it before school started. Charles was relieved to be done with helping at the store, but I often still tagged along on mother's trips to town. Whenever I was in town, I would also stroll down the main street to visit the other tourist shops to see what kinds of things were being sold.

The one I visited first was owned by Jiggs Throckmorton. This man, with critical eyes and black curly hair, kept an immaculate shop. Almost immediately upon entering the store, I sensed that he didn't care for children as customers. He only looked up briefly when I passed his front counter, but when I peeked back through a gap in the shelving, I could see his cold stare following me around the store. He wore a well-tailored button down western shirt and the tips of his leather cowboy boots were visible from the bottom edge of the counter where he sat. The store was stocked top-to-bottom with glass blown objects, silver jewelry with inset stones of all colors, racks of picture postcards, western wear and many things carved out of wood. The way this man displayed his wares was attractive and interesting to me. I couldn't wait to tell my parents the details which they could use in arranging their new store. As I poked around, two middle-aged men walked in.

"How's business?" the first one asked Jiggs. He was wearing a dark brown business suit and looked like an old fashioned gentleman to me.

"Was busier a few months ago, but these days it's been real slow," Jiggs answered.

The second man, quite humbly, said, "In my grocery store, doesn't matter much how tourists run in and out during summer season. Local people gotta' eat so, it's pretty steady for me all the time."

"Since that Hansen couple moved in, they've tried to open a duplicate of every business we already had going here," Jiggs said.

"Come on," the first gentleman returned. "You can't blame your slow sales on competition. Competition's good. You'll have to pick up your standards." He arched one eyebrow and smirked as he added that, as if he knew it was provoking.

Raising his voice an octave, Jiggs said, "My standards are higher than any business in this town, Johnson. And, being a friend of mine and a fellow business owner, you ought to be concerned. They've got a tourist shop, same as I do and a general store which could put a hardware store like Sam's out of business. They're selling groceries there, too."

"All I'm sayin' is that them being here hasn't affected my business," said Johnson the grocer, stuffing his hands further down in his blue jeans pockets.

Jiggs stood up from his chair behind the front counter and leaned closer toward his two visitors. "Of course, they have the right to do whatever they want," he stated matter-of-factly. "I simply find it peculiar that the man and his wife come out of nowhere and are trying to have a monopoly on our main street business."

"They're not," the gentleman in the suit said. "They're maybe just overly eager. They'll find out like the rest of us, that business in this part of the country is different than back east." He withdrew his old-fashioned gold pocket watch from an interior pocket and checked the time as if he were expected somewhere.

"I heard that the guy never had his own business before," Johnson cut in.

"You don't say...so what'd the guy do...what was his background?" Jiggs asked.

"Dunno."

"Find out, will you?" Jiggs said. "We should know the facts about these people."

"The woman inherited the property from her mother, who hadn't lived here since the 1950's, aside from weekend visits in the summer. They got money behind them somewhere. The renovations to that ole building don't come cheap," said the gentleman. "I heard they're from Chicago."

"Chicago," Jiggs confirmed, shaking his palms up and forward as if begging for more information. "Well, that's something we know now. Sure you didn't hear anything else?"

"Minneapolis, you fools," I thought, mulling over how I was going to exit.

"We need to find out; you're right about that for sure," Johnson said, nodding to Jiggs.

"I've gotta leave you two," the gentleman said. "See ya' in the morning for coffee." With that, he turned and left.

I couldn't get out of there without going around Jiggs and Johnson, so I waited a few minutes. Eventually, they moved away from the front counter to the far side of the store. When the door cleared, I bolted out and ran down the street towards my parents' general store. Bursting through the front door, I promptly told my mother how the men were discussing our family.

"Don't worry," she said, affectionately. "They'll find out we're regular people."

If she had been there, she would've understood better that the men were against us. "Are they going to treat us different because we're not from here?" I asked. "Why would they talk about us instead of coming over to see what a nice place we've made?"

"Listen, Laura, some people constantly talk about others like that either way," she laughed. "No matter what we do, they might just be talkers. We won't let it bother us. Besides if they're talking about us, they're leaving someone else alone."

Then, I told about the way Jiggs made his displays, how intricate and eye-catching they were.

She listened, genuinely interested. "You know," she said. "You've always had a creative streak. If I have the carpenters build a big stand behind the two glass windows, we could make a window display there with lighting and everything, like we used to see in the Minneapolis mall. You could try your hand at decorating it—make it special. I'll let you choose whatever you want from the store that you think should go in it. Maybe yours will be more special than this man, Jiggs'."

This was an illuminating and exciting idea. Not only could I show up those businessmen down the street by making our store look better, but I was doubly thrilled that my mother had put her confidence behind my artistic ability. I was only thirteen years old now and I was going to try my hand at promoting my parent's business. During the building of these display window boxes, I hung around the workmen watching how they put it together, and made a general pest of myself trying to hurry them along. As I waited, I set out to draw a rough drawing of my ideas, listing materials I thought I needed and choosing items from the store that we could feature. I was still only a child, so I had no idea what I was doing, but it was fun to imagine what it could look like.

In the course of seeking inventory for the general store and the tourist shop, my parents were put in touch with a Sioux Indian man who sold handmade wares of all kinds. I happened to be in the store on the first day he arrived.

Charles bolted into the back office like a crazed rabbit, breathlessly announcing to me that a real Lakota Sioux was standing in our store. Positioning myself nervously nearby, but out of sight at first, I observed my father overcoming his discomfort with the rumors he had heard in town about dealing with Indians. This large man with two long black ponytails adorned in beads was like no man I'd ever seen in Minneapolis. Nor was he like the Indians I had read about in books. He wore blue jeans and a fringed leather jacket. His skin didn't look red, but rather a rosy tan with a ruggedness telling he had spent a great deal of his life outdoors. He didn't smell bad and seemed educated. When he spoke to my father, he looked straight into his eyes, which was a trait I knew father liked. I began to wonder if he were really an Indian at all.

In the days that followed, I witnessed many preliminary conversations between the two of them, until father felt comfortable enough that they were ready to establish some kind of ongoing business together that could be mutually beneficial. His military years had taught him to make allowances for what he called 'alternate scenarios', and I can still remember them talking over many conditions for their association. Being only a child, I did not understand the importance of this until later. Once their understandings were in place, it seemed like an easy working relationship, right from the beginning.

This man gradually brought both my parents into an agreement that he would be their sole source of a variety of Indian artifacts and handmade wares. They in turn, had agreed not to purchase Sioux Indian wares from anyone but him. I eased myself into these early dealings by standing around yet saying very little. I couldn't pronounce his Indian name, even after he had repeated it several times to me. He translated it into English as "Old Iron Eyes".

In the large wooden boxes that he unloaded from the back of his vintage Ford pickup truck, there were drums of stretched leather and wood that were painted with symbols and there were headdresses loaded with bright colored feathers. There were long-necked pipes of a speckled red stone and abruptly carved wood wrapped in both leather and multi-colored beads. He explained to us how his people smoked these red stone pipes in ceremony, a long time ago and even in current times. The bowl would be packed with kinnikinnick, a mixture of tobacco leaves and tree bark. They would present the pipe to the east, west, north and south in prayer, then readying it to smoke, pass the pipe around a circle of people letting everyone share.

One day, when we went out to his truck to help him unload another box of items, an elderly Indian woman emerged from the front cab. Old Iron Eyes introduced us to his mother. Her name, translated, meant "Kills Enemy". She had waist length grey-black hair, worn unkempt, and it danced with the slightest breeze like bolts of lightning. Her skin, though broadly wrinkled, did not reveal her age. I thought she looked like a wild animal, sleek and strong, and something was distrustful of us in her voice when she spoke. Old Iron Eyes took her aside in consultation before the closing of any final deals with my father. It seemed funny that such a slight framed woman would have such a tough sounding name. Barely over five feet tall and weighing around ninety pounds, she and I were almost the same size.

When everyone returned to the inside of the store, Kills Enemy stayed quiet, poking around the store and looking at the wares in every showcase and on every shelf, while her son took care of business with my father. I wanted to start a conversation with her but I couldn't get past that name. I even found her quietness intimidating.

At last, I gathered up my courage. "You guys live in tipis?" I asked quietly.

"Oh, we have two," she answered. "One for our whole family to live in. The other to park our truck."

"Really?" I said wide-eyed.

"No," she stated flatly. "We live in a big lodge made of cut timber and stones. It's five miles from here and, we own a few rental cabins around it for white tourists. On the property, there's three real tipis for camping out in." I knew that she could see my embarrassment. "You come look at them sometime if you want," she said. Then, she noticed the necklace I was wearing. "Where'd you get this thing?" Her hand examined it without asking.

"We got to pick out souvenirs when we were driving here. This is a thunderbird."

"I know that," she said. "Not a very good one. Not genuine Lakota beadwork either."

"The sticker on it said it was made in Japan."

"Junk," she said angrily. She shook her head and closed her eyes for a moment. Then, she looked at me sincerely. "You come see our lodge, okay? Ask your Mom." With that she turned to follow her son as he left the store.

"I don't think they'll let me," I called after her, but they had disappeared just as abruptly as they had arrived.

This invitation intrigued me. However; my parents had always been protective of Charles and me when it came to strangers. They wouldn't even let us go to sleepovers at friend's houses in elementary school. Meeting Old Iron Eyes and Kills Enemy had left an indelible impression on me though. After meeting them, I longed to see and hear the history and culture of these Indians, from them directly—not from books. My parents were so busy at the stores I doubted they'd ever have time to take me to see their lodge. Inspired by this new interest, I threw away my previous pencil sketches for the window displays and started over with them in mind.

During this time, father announced his idea to build another building on the east side of our existing store and open a sort of a makeshift museum. Mother was wary of the idea since this time, if it didn't turn out the way he planned, it wasn't only our family who would be set back. He had consulted with several local families about his plans even before he told mother anything. It was surprising how he had managed to overcome the suspicious nature of the town in general and convince so many people to join his vision. These families had already agreed to bring their time, personal histories and financing with them to back his proposed project.

My parents' plans were undoubtedly ambitious. Charles and I felt important being only children, when they talked everything over with us too. They felt it would be helpful in promoting the museum, for our whole family to understand exactly what we were trying to accomplish. Reviewing the details was also a confirming practice for my father who had pitched his idea at least ten times by then.

First, he planned to cast a wide net locally, to pull together a collection of artifacts, historical letters, news articles and some recorded interviews with elderly residents. The interviews would tell the local history; the backgrounds of its residents, their lives and loves, how they survived, even the unique geological features for which the town was known.

My mother, although reluctant at first, suggested that the museum should avoid being just another tourist trap based on locally infamous outlaws or the historical Cowboys-n-Indians battles. There were plenty of those scattered across the west. She envisioned a museum that would tell another, more intriguing, side of the west and share the lives of the original residents who emigrated from all parts of the globe to this town. It would span over two hundred years of history up to the current year. The residents would create the crux of the displays through their keepsake contributions such as personal albums, letters and stories; including the documentation from my great grandmother's life.

CHAPTER FOUR

When one was down with any kind of illness, my mother was not always nurturing. She preferred to let a minor sickness run its course without interference. If the illness grew beyond what she could manage, it then became a mad rush to see a doctor. During our first fall season in Hot Springs, I became sick with a high fever that lingered for two days. As I lay abed at the far end of our upstairs efficiency of the general store, mother monitored my illness while she worked. My sickness had lingered long enough that she was on the fence between letting it run its course and pushing the panic button for a doctor's help.

As I rested, I observed six or seven crows outside my window who were holding a meeting. I was immensely interested to see this as I had read in a science magazine about how these birds communicated and that if you watched them closely, they could tell you things. They were gathered in a circle in the trees outside my window, but I couldn't make sense out of what they were doing. I grew frustrated because I wanted to glean something more from witnessing this, but with the annoyance of my fever, they just seemed like a flock of noisy birds.

Charles poked his head inside the room for a split second. "Those Indians are coming by this afternoon to sell artifacts for the exhibit," he announced. "Dad talks about building this museum, on top of everything else, but for all we know, it's going to turn out--like your treehouse project back home--never quite finished."

"The building's already being built. I think he'll finish it," I said. "He's excited same as we are. He's going to do it, Charles, and you and I can help too, can't we?"

He pulled up a chair to my bedside and looked me over as if he was determining for himself how sick I might be. "Too bad you have this flu and have to miss the Indians. I know you like to see them up close. Mom and dad best not be counting on me to keep them entertained because I'm leaving right now to hang out with some guys I met. I'm not even slightly interested in their visit. The locals told me that crazy guy and his mother are gonna' be a problem down the road. I told Dad we've been warned and he just shrugs it off. Doesn't question any of it. Thanks to him, Mom is up to her neck in extra work around the place."

I had noticed how Charles skirted the issue of helping our parents set up the museum. I wasn't going to let him get away with it while he declared his concern. "Why don't you at least go down and help them in the store?" I repeated.

"Say that again so they hear it and put me to work, and I'll..." he ran over to me and with both hands, tangled my long hair up playfully as I fought back, helplessly sick.

"Never mind," I surrendered, and forced myself to climb out of bed to go to the bathroom.

Charles bounded down the hall, slamming the back door on his way out of the house. I shuffled into the bathroom for a minute and puked again before dragging myself back into my room. I pulled a local magazine out of the stack beside my bed to take my mind off of things. In it, I found an excerpt that had been reprinted from the town's original newspaper, about Indians. The paper was brown with age and it was printed in the old-style lettering.

"The writings of Meriwether Lewis of the great Lewis and Clark Expedition Tells of their account crossing the Dakota territories.

On October 8, 1804, the expedition made contact with the Arikaras, and stayed with the tribe for five days. Relations between the Corps and the Arikaras were warm. Keeping with the directives of the expedition, the Corps observed and recorded descriptions of their hosts. Arikara men wore buffalo robes, leggings and mocassins, and many warriors wielded guns that they had acquired in trade. Women were clad in fringed antelope dresses.

I imagined myself, as a grown woman, wearing a fringed antelope-skin dress running through the wide open fields. Then, I remembered what my grandmother had taught me. It certainly wasn't carefree for pioneer women on most days. I fell asleep, half-dreaming about the first settlements in the Dakota territories and half-listening to the noise of the construction equipment across the road as a cement truck poured the foundation for the new museum. I was proud of what my father was trying to do. The five-person volunteer board he had assembled came from various backgrounds with one common trait; they were all determined to preserve and balance the history of the area. There was more riding on the project than the building and the collecting of local artifacts. We were staking our family's name in what was now our hometown.

Hours later, when it was dark outside, I awoke to the face of the old Indian mother standing in my doorway, watching me. Even while remembering that her name translated, meant 'Kills Enemy', there was nothing about her now which scared me. I could see that her eyes were measuring my sickness. She walked directly over to me without asking my symptoms, and heaped a warm salve on my head made from some type of wispy yellow-white flowers that she had boiled into a mush. It was dripping and had a sweet spicy smell that helped ease my stomach which threatened to turn itself inside out again at any moment. There was no soft, "How are you feeling?" type of questioning, no "Where does it hurt?" Yet, in glances and gestures alone I felt a tremendous amount of care flowing from her to me.

Before leaving the room, she said, "Take the messy stuff off after an hour. Then rest."

Even now, I remember how pleasing my sleep was that evening, despite my illness. By the next morning, I was up on my feet again. My first thoughts were to continue gathering the materials for making my window displays. Perhaps, it was the flowered mush from Kills Enemy which had healed me so quickly or perhaps it was my ambition to make our store windows the most interesting the little town of Hot Springs had ever seen.

The following evening, I set my alarm clock for three o'clock in the morning. I had a plan to slip out of that small upstairs apartment and into the general store to work some magic in the middle of the night. Inside the store, I checked for gaps in the thick brown paper covering the window, in case anyone passed by before the front door opened for business, they wouldn't see my unfinished work. I had decided to create a modern looking role reversal with a white American family living in a tipi and an Indian family living in a well-furnished home. My heart and mind were humming with creativity. It was the first time in my life that I actually noticed how much I changed inside myself during moments when I was creating.

Although I should have asked first, I had already borrowed an original oil painting off the wall of our living room at the house, along with an old crystal chandelier that the workmen had taken down for me to use. My parents called the chandelier 'baroque and garish', but to me it was a real treasure. A white sheet, wrapped around three wooden poles that were tied at the top with a rope, made a tipi. Trying to keep the costs down, as mother had given me only thirty dollars to do both displays, I had collected whatever we had readily available to complete my vision. Father had recently purchased the contents of an abandoned warehouse at an auction, which included taxidermied animals, wooden store mannequins, some metal café chairs and other miscellaneous junk that I had sorted through and put in the large storage room at the back of the store.

As each hour passed, I worked out every detail in the hopes that my final project would match my drawings. It was nearly sunrise when I put the finishes on the window displays and peeled off the dark paper. Soon, my parents would arrive to open up the store. I wanted to be there to see their reactions, but by then I was dead tired. With expectant anticipation, I walked outside and gave the artful vignettes one last inspection from the opposite side of the windows.

In the first one, there was a living room containing the mannequin of an Indian man with long black braided ponytails. He wore my father's best suit and leather shoes while sitting in a comfortable chair reading Steinbeck's 'East of Eden'. The baroque crystal chandelier hung overhead. The oil painting behind him depicted an English Fox Hunt and the rug on the floor was Persian. To finish the scene, a stuffed hound dog sat at his feet and his new fishing rod leaned into one corner. On the table was a place setting of fine china, cut crystal glasses, silver utensils, a loaf of bread, a wedge of cheese and a bottle of wine. In the foreground, lining the front of the glass and pulled back with braided rope, were fine blue silk curtains. We wouldn't need them until the final renovations were completed at the ranch house which was months away. They had become a perfect frame for a domestic scene.

I walked over to the second window and looked through full-sized birch tree branches in the foreground at the white man and woman mannequins, each wearing plaid flannel shirts and blue jeans from our store. They sat on tree stumps while they fished using only a stick and a string dropped into a shallow pond in the center of the scene. I had cut out the dark blue pond from a sheet of vinyl material left over from the construction site at the museum. The man and woman wore no shoes and the hair on the woman was fastened into ponytails which were adorned with beaded medallions. A taxidermied coyote stood at their side. Behind this domestic pond scene, sat a bedsheet tipi.

It glowed from the inside which helped to further backlight the people in the scene. I had also propped up tree branches in the background and, on these sat flocked plastic birds as onlookers. Lined up in front of the forest scene was a sampling of the camping supplies that we carried in our store.

Content that both of my displays had turned out as beautifully as I had envisioned, I cleaned up the mess, locked the door on my way out and hurried back to the apartment. As I slipped into my bed, pulling the blanket up around my shoulders, I could already hear rustling in the kitchen. Mother was making the coffee. Soon, my parents would be going to work for at least ten hours. My novice contribution suddenly didn't seem like much by comparison. I hoped they would like what I had done.

There were many visitors to the general store that day and in the days that followed. Many locals and tourists began to comment on our unusual window displays. Some said that we should not encourage Indians to want to live like we did. Father told me that one man said the ideas these window scenes envisioned were too 'big city' for the town of Hot Springs, while others had commented that they were 'artful'. My parents were delighted with the attention, even if it became controversial, and promised that I could make the window displays whenever I wanted. We had drawn many more people into our business and that is exactly what we wanted. I was more than proud. I was elated.

Father had heard from several people he met around town that there was much speculation going on as to how our citified family was going to fare living on a Midwestern inherited ranchland and starting up businesses. A few of the merchants had been bold enough to probe further into our plans and finances than he wanted to go which was becoming an irritant.

Jiggs Throckmorton had lodged a formal complaint with the city about the display windows within a week of their completion. He didn't like how they jutted out onto the sidewalk, instead of being flat against the exterior of the building. On the same day he made that complaint, he walked up the sidewalk and into the store. "Why can't you do things like everyone else here?" I heard him say to my father, in a tone that begged confrontation.

"The idea for us is that we're bringing new ideas to this town," father told him, keeping his temper in check. "Do you think it was neighborly of you to file a complaint?"

Jiggs didn't answer, but instead kept studying the construction of the display window. "What is this...this shit showing the Indians living in our houses? It doesn't take much to set these people off, start down the warpath over stuff—you'd better be careful. They keep talking, these savages, about reclaiming the Black Hills as their sacred territory again—like forcibly removing us from our properties. It would affect your family too..." his voice tapered off as if he were giving up on trying to persuade him.

I wondered why my father didn't throw him off of our property. Instead, he tried to discuss the matter again while ignoring the man's comments. "As our neighbor, you could've walked up the street and talked to me about your concerns."

It seemed to unnerve Jiggs that my father kept talking to him in a civilized manner when it was obvious that he was agitated. "We're not neighbors," Jiggs stated monotone. With another uptight sniff and a furtive glance around, he turned and promptly exited the store.

We all understood that our business success would be indelibly associated with our family. Even though I was only a child, it was beginning to make me feel concerned that my parents might be on the wrong track.

On school days, instead of riding the bus home to the ranch, I nearly two miles into town to spend time in the store. At the big house, Charles would stay for about an hour before taking off somewhere with his friends. I was seeing less and less of my parents, so I wanted to be where they were. Besides, I was beginning to find the local characters who came to our store very interesting. If there wasn't much going on, I'd go into the back offices where there was a large workroom. I'd spread out various containers of glass seed beads and leather scraps I had bought in town. I had also bought a book called, "Indian Beadwork for Beginners", and a red plastic loom. The idea of creating beautiful pieces of beadwork myself turned out to be more complex than I had ever imagined. Over and over, I would spend hours trying to make a piece of jewelry, only to end up taking it apart when it became a tangled mess of string and beads. The process was frustrating me but I was determined to keep trying.

CHAPTER FIVE

It was always a grand surprise, to get out of school and wander up to the store to find Old Iron Eyes there. I had been trying to insert myself between him and my parents as they discussed business things, but so far I'd been only a secondary concern. He didn't seem to notice my interest in him at all. Mostly, he was intent on selling his wares, explaining every item with great care. Sometimes though, he would stop by for no other apparent reason than to chat with my father for a while.

I skipped through the front door of the shop wearing my best school skirt and my thunderbird medallion necklace. Old Iron Eyes saw it and looked at it with the same disdain as his mother had so many months before. "It isn't real," he said, pointing to my necklace as I got closer.

"I know. Your mother and I already talked about that," I admitted.

He pulled up a wooden café chair and sat down in front of me. "She told you about thunderbird?" he asked.

"No--just that the necklace is a fake. It was a powerful mythical bird, right?"

"Wasn't mythical. Maybe legendary, but not mythical," Old Iron Eyes said. "Thunderbird was and still is, real. Just because you haven't seen one doesn't mean it isn't real."

My father walked over and handed him a cup of coffee. "What he means is that it's symbolic for his people," he said. "Not that it really lived."

"Not so sure about that," Old Iron Eyes said. "Our people told about experiences a long time ago, long before white man came to America. There was a group out hunting for food in the granite cliffs. They were far away from camp when a great storm came up. There was a loud thundering and the earth shook." He took both of my shoulders in his strong hands and shook my body for a second like the rumble of thunder. "When they looked up they saw the shape of a giant bird falling to earth. They ran to the place where they saw this bird fall. There was nothing left but its bones. It fell so hard the bones sunk into the rock. They described the wingspan as big as four tall warriors standing on top each other. This bird had fierce claws on its wings and feet. It had a long sharp beak. On top its head, there was a bone standing up. They never seen this bird before. This story has been told for thousand years and is still told, so we don't forget."

Father had another suggestion. "Maybe it was a large eagle. Maybe the bones in the rock was what we call a fossil. Maybe these brave hunters were young and their imaginations got the best of them?" He quirked one eyebrow skeptically at Old Iron Eyes. "Science proved that dinosaurs--basically what you described--didn't live at the same time as man. They were all killed off a thousand years before man."

"Lakota are not agreeing about your science," Old Iron Eyes said. "This creature was real and was no eagle. These warriors were great hunters. They knew what an eagle looked like. Many tribes passed thunderbird legends from one generation to another, from person to person. They also told stories about large birds who brought thunder with them. There's places around the base of the Black Hills where fossil hunters have found pterandon bones--large birds from dinosaur days. They lived in dinosaur days but it's possible they flew during the time of man too."

I studied him carefully as he spoke. I wasn't sure what to believe.

"There's controversy, even in our own tribes, about whether this existed as an animal or if thunderbird represented thunder and lightning. It's not only Lakota who told this story for so long. People from other tribes far away, like in other countries, have told stories close to this one. They drew pictures on walls of caves—pictures of something like thunderbird. They saw it. Whatever he was, it's certain that he was. That's proof for me."

"Me too," I said. "I believe in thunderbird, but I think it was a pterodactyl."

"It's all a crock," my father said, giving a hint of a snicker. "Furthermore, it's my understanding that if a fossil hunter finds prehistoric bones or relics he has to relinquish them to the state."

"Not in my case," Old Iron Eyes said. "I'm exempt."

"Really?" my father asked suspiciously.

"Really," Old Iron Eyes answered. "My family was here before your state anyway."

For a moment, I thought that my father might argue in defense of the government, since that was his nature. However; he let the information settle into his thoughts carefully. "Interesting," he said.

I left them to finish up their business. There were several large boxes of merchandise to put away, so I dragged them to the back office to begin unpacking them. I marked the items on the inventory list as I had been taught to do and continued by pricing them with handwritten stickers. It was only our first year in business and I had learned so much about running the store that I carried out these tasks without anyone asking me. Charles had learned much too, but what I called fun he called work.

Within that first year, my parents had learned what particular items sold better than others which helped them establish their overall inventory. One of the more popular items that Old Iron Eyes' craftsmen made and sold to us, were chest plates of long rice-shaped bone beads that were decorated down the sides with intricate beads of silver and glass. These chest plates were designed to slip over a man's head like a sort of vest, covering the torso on the front and the back at the same time. Apparently, these garments symbolized that the wearer was a strong and important man. At thirteen years old, I used to try these on when no one was around and, holding up a couple of painted gourds which were loaded with rocks, I would dance up, down and around as vigorously as possible, making the beads, bones and rocks rattle together to make music. The ballet lessons I had taken for five years preceding our move from Minnesota, had become worthless to me after mother was unable to find a dance studio within a hundred mile radius of our house. Nothing had inspired me to dance again until then. The boisterous sounds I could make with these colorful items left me feeling incredibly elated. It wasn't long before I began borrowing the chest plates for a hike in the mountains near our home or for an impulsive dance right out in the front of our store. If anyone thought it was odd for a young girl to do this, they never said it to me. There was a reason that Indians felt powerful wearing these pieces of armor or dancing in colorful beads. I wanted to feel that way, too.

The steady stream of tourists passing through the state all wanted souvenirs of the great Sioux Indians, but that was a name given to them by the government, not what they called themselves. I was now being taught both versions of the various battles that led to my country claiming tribal lands as our own; the version taught at school and the version told to me by our Indian friends. One thing I noticed was that while people loved to discuss everything they had learned about these native people, most couldn't spell "Sioux" correctly. I rather enjoyed correcting any mis-spellers with my own observation: "Remember," I would say impudently, "that when you think of the Sioux, put an 'IOU' in between the 'S' and the 'X'. It was my first memory of ever making a political statement and I knew that at this age, anything further might get me into trouble.

Why any regular white American tourist chap wanted to buy these authentic things from another culture for which he had no real understanding, was beyond me. Would he wear a genuine eagle feather headdress for his friends back in Parsippany, New

Jersey or pull it out when he battled his own local government bureaucrats just for special effects? Would he don it bravely poolside in a mansion in California to entertain his spoiled children while doing his impression of an Indian himself? It was a strange business catering to the wants of the tourist and I was starting to see the absurdity of it.

* * *

There was a particularly wicked week-long blizzard on our first Winter in town. It ushered in the beginnings of a lifelong blessing for me. Almost everyone in Hot Springs ended up without power due to heavy ice on the lines. Since the magnitude of the storm had been so relentless and unpredictable, many people didn't have enough gas in their storage tanks to keep their heaters running. Our heater ran out of fuel after the first day and there was a larger blizzard reportedly moving in our direction. With no access on the main roads for deliveries, men from the Army National Guard were dispatched via snowmobile to check on each family. When a pack of three of them arrived at our house, my father told them all too soon that even though we lacked heating, we were fine and didn't need help.

Later, the temperature inside the house reached nearly twenty degrees below Fahrenheit. Before nightfall, our water pipes burst. We spent the evening bundled up on our beds in sleeping bags in an attempt to stay warm. The next morning, to pass the time, we all ended up in the living room wrapped in our sleeping bags and blankets, talking about things we could put in the shops and the museum to take our mind off of the dire situation. Despite

54

increasingly freezing conditions inside the house, we spent those hours sharing stories and ideas, before there was a knock at the door. My father opened the door and, to our surprise, there stood Kills Enemy and her son, Old Iron Eyes. They were covered in snow and round ice rivulets hung from their coyote-fur-trimmed parkas.

"Come in. Come in," father said, stepping aside to make room.

They entered, unconcerned about tracking chunks of snow, until they had reached the edge of the foyer, then stopped. "We came to offer you the warmth of our lodge for a few days," Old Iron Eyes announced.

My father poked his head outside for a moment, looking all around. "How did you know we needed help?" he asked. The wind tugged open then pushed closed the door as if struggling to find its direction.

"Ran into some Army guys on the road leading into town. They warned us we shouldn't be out on horseback in this terrible weather. We laughed real hard, seeing them freezing on their metal snowmobiles."

"My wife and I have to stay," said my father, struggling to shut the front door against a sudden burst of frigid air. "But, it would help if we didn't need to worry about the kids staying warm enough."

"We take the kids up to the lodge then," Iron Eyes said, turning his attention to my brother and me. "Get your travel blankets, your sleeping bags, extra clothes," he ordered. "Roll them up in a bundle and tie it so it doesn't open up. Meet us at the horses outside."

"Horses," I echoed from the protective shadow behind my father's long coat, wanting Old Iron Eyes to tell more about how we would be safe traveling out in the severe cold, but he had already walked away without another word to our parents.

Racing to my room, I threw my duffel bag up on my bed, stuffing things into it without much thought to practicality. If I hesitated, I worried, maybe my parents or our friends would change their minds and I wouldn't get to go. I opened the top drawer of my dresser and took out my new little container of beading supplies. Since we were going to be staying with real Indians, I hoped one of them could teach me the proper techniques that I wanted so desperately to learn. Wearing my dark blue snowmobile boots with the woolen liners and my calf-length brown leather coat with the fake fur trim, I bounded toward the front door.

Outside, the frozen wind blew fiercely like an angry white monster. There were four horses and riders, already mounted, waiting for my brother and I. I pulled my knit hat out of my pocket and put it on, then wound my knitted scarf around my neck twice before pulling it up over my nose. Snow wrapped around me in sheets so thick I could barely see the stirrups on the horse I picked. I placed my feet firmly in the stirrups which were behind the leg of the man already occupying the saddle. I grasped the back of the saddle just as I had seen cowboys doing in the movies and pushed myself off of the ground with my other leg. A strong hand grabbed my coat, lifting me up behind him. After a short minute, we began moving forward one step at a time.

Thinking back on that afternoon, it seems almost unthinkable. Most parents wouldn't let their children travel with another family without accompanying. To this day, that event stands as a testament to how much my parents had grown to trust our newfound friends. I knew the emergency weather conditions must have been more serious than anyone was saying at that moment, for there had been no debating the decision to get us out of the unheated house. Out of this crisis, came the most beautiful ride I have ever taken through the outer edges of the great and majestic Black Hills forest, riding on the back of a colorfully blanketed horse sitting behind one of Old Iron Eyes relatives, holding on to him for warmth as much as for safety. On up past Angostura Lake we trudged, the snow falling like white downy feathers from an enormous pillow fight. The terrain was unstable in places and the horses stumbled tediously along the way as the layers of snow grew deeper by the minute.

Our horses were side-by-side when I looked over at my brother Charles, sitting behind Kills Enemy and he didn't seem to be enjoying the snowy forest trek as much as me. As a matter of fact, his face looked downright terrified. The fact that the trip was on horseback under a still-snowing sky, to me, made it all the more awe-inspiring. I had heard through local hearsay and former guests that the lodge was the best establishment in the area and I was excited to finally get to see it.

For five miles more, the horses and their riders trudged up a gravel road that had been cut in by loggers deep into the stately forest to the site of the Lakota family's great lodge. In addition to the lodge, they also owned ten cozy log cabins that they leased to tourists throughout the summer months. I had expected to participate right away, in special ceremonies or something else fantastic, but for the first two days everyone seeking refuge there remained strictly concerned about the weather. The overall mood was quietly somber. We were allowed to do whatever we wanted to keep busy and my brother and I were assigned certain small chores like helping with setting tables for meals or washing dishes. Most meals were quite simple, but at dinner we were treated to buffalo burgers, rainbow trout and various bean or corn soups. Kills Enemy would tell me to stand beside her and watch her cook, but didn't offer to let me participate. She didn't talk much then, so I remained quiet and watched.

While dinner was being prepared, Charles joined the men who were working diligently to chop cords of firewood. They came and went from the lodge carrying in supply for the enormous fireplace while I sat near the four-inch-thick slate hearth. When the heavy work was done, the men took orderly rotations through the three bathrooms for showers. After his turn, Old Iron Eyes emerged in grey sweat pants and a red flannel shirt, his hair soaking wet atop a towel draped around his shoulders. He seated himself on the large blanket near his mother and I who were sitting cross-legged near the fire.

"You smell like perfume again," she commented.

Twisting his long black hair over his shoulder and pressing it into the towel, he smelled the ends of his hair. "Used my wife's shampoo. It's got herbs and flowers. Men appreciate the smell of flowers too."

"It's too much perfume," she said. "You smell like a lady."

Pushing his abdomen out as far as it would go, he wiggled his body. "Do I look like a lady? I'd be mighty big if I were. Or very pregnant."

"Stop fooling around," Kills Enemy said. "You will make our guests think you're crazy person."

He sat down obediently. Even with his substantial height and weight, which made him look intimidating to most, he was still underneath it all, his mother's son.

In the late evening hours on the last two days, I waited until the others were away from us and asked Kills Enemy if she would teach me how to do beadwork while we passed the time. "I've loved the art of native beadwork since the first time I saw the pieces that Old Iron Eyes and you sold my father for our store. I've tried to do it on my own, but there's much more to it than I thought. I want to know how to do it the right way," I said. "If you could teach me the right way; it'd make me so happy."

"You're willing to work hard--stick with it, even after we leave this place?" she asked.

"I'll listen to you as long as you'll teach me," I promised. "Please, say yes." I was ready to cry to get her to do this, if I had to—truth is, I felt like crying at the thought of her teaching me. I knew how guarded the Lakota were over their culture.

She studied my face, waiting half a minute before answering me. "Since this isn't a passing idea of yours, I'll do this," she said.

I fetched my box of materials and placed the whole lot in front of her. She poked around in the box pulling out a selection of supplies we could use.

"There have been many varieties of this technique, over many years," she said as she began selecting beads from my plastic container. "But, it's a definite style of our people which you have to understand if you want to do this. And, don't ever hold out your final piece as real Indian beadwork. Even if you can make it in the right tradition, if you're not Lakota by blood, you cannot say it's genuine."

"I'll respect that. Of course," I agreed, knowing that I'd never be able to create artful things comparable to the level of their wares anyway.

"Let me get some of my own supplies," she said before leaving me for a few minutes. When she returned, she was holding a tin bucket. "Here we have buckskin," she said, laying out a piece of thin soft leather onto the table. She held a pair of heavy scissors and began clipping the leather into a circular shape. "We'll make ties for your long hair, Laura. Without confirming that I wanted to do this, she roughly divided out a section of my hair in her hands. She moved it forward covering my earlobes, gripping it in a bunch. "You tie the beadwork here, see?" She let the hair fall back into its natural place. Next, she unrolled a line of heavy thread off of the spool. "This long. Start here, in the center, on the meat side of the leather."

"How will I know what side that is?" I asked.

"See that it's more rough than the skin side?"

I rubbed it with my finger and nodded.

"We poke it through here." She took my needle and thread from me and examined it closely before sticking it through the center of the leather. "Who told you waxed thread was the thing to use? If you want to be authentic, you use sinew."

"What's that?"

"Animal gut."

"Gross! I don't wanna use that," I shuddered.

She eyed me as if I were defective. "Okay. We'll go with this since you have it." She expertly threaded the needle with the waxed thread, then held up her hands closer to me. "This is called the lazy stitch but there's nothing lazy about it. Takes time. Takes patience. Many lanes of beads, eight at a time. Can be very hard on fingers to do for days at a time. When you get to be an old lady like me, you'll have hands like this if you want to do beading." She placed her twisted fingers out for me to see.

I took her hands in mine and felt the knots in her knuckles and studied the rough texture of her skin. I admired her even more now. "When I'm older," I stated. "I want my hands to look and feel just like yours."

Withdrawing her hands, she redirected my attention back to the piece. "Patience to space the rows correct—'parallel' is the English word--is really important to get the hard ridges. You need to pull the thread tight to avoid sagging or the beads moving on the piece, too. The thickness of the sinew or thread should be so that you can send it through the bead twice and it will fill the hole."

She looked up from the piece directly into my eyes. "You are getting this, right?"

"I'm getting it," I answered.

"Use only the right size bead and the right colors. Most beads I use aren't the old glass beads our people used—most come from Japan and places in Europe now that I never heard of." She nodded toward the open kitchen area where Old Iron Eyes stood talking with visitors. "I think the new beads I got came from France, but my son, the one there with the women's flower hair, orders them by mail, so I'm not sure. He fixes the business things for me now." When he looked back at us, we both started laughing at the same time and a confused look crossed his face.

Kills Enemy waved away our temporary distraction to help me start the pattern. I did exactly as she said while she pointed to each place I stitched along the way. When it seemed that I had made sufficient progress, she let me take over the piece by myself. As I worked, Kills Enemy gave direction only when needed before finally leaving me alone. Sitting there next to the thick stone hearth and roaring fire, I was contented. Even with the blizzard outside dumping what would become a final total of six feet of snow before sunrise, now that I was creating something wonderful, it was a perfect evening.

Two days later, when the snow no longer fell and the roads were becoming passable, a truck arrived bringing supplies and a message from our parents: They'd be coming to get us the following day. When our hosts told us, I was relieved that my parents were fine, but I wondered if we might ever get to visit the lodge again. Charles had remained mostly isolated in a corner playing board games with other children during these days. He didn't seem as intrigued by the whole experience, but I would have liked to stay for a little longer.

Before our parents arrived, Kills Enemy presented me with a special gift. She handed me a two-inch-long beaded lapel pin in an unceremonious manner. "This lapel pin was given to a new mother fifty years ago. It's shaped like a papoose, the board a Lakota mother uses to carry the baby in. Don't ever lose this or give it away, alright?"

I glanced down at the leather and multi-colored glass beaded object she had placed in my hand, folding my fingers around it and holding my hand tight in hers for a moment longer.

One of the photographs that my grandmother Kate had shown me a few years earlier was of a baby wrapped in a papoose. I remembered the story she had told me about an Indian woman who worked for my great-grandmother making it out of wood and leather as a gift to her. I remembered taking a magnifying glass toward the photograph for a closer inspection of the adornments of beadwork and feathers hanging from it. Now, I was receiving a miniature hand-beaded heirloom of my very own, from an Indian woman all these years later. I already knew of the sincerity behind items given in this way and felt a stab of guilt for the fearful thoughts I once held for the Indian people as a younger child. "I promise. I'll keep this always. Thank you for this gift," I said. "I'm honored."

That tiny treasure meant the world to me at that moment and I have kept it just as I promised. I felt sadness at the same time knowing that I had to return home. Of course, I had missed my family's home, but from that day on whenever I visited this family a part of me stayed behind wherever they were.

CHAPTER SIX

I left the house one day, during the summer of 1974 for my usual weekend trek into the forest. On this particular day, I purposely took a different and longer route than ever before. I wanted to explore the farthest end of the Cascade Creek where it narrowed and the forest thickened. There was a place Old Iron Eyes had mentioned during those days when Charles and I stayed at the lodge. He spoke of a place where a Nakota tribe of approximately six hundred members had lived for a couple of generations before moving further north, almost into what was now Canada. There was a legend too, that before humans ever lived there, giant mammoths and monstrous bears were roaming this area.

After hearing that, Charles and I had already dug deep holes around the places we knew nearby and we spent hours sifting sand trying to find fossils. We were lucky enough several times to find petrified wood or snails and a few large angular teeth. Old Iron Eyes had described, in detail, exactly where the main part of this old Nakota settlement laid and what the surrounding area looked like. I had absorbed all of it and on this day, I was determined to hike deeper into more treacherous terrain to find that spot.

I was feeling a tired on that day, as if I were coming down with some ailment. After only two hours into my quest, I had hiked for as long as I could physically stand it. In the distant sky, giant layers of uneasy clouds cast a dark blue tint onto the acres of long gold grasses below them. I gave a quick thought to the idea of turning back for home, but instead I impulsively pushed myself to run full speed down a ravine alongside the narrowing creek bed. Then, I ran for about a half-mile more through a thicket of trees where the earth sloped abruptly and there laid at the end of it, a wide open field. The high rocky walls on both sides appeared to have been cutaway by hand allowing direct access to the hidden enclave. One could only wonder how many footsteps were embedded in history here, how many warriors might have lost their lives defending their families from invaders or to the harsh winters and incurable diseases.

I followed the pathway to where it recirculated around the perimeter of the only wide-open area just as Old Iron eyes had described. I doubled back to where I guessed that the tipis could have been set. There were still-splayed circles of stones, stacked by unknown hands, which proved that there were people living there once exactly as Old Iron Eyes said. Probing around in the hard dirt and the underlying layers of clay with sharp edged rocks, I found traces of a tribe—long oval-shaped bone beads, some carved stone tools, the broken handle of a white man's gun.

An eagle flew, screaming overhead, as if I were an intruder, as if to say that I didn't belong there. As a white person almost a hundred years later, I felt in some way as if I didn't, but as a human being with a spirit too, I did. However; I had no desire to own this land, as my mother had come to own our family's ranch, by inheritance. This American landowner concept, incomprehensible to the nomadic Sioux nations, made me question it in my own heart also: *"How can anyone own land? The earth does not belong to us. We belong to the earth."* It was Chief

Seattle of the Duwamish tribe who had asked that. I remembered reading it in a book at the school library. After resisting offers from the American government, who he referred to as 'the Great Chief at Washington', he agreed to sell land believing the government's promises of protection, goodwill and friendship. Even while he didn't feel his people could really own land, he wrote in his famous letter: *"So, if we sell you our land, love it as we have loved it. Care for it, as we have cared for it. Hold in your mind the memory of the land as when you receive it. Preserve it for all children and love it as God loves us."*

Even if he wasn't part of the Sioux tribes, I had learned that most native people's beliefs were the same. At that moment, I could almost hear the ancient spirits whispering on the increasing wind, urging me to pay greater attention to this place, to absorb it into my being, to make it part of me. I hoped someday that America would return some of the land back to its original caretakers. They seemed much better at respecting it than we were. My thoughts were lost in the history of the place, but I knew, even in my naivety, that the idea was unlikely after all that had happened.

A violent gust of wind suddenly swept up as if to caution my thoughts. It lashed at the birch trees and rattled their branches. Suddenly, the sky turned a greyish-green and I could hear a rumbling in the distance. A great swirling mass of darkness was closing in from the west. Although I'd never seen a tornado, I knew by instinct that the rapidly approaching dirty white swirl was one. At the same time that this realization struck me, I noticed a child, about eight years old, standing in front of me. He looked at the tornado then back at me and I could tell that he was scared. I moved quickly towards him holding out my hand. Without hesitation, he held it and we headed for the lowest spot in the broken landscape.

We had barely laid flat against the ground before the sound, like a giant growling bear, approached and rain began to fall. I felt the boy's hand in mine, but I could no longer see his face for all of the debris blowing between us. The wind was fierce and loud. It appeared to me that we were on the outside fringes of the tornado. I tightened my grip while the sand pelted our skin, wanting to cover my ears, but I couldn't let go of the boy. I sensed that he was crying out but I couldn't hear him. Pellets of pea-sized hail mixed into a heavier rainfall and began to hit us. Then, as quickly as the tornado had arrived, it left, and we both stood up in the decreasing rain without speaking. As it fled to its next destination, the storm threw dark debris up into itself like a ragged upturned skirt, before disappearing into the distant horizon.

Brushing off mud and wet dead grass from our faces, we eyed each other. The boy stared at me amusedly which made the situation lighter for a moment. I realized he was an Indian child. Thinking I should be the first to speak, I said, "Hi little guy; I'm Laura Helena Hansen."

"Dennis," he said shyly, placing his hand over his heart. "Was that a real tornado?"

"I'm sure it was and I was lucky you were there to help me. I was scared."

He took a deep breath and puffed his chest out. "I can't wait to tell my family," he said.

"That's your real name—Dennis? You're an Indian?" I was used to their first-name-only introductions.

"I am Lakota and that is my real name. Very American, isn't it?"

"You have an Indian name too?"

"They gave me one to use with my family, but there's no reason to tell it to a white girl. You won't be able to say it."

"You're right," I said, concerned that someone might be looking for him. "You live close by?"

He pointed down a dirt path winding up to a mountainous road in an area that I had hiked before. There was an expansive old millhouse up there about two miles up the road where several Indian families lived. The local people had tried to stop them from living there by reclaiming the property based upon its historical significance from the gold mining days. At one time, it was the main millhouse for the towering pine timbers that were floated down the river to be milled for use in the town's original buildings.

There had been a full-fledged campaign a few years before, complete with committee members and a flurry of meetings over several months aimed at taking over or purchasing the millhouse for a county property for another proposed museum. However; it was acknowledged that the current owner had a legal right to let whomever they wanted to reside on the property and the owner had made an agreement with the Lakota families to stay there. A judge concluded that without adequate funds by the county to purchase the property and without enough governmental support to take it, the issue was closed.

Seeing my brother's friend, Paul, driving his father's old pickup truck in our direction, I waved him over to us and asked if he wouldn't mind giving me and my newfound friend a ride. Eyeing the Indian boy and murmuring, he looked off into the distance without answering me. I was remembering what Charles had said about Paul, that he was older than him and sort of a bully at times.

I tried again. "It's only about two miles down the road to the millhouse," I said. "We just got caught in that tornado that came from the west. I need to tell his family what happened. It's only two miles," I repeated, looking at him like he was stupid, which I thought he was.

"Alright. Tell the boy not to touch anything inside my damn truck." He reached across the bench seat to unlock the door on the passenger side.

"He understands English perfectly," I noted. "I'm sure he won't be any trouble."

As I pulled the door open the boy politely refused. "I don't need to ride," he said. "I can walk back the same way I came."

"You will not!" I said, looking at Paul with disappointment. "He's only a boy and he might be injured," I lied.

"It's no trouble," Paul stated obligingly. He gestured for us to climb in. I slid a stack of dusty papers and a pair of leather western boots out of the way and we settled into the cab. My bare arm touched against Paul's and I felt him lean closer into my space. He smiled at me and I put my arm around Dennis to comfort him. As the truck bumped along the narrow road, I glanced over at the boy many times to smile with only my eyes. His dark eyes returned the same gesture under layers of messy hair. Neither of us spoke until we had reached the millhouse.

Three men were sleeping on the front porch; one sprawled out on a blanket and two sitting up in chairs. Hearing the truck, they jumped to their feet, appearing ready to confront its occupants. When they saw me step out with the boy, they eased their stance. "Thanks for the ride," I called out to Paul, who departed without a word or a wave of the hand.

Dennis ran up to his father. I recognized the man immediately as the main stone mason on my father's museum building project. As I reached the stairs, he recognized me too. "Laura Hansen, what are you..."

Dennis cut in before I could speak and told a detailed version of what had happened to us in the field. His father and two uncles, who had walked over, listened intently without interrupting. When the boy finished his father noted, "Very good and quick decisions," addressing the uncles as well as us. Dennis stood waiting for agreement from the two other men and when they nodded, he gave my waist a slight hug then disappeared up the stairs and into the millhouse.

"You guys slept out on this front porch all night?" I asked.

"Sure," answered the boy's father. "Why not? Was a clear sky. Nice and cold."

"Aren't you afraid of coyotes or maybe a wolf sneaking up on you?" I asked cautiously.

Bursting out in laughter at the same time, two of them made pointing motions towards the oldest one.

The oldest one finally said, "You think it's funny the coyote wanted a bite of me? After that bite, he knew I was too tough. He ran off scared."

The father spoke up first. "He might have been thinking that you were too heavy to drag away to his den." More laughter...

"What's that about?" I prodded.

"Another time, Laura; some other time." He said, putting his arm on my shoulder to lead me back towards the driveway. "Thank you for protecting my son," he said. "You should be careful out hiking the forest by yourself too. Stay away from those old gold mines up in the mountains. Once or twice every year, a child or a tourist wanders out there, gets lost or falls down in one. They're dangerous."

"I've never found a gold mine," I said. "I wonder what one looks like inside."

"Better you don't ever see inside one. I hope you listen to what I'm telling. Meantime, you ever need anything, let me know. Come visit again sometimes then? My wife and my daughter could meet you too."

"I'd like that," I said.

He opened the screen door on the porch and grabbed a leather ring of keys. "I'll drive you home now to your family, if that's alright."

After what had happened I didn't have the energy anymore to walk home. "That would help. Thanks," I said. It dawned on me his name then. "You're Dan right?"

"That's me," he answered.

"You're the guy who did masonry work at the museum. My father mentioned you just yesterday. Said he has a big old sea chest he wanted to show you," I said walking with him out toward the truck parked down the sloped driveway.

"Why would he have a thing like that in these mountains? What use is that if it's to use at sea?"

"He picked it up in his younger days as a Navy man."

"But, why would he want to show this thing to me?"

"Not sure. My dad lives in the past with Navy stories. He mentioned what great masonry work you did and he said you liked seeing neat stuff from other places."

"Could be interesting, I guess. I'll never see the sea," he said thoughtfully. "You know, he's the only military man I ever met I halfway trusted." He opened the passenger door and I took a seat inside.

"You trust my father?" I asked as he started up the truck.

He paused before putting the truck into gear, and looked at me seriously. "I said halfway."

That memorable day launched my regular hiking trips in the direction of the millhouse, walking the rocky road up to the top of the hills, showing up as if I were in the neighborhood. I didn't like having to invite myself, but if I waited for them to ask me I might count on only special occasions. I had already learned that once these people invited you, they didn't want to have to keep calling you to come over. They were warmly welcoming and I started taking these walks earlier in the day each time. At first, mother didn't like the idea, saying that it seemed like I preferred to be at their house more than ours. We had the love of family in our home, but there was no way to explain why our life seemed boring by comparison to the Lakota.

Often the daughters at the millhouse would invite me to stay overnight there to listen to the women telling stories and to learn the traditional dances along with the other children. I'd always phone my mother for permission which was usually granted. She had come to understand how enchanted I was with these visits. I loved sitting on the wooden benches outside the wide circle in the grass, watching the women dressed in full costumes and jingle dresses, stepping gracefully while the layers of fringe swayed with a life of their own. The older brothers helped to craft wooden toys for their younger siblings and they would even help sew beautiful dancing costumes for their little sisters. My eyes had been forever opened to a new way of life.

One evening, our parents were attending a community business owners' get-together. I had been restless the entire day, knowing they'd be out of the house later. After getting permission to go to the millhouse for an overnight stay with my Lakota friend Mary, I walked the long road up to it alone. We spent the time telling stories and baking bread and the next morning, I woke up shortly after sunrise. Looking out the huge front window, I noticed that one of the Indian mothers named Lucy, was planting seeds in the dirt—barefooted.

I went outside and walked up beside her. "Guess we're the only ones up so far. Where are your shoes?" I asked.

She looked up for only a moment. "Hi, Laura." Then looking down at her feet, she said, "I like to garden with my feet feeling the ground."

"What for?" I asked.

"I feel for cold spots where the seed might not do well or hard places where soil isn't right. I don't know if it matters; it's what I like to do."

"I've never grown something from a seed," I confessed. "I couldn't tell a corn seed from say, a bean seed."

She looked at me in a puzzled way. "You've ate corn, right?"

"Sure," I said.

"Then, you at least know it's yellow. The seed is the kernel. But, if that seed's cooked it's not going to grow. Or, if you store them wrong and they get bugs in 'em." She continued to work without looking up. "You got to take care of seeds from season to season, so they stay strong. Make a big crop. Weak seeds will sprout, then wither. Weak people do the same; they stand big and over-proud, but there's nothing inside to let them be great. They will wither in health or fate or spirit too, the same."

She placed her hands on her hips and stretched, catching her breath for a moment. "That boy you drove up here with the first time--Paul. He's an example. Earlier this year, it was said his mother run off with another man...left town. Wasn't a surprise she might try because the husband used to beat hell outta her—left bruises on her face and things. Then, she returns again after a while, but then her body was found a few months ago in a burned-out barn. Maybe the husband did this, maybe another man or just an accident. No way to tell, but tragedy can have bad effects on young men like Paul. He'll have to pull himself out of this bad start. He's only being raised now by that horrible father of his. If he gets strong in his spirit though, he might be okay. Either way, he's not the one for you."

"I don't like him as a boy," I said a bit embarrassed as I had never talked about liking boys as more than friends. "I asked him for a ride up here on the first day I met little Dennis because he was an acquaintance of my brother's. I'm only fourteen and a half. I don't have a boyfriend yet."

"You will. Little Laura, with your qualities they'll be running to you before you know," she was smirking like a cat. "Wait 'til high school. That's when drama starts."

She took my hand in hers and unfolded my fingers. Placing a single white bean in the palm of my hand, she said, "What's amazing about this bean is that he has the same intelligence God has given each of us. Like a miracle by itself." Crouching down and dropping another seed into a tiny hole about an inch deep, she pressed the soil firmly over it.

Glancing down at the bean in my hand, I felt genuinely stupid because I didn't get it. By the look on her face, she was satisfied that she had pointed it out. "Okay," she explained. "We all have to find out what we're supposed to be doing here on this earth. The bean, he already realizes, even as just a seed, that his purpose is to be a beanstalk and grow more beans. The bean has its own mind."

I laughed aloud because I'd never contemplated that a bean would think anything.

"That's another problem. If you laugh at an idea, you might never grab a deeper meaning. White people are like that—too busy to stop and think about important things. Easier to laugh it off."

I was unsure of how to react, so I said nothing. For several minutes more she continued to plant her beans. I had picked up another seed pouch to hand one to her now and then as if I were helping. Feeling useless, I wanted her to see that I did appreciate the meaning of important things. "I guess I don't wanna' think too deep about what I don't understand because it takes every effort I have to make decent grades in my classes this year," I said as I followed along behind her.

"You people put too much weight on grades. Teachers try making everyone the same, but they're not. Some are smart calculating numbers. Other people are smarter to tell stories. It's not right to try to make all children be the best at things which might not be their talent."

I thought about this then said, "I wonder if I'll ever have a talent." I realized for the first time, that I had never needed one.

"You do, Little Star," she said. "Everyone has a true talent."

"Why'd you call me that?"

"That's what Kills Enemy calls you."

"I didn't know that."

"There's a lot you don't know. Try harder to pay attention to these experiences which come to your life. Recognize which ones stand out—not in your mind, but in your heart. You'll be a young woman soon. You're going to need to understand why you were put on this earth."

My mother never talked to me in this way. Perhaps it was because she too, didn't pay attention to things with her heart, but rather with her mind. Her goal was to feed our minds rather than our hearts. I couldn't wait to get home that day and tell Charles what I had learned from Lucy.

Unsurprisingly, when I told him, Charles glazed over Lucy's advice because he was more excited to tell me about a cave he had found. He also couldn't wait for us to explore it together. At first, when he asked me to hike up four miles into the mountains with him, I said no, but after much ribbing from him about my scaredy-cat nature, I relented. He led the way through the forest and up into the steep mountainous edges of the Black Hills before we arrived at Charles' cave.

The mouth of the cave was hidden by thick bushes at the base of a steep hill. Its entrance angled sharply towards the underground, barely visible at first glance. Neither of us had experience exploring caves and I knew, without asking, that Charles hadn't bothered to consider anything about safety before we entered. The low walls inside felt much colder and damper than the outside air had been. By crouching low, we navigated the first narrow space before it forked off into two separate directions.

We decided to take the left branch first and, after several hundred feet, we came upon a large dark hole. Straight above this hole, on the roof of the cave, was another hole. It seemed as if something had plunged right through the surface of the hill and continued for an unknown distance down into the hard underground below. We lit up our flashlights and, standing on a narrow ledge, shined them into sheer darkness. Since the hole was fairly small in diameter, we could only make out another narrow ledge about fifty feet down and more darkness below that. Carefully, I backed away from the ledge and, finding a loose rock, I cast it down into the hole. Charles and I watched silently as it disappeared.

After nearly half a minute, there was the splashing sound of water.

It was never easy to reason with Charles at times like this, but I knew that we were unprepared for exploring this cave further. "If we turn up missing, nobody will even know where to look for us," I warned.

"Alright," he said, proving that he was wiser than I assumed. "But, we're coming back here next weekend with some kind of equipment. Or, if you don't want to go with me, I'll go by myself."

"I'll go with you," I promised. Although I was still scared of whatever might be at the far end of that cave, I wanted to do more challenging activities, even with a possibility of danger. Charles was right about my timorous nature and I intended to change it.

Charles laid stones in a half moon pattern on the ground near the entrance to help us find the spot again when we returned. "Don't tell anyone about this place," he said. "I found it. It's my cave. We're going to check it out before anyone else."

"I swear," I said. "I won't tell and we'll name it Charles' Cave."

CHAPTER SEVEN

One afternoon that summer, I was finalizing the planting of my vegetable garden at the east side of the ranch house. When deciding where to place it and what to plant, I imagined where one might have been in the past. I turned to my great-grandmother Laura-Helena's scrapbooks and journals, scouring photographs with a magnifying glass, trying to identify her plantings from many years back in time. Our family's hired hands were already preparing to grow a large crop of corn, wheat, beans and millet, but my garden wasn't being planted with the same intent. My garden was a challenge to myself--could I actually make it flourish? The only knowledge I possessed, had been gleaned from books or from questioning anyone with experience in gardens. I doubted myself and the unforgiving Midwest weather too, fearing that a snowstorm might come early and freeze my ambitious little crop.

"You ought to put shoes on doing that kind of work", a voice said, breaking my thoughts.

I turned to see Paul walking up to our house. "I prefer to garden in my bare feet," I returned.

"Nobody gardens barefooted. You'll get all kind of disease from the ground."

"The ground won't give you disease, stupid," I said before I thought it through. I knew that Paul sorta' liked me, but I also knew that my brother had seen him being mean to other girls.

"Stupid, huh? I'll remember that, Laura-Helena," he said.

"What're you doing at our house, anyway?"

"I'm here to talk with Monroe about doing some work around his store or the museum. Maybe I'll tell him what you just said to me—see what he thinks of his daughter's manners."

"Sorry, Paul," I said, uneasy now.

"Too late for sorry. Better put your damn shoes back on now like I told you."

I stood up and put my hands on my hips. "Wait a minute," I defended. "You *might* go to work for my dad, but it doesn't mean you can instruct me. Besides, if I wore shoes they'd get dirty and I keep them clean."

He walked closer to me and looked me over. "Ain't nothing clean about you. You're nothing but a dirty little girl who thinks she's a Sioux Indian." I wanted to think he was teasing, but I could see that he meant it.

I had heard the gossip about Paul's poor upbringing and his sharp tongue. In the past, he had shown signs of having manners, so now I tried to be nice. Still, I wanted him to know how I felt. "I'm a Hunkpapa Lakota in my heart, not a Sioux," I corrected, standing proudly. "Go tell my father what I said. I'll tell him you're lazy and he won't hire you."

He walked a straight line through the tall grass and across the sidewalk to where I stood. He lowered his voice. "You made a mistake girl," he seethed and twisted his fist into the palm of his other hand. "I'll get this job and someday you'll be working on these properties for me."

I raised my hand spade up in front of me and pointed it at him so he could see that I wasn't defenseless.

My father emerged from around the corner of the house. "What's going on here?" He saw that I was confronting Paul.

Paul stepped aside to shake my father's hand. "Your little Lakota is planting her corn," he said straightening up his posture and smiling.

"Go to hell!" I snapped, pitching the hand-spade down so hard that it stood up in the dirt very near his feet.

Before I could say more, my father took my arm and yanked me around to face him. "Don't let me hear you talk like that again, young lady or I'll slap your face! I've had enough of your disrespect of people these days. If you can't be civil, perhaps you want to be grounded to the house for a few days?"

Saying nothing, I wriggled my arm free and ran quickly to the house, not turning around because I didn't want Paul to get the satisfaction of seeing me cry. Surely, my mother would listen to me and insert her common sense into any conversation about hiring a no-good illiterate like Paul. That evening I learned that my father had hired him.

That next morning, I got up ahead of everyone in the house and hiked several miles up to Angostura Lake. I was angry and I wanted to be as far away from any other person as I could get. The cold early morning mist cloaked me and my thoughts like a thick grey blanket. It wasn't a smart idea to go that far alone, but at the time it was either that or stick around home and be moody.

Circling the north side of the lake, I walked out onto the half-bridge. The end of that bridge jutted out over the smooth lake right at the point where it tapered off and then ran in a rough tumble, gurgling over enormous rocks. Several hundred yards away, the water dropped down several levels into a fast-running stream. On any given day, I knew that there would be schools of at least twenty decent-sized rainbow or brook trout at a time passing underneath. When Charles and I had first started fly-fishing there, we could drop our lines directly over the fish, easily catching one within a few minutes. After some months though, I stopped fishing like that because it didn't seem as sporting as fishing from the side of the lake. Before leaving the house, I had folded my new Cortland fiberglass fly rod and put it in my pack with the reel in case I wanted to fish, but I was having trouble getting started.

I opened the pocket-sized tin box that held my fishing flies, seeing the tiny black gnat, the caddis nymph and the royal coachman—all lined up, waiting to be chosen. I took pride in the fact that the whole box of these insect imposters had been tied by me. During my first year in the mountains, I had learned the art of tying fishing flies, and yet I couldn't seem to reach the same level of art in beading. That was what I wanted to master most of all. Recreating the exceptional pieces that I had seen seemed impossible for me. This impossibility made me want to try harder than I ever had at anything. I didn't want to sell the things I made, as merchandise, as Kills Enemy did. I wanted to create real beaded art pieces which I could simply admire for their intricate and accurate detail. Possibly, I would have a relative many years into the future who might appreciate having a beautiful heirloom piece created by me. For whatever reason, the Lakota beading tradition had taken hold of my heart and with this sincere longing came the frustration of believing that I'd never be good enough.

Since the day our family moved to our new home, I had tried to sink my roots as far into the rich volcanic earth of Hot Springs as they could get. Still, I had the distinct feeling of being lost. Not lost in the place itself, since I could navigate the lake, the trail back home and everywhere in between, very well. I felt lost in my spirit, but I knew that if I were truly lost, there wasn't any better place on earth to be. I stared out at the water, smooth and glassy, reflecting the sky overhead of the purest cornflower blue. Confused thoughts rushed over me like the swarms of newly hatched bugs which were skimming the top of the water. I tried to catch them with my expandable pocket net to make out what they were, in order to choose the right fly for fishing. After half-heartedly studying the insects, I gave up. My focus just wasn't there for fishing.

If I returned home, I could call my new best friend, Berit. I'd ask her if she wanted to stay over for the weekend. Berit was like a bright light who never thought about anything too deeply. In one way, I wished she did; in another way, she was the best person to be around when my heart was feeling muddled. She could narrow life down to only a few vital pieces very quickly. I walked back to the end of the bridge and headed up to a new gravel road towards the mountain wondering if I could find a new shortcut home. Walking along the road, I identified many wild herbs growing along the barbed-wire fence line. Then, I was instinctively distracted. I turned to face the fence.

On the other side, through the low grey mist, I saw a hulking brown shadow and I smelled him. If you've ever hung your rugs outside and forgotten them to the rain; this is the smell. If you can imagine packing cheese inside your shoes then putting them in the cupboard for a week; that is the smell. Horrid. Simply horrid and floating on the gentle wind in my direction. All at once, he breathed out and a great churning fog encircled his massive head. I stood frozen staring with a combination of panic and wonderment. The urge to run was great, but it quickly left me. I could only stand quiet and still, in awe of the colossal buffalo.

Making sure that my movements were meek, I moved stealthily behind the nearest pine tree. Hoping that he wouldn't see me and run away, I pulled myself up into the branches of a birch tree. I sat there, watching him graze below for nearly an hour before he wandered off and disappeared into the rolling hills. When I returned home, full of excitement, my father was sitting at the house with Old Iron Eyes. I told them about seeing the buffalo.

"Weren't the buffalo a holy animal to Indians back when Indians lived wild?" I asked Old Iron Eyes.

He immediately corrected me. "What does that mean? That we used to be wild? Now, we're not? You mean wild like uncivilized or wild like free?"

"I didn't mean..."

He let it drop, but not before I saw his disappointment. "I wouldn't say buffalo were holy," he said. "They provided more than food for the people, but not exactly holy. You're thinking things like buffalo spirits—like that. Some animals, in certain circumstances are wakan. That is, they have power. Everything has its spirit, even rocks do."

"That's a bit far," my father remarked.

"No. It's true, Monroe. Laura asked me so I'll try to explain. She wants to understand how Indians think on these things. This 'wakan'—it's not just holy, it's more like supernatural. It happens in formations of stars, signs in the earth, people and yes, buffalo too. There are weak and strong spiritual powers. Sometimes, the weak is so slight, it's not noticed, but when you meet a strong wakan power you react to it. Lakota believe that there are beings or Gods outside of earth which place wakan into things. If you smoke pipe or hear music that affects you deeply, moves your spirit, that's wakan. Plants and animals with poison, drinking alcohol and things that change a person drastically like that have strong wakan too. Mostly, the way my people think of it is in good wakan which everyone needs to walk through life the right way."

I whispered aloud to myself, "Walk Wakan," liking the way it sounded. I knew then that I wanted to walk wakan in my life, even without fully understanding what it meant.

Old Iron Eyes stepped closer, squatting down to be at eye-level with me. "Yes," he stated in a more serious tone. "You should—always walk wakan," he said. "But, every person has to figure out what that is for himself."

Father seemed increasingly uncomfortable. "I've never been one to question someone's belief," he said, clearly getting ready to question all of it. "To each his own—as they say--but there's no power in a damn rock that I can see. No holiness in buffalo. As you said; he's only meat."

"Sorry, Monroe. That's wrong," Old Iron Eyes said. "I think you are very wrong, my friend."

"Maybe so," my father said. "Isn't going to change a thing we're working on today." He looked at me bewildered. "Why don't you visit with Iron Eyes later? He's going with me and Paul to work on the fence line. We've got missing cattle and three guys off sick. There's too much to do for us to sit around talking about holy buffalo and rocks."

"Can I help?" I asked.

"Fixing a fence line isn't work for a girl," father said. "Stay here and wait for your mother to get back."

I was more than offended for being left out simply because I was a girl. If only my father could free himself from the business and projects they had going on sometime. If he came along with Charles and me on one of our hiking trips, he'd see that I was becoming much more capable. I wondered if he was annoyed more by Old Iron Eyes' extreme ideas or by my endless admiration of the Lakota people.

At dinner that same evening, my father announced that our family of four would take the weekend off, for a driving tour. Apparently, after my description of seeing the buffalo finally sank in, he had developed an interest in seeing one up close for himself. Higher into the Black Hills and the surrounding towns, he said there were places where we could look at herds of buffalo living in the wild. My mother found the idea amusing and completely out of character with my father's usual stoic nature, but cheerfully agreed that we should go. From the first day we had moved to our new home, she had worked diligently in the businesses and at our ranch house. She, no doubt, saw that a break could be uplifting for everyone.

On a clear Saturday morning, we drove thirty minutes away from our property to Wind Cave National Park where buffalo herds roamed the hills in the wild. There, we viewed groups of these dark brown thick-coated denizens numbering fifty or sixty at a time, grazing passively in open fields. Charles and I were glued to the window in the backseat of the car, continually passing a pair of binoculars back and forth between us.

At the park office, there was a humble exhibit and a single ranger to show us around. We learned from him that Wind Cave had been known to the native Indians for centuries, but the first record of its official discovery was in 1881. Two white miners, who were brothers, had hiked near the cave when they heard an anomalous whistling noise. To their amazement, a wind blasted fiercely out of the cave's entrance blowing off one brother's hat. The next day, when they returned with friends to show what they had found, the wind coming from inside of the cave had switched directions. On that day, the hat was sucked into the cave.

Father pointed out that the phenomenon was caused by a difference in atmospheric pressure between the cave and the surface air, which put a disappointing end to the marvelous mystery of it for me.

Still, he was intrigued. He absorbed the view standing next to mother. "I don't believe I've ever been in a cave," he noted.

Then she said, "Neither have I."

Charles shot me a conspiratorial glance, smirking. "Same for me," he lied. "Aren't they great?"

I poked him with my elbow when they weren't looking, but said nothing about Charles' Cave. Ever since Old Iron Eyes told me about things which were wakan, I had been searching for examples. So far, nothing appeared wakan at all. It occurred to me that whatever the Indians were unable to explain, as we could through science, they would've looked upon as wakan.

After seeing the cave, my parents and my brother wanted to go for an hour-long walking tour. I stayed back at the park office to wait for them. I had brought along my sketch pad and while they were taking the walk, I sat outside the park entrance and made several memorable pencil drawings. To me, the harmonic sounds we had heard in those mineral-rich caves filled with spindly stalagtites and stalagmites, were like nature singing hymns. I wondered what it must've been like before the original mining men with their homesteading claims blasted a separate entrance, installed wooden stairways and enlarged the interior passageways. Did they appreciate the find as wondrous or did they simply realize how it could make them rich?

According to our guide, bad luck, bad health and business feuds befell that original family's ties to Wind Cave and it was withdrawn from their legal claims. Control of it reverted to the Department of the Interior and in 1903, President 'Teddy' Roosevelt officially established Wind Cave National Park, America's eighth national park and the only one in the United States that formally protected a cave.

Later, the American Bison Society re-established a bison herd in the prairie habitat around the park by importing a small number of elk from Wyoming and pronghorn from Alberta, Canada. The park needed to be constantly reseeded with native grasses after that due to overgrazing. What was once a perfect ecosystem hundreds of years ago, managed by nature itself and hunted precisely by the native people, now had to be maintained the same as our family did our ranch lands. Even with its mystery somewhat diminished by the money-making tours and the selling of souvenir pieces of the cave's formations, our family had a new appreciation for this natural wonder so close to our home.

On our return trip, we drove through other wondrous natural rock formations, like Needles Highway, where spindling austere rock formations stood on either side of the highway like enormous sentries guiding our way. The air at this higher elevation, even in late summer, was cool and I breathed it in hungrily. Along the way, we cupped our hands to catch and drink the mineral water which trickled out of the rock walls. It was much better tasting than the city water back in Minneapolis. We explored the area for a couple of hours more before finding a roadside table where we enjoyed a picnic basket of food.

"Is it any wonder the Indians believed this is where God himself lives?" mother asked, being uncharacteristically philosophical. "It's so beautiful." She never dived too deep into religion, but the inspiring views were affecting all of us.

"God doesn't live anywhere in particular," Charles said. "Weren't we taught at Sunday school that he lives inside you and everywhere at once?"

"Maybe it's not exactly a holy place, but I don't doubt that it's a special place," she added.

When we returned home that day, I could feel that something had changed in each one of us. We had a new attachment to the lands around our properties and businesses. I didn't know where I would go in the future, but I did know that the spirit of these great lands would go with me.

* * *

When school resumed in August, I hung out almost exclusively with my friend, Berit Biermann. Like me, she loved creating things and as budding artists do, we clung to each other as best friends both in and out of school. Mother had met Berit's mother, a congenial middle-aged German lady named Millie Biermann and hired her to help with various tasks

92

around our house and at the store. Father said that in German their last name meant 'beer man'. He said that the gossipers in town had made reference to that last name a lot when telling how Millie's husband had a reputation for living his life in a bar. Eventually, he left town, leaving her with two children to support—their daughter, Berit, and a son named Michael.

Even the school staff had begun to share in the excitement of the town's new historical museum, mentioning it frequently in the classrooms. Some teachers would put me on the spot with history questions, as if I might know everything to be housed in the exhibits. I was torn between pride and embarrassment to be singled out. The impending grand opening was to happen soon, on a Saturday night. It was becoming a reality.

During this time, my father was on fire with an added enthusiasm for the local culture, the land and its history. We had all contributed our ideas which made the undertaking very much a family business. Mother commented to Mrs. Biermann one day that she had never seen her husband so inspired by anything. Even Charles was saying encouraging words to him about the future of the endeavor. Father had found his talent, as Kills Enemy would say. The other properties and the museum business had pulled him out of the retirement blues that he had felt in our former life and had given him a multitude of new interests.

Each part of the grand opening was being carefully timed down to the last few minutes. A team of volunteers came and went that entire week, moving things around and making exact adjustments to the displays. Paul was in the middle of it, playing the role of a supervisor, even though my father hadn't authorized him for anything, except general help. The glass-topped display counters had been filled with items which had been catalogued and labeled.

All sorts of interesting historical items and corresponding informational signs hung on the walls. Various crews performed last-minute checks of the audio tapes that coincided with each designated area.

There was such a volume of loaned and donated items that many of them became duplicates or simply couldn't be used. I was assigned the task of tracking down the owners of the things which weren't usable and updating the ledger to track them. After that, I had to make arrangements to return them. In the storage room, I sorted through a fascinating assortment of treasures. Many families had lent the museum huge volumes of photographic journals, very much like those made by my great-grandmother.

In a corner, I spotted an odd wooden cabinet with two drawers and a wide metal bar at the bottom. After looking at it closely, I found an antique sewing machine folded up inside of it. The machine belonged to Mrs. Biermann. At my parent's request I had sent a message through Berit that we didn't have enough room in the exhibit for the piece and that her mother should pick it up. Some days passed, then Mrs. Biermann came to the museum and we pulled it out of its corner together. It was heavier than it looked and the wooden drawers needed fixing. I suddenly had the notion that maybe if I could learn to sew on it, I could save my earnings from the store and later on, buy a newer machine.

While we discussed the sewing machine and its history, Mrs. Biermann wondered aloud about our absence from the store when we had taken our driving trip. "I was surprised to find both your shops closed," she said. "I've never seen that since your family arrived here."

"Our family took a driving tour way up into the mountains," I said. "We needed a break from working so much."

"First time you went there?" she asked.

"Yes. For all of us. It was a long trip."

"You saw the wild sheep?"

"Missed those," I answered. "But, we saw the buffalo at Custer and of course, lots of prairie dogs."

"I have those in my back yard even," Mrs. Biermann said, shaking her head. "Love them, but they've gotta' go. They ruin a garden in no time. What else?"

"Needles Highway with those weird tall spindles of rock formations. Granite, I think. Looks like they could break off--some are so thin."

"The Sioux believe those mountains are sacred," she said in a serious tone. "There's been tremendous turmoil on that land since we decided to take it from them many years ago. Problem is, it's said and done, yet they still want it back. It's a struggle to reconcile in my mind, since I own a house here. I do question if it's right of us. Respecting sacredness, you understand? My people were from Ireland and it's the same there. So much is being lost." She was visibly uncomfortable saying this.

I had noticed that people in town didn't always use caution when talking about their personal opinions on Indians. "I understand how they feel," I offered. "A place doesn't stop being sacred just because someone else suddenly claims it belongs to them. Wouldn't it be great if we shared land like they did way back when?"

"Not practical," Mrs. Biermann said. "First of all, they fought over this land too, amongst the various tribes. Still, Indians knew things about this land that we aren't ever gonna know. They do understand hidden things because they're spiritually, I think, far more advanced than we'll ever be. The Sioux called the Black Hills themselves "Paha Sapa", meaning 'heart of the hills'."

"I've seen it on tourist brochures."

"If you want to think about something crazy; that's it. They were convinced it was the most sacred place on earth. Literally, the heartbeat of the entire earth—right around Harney Peak to be exact. That peak is over seven thousand feet high. Higher than any mountain in the Alleghenies or Appalachians. If you traveled east from Harney Peak, you wouldn't find a higher point on any mountain until you reached the French Pyrenees."

It wasn't the craziest thing I'd ever heard, but I was fascinated to hear Millie telling what she knew about the Sioux too.

She continued: "Before us immigrants got here, the only visitors to this place were Indians. When white men came to take land, their struggle to keep non-Indian people from owning this area was intense. They fought more savagely over those dark mountains that surround us than any other lands. As a shock to everyone, long after the Paha Sapa was taken and after the invention of airplanes, when flights began to go over the region, it was discovered what the Sioux had said from the beginning of time, was absolutely true. The geography of its mass of dark evergreen trees, where the prairie borders it, forms the perfect image of the human heart."

"Wow!" I said. "Shaped like a heart?"

"Not like the one we draw for a silly heart valentine, dear," she said. "The shape of a human heart which isn't that of a valentine at all. They knew this--what it would look like from above--centuries before we even had airplanes flying above it."

Paha Sapa," I repeated. "Harney Peak. Do you think I could hike up there?"

You prepared to climb five hours to the top?"

I scoffed at her doubting my resolve. "I don't care how long it takes," I said. "Do you think I could make it? Am I strong enough to get to the top?"

"I couldn't guess, dear," she said studying my small frame. Then, as if she wanted to offer me hope she added, "If you hike up it, best go with others too."

I said, "My parents say I'm too gullible about everything that the Indians have told me. Father says 'take what they tell us with a grain of salt', but for some reason, I believe them even if I don't get it. Kill's Enemy, you know—the one who teaches me beadwork?"

Mrs. Biermann nodded. "Right; I've met her."

"She says white people only listen to themselves and not to everything around them."

"Probably true," Mrs. Biermann said. "You think quite a bit of her, then? She's a good one?"

"She's my favorite person ever," I answered.

CHAPTER EIGHT

Millie was snapping our house into shape, cleaning and doing various sewing projects. Running the businesses in town was an extra burden on mother and me, and our household chores had suffered for it. None of us had minded pitching in, but it was always relief when Millie came to help. Since Millie didn't own a car, I'd ride along with mother to pick her up. A couple days each week, Millie would cheerily accept an ever-changing list of tasks prepared for her arrival. Whenever possible, we'd bring Berit and her little brother, Michael, along too. With all there was to do running businesses in town and helping at the ranch with my father, mother was visibly relieved to be free of the domestic tasks.

It didn't feel right, seeing the mother of my friend doing chores in our house, especially when her daughter was there visiting with me. So, I'd hang around Mrs. Biermann when my mother was out and Berit and I would do what we could to help. Millie was often tired since ours wasn't the only house she worked for.

One day, she brought up the old Singer sewing machine again. "I don't have room in my house for that machine," she had said. "Will you ask your mom if she knows anyone who'd buy it from me?"

I had already thought about it since the day I saw that sewing machine. "Could you teach me how to sew on it?" I asked.

"If you want to learn," she answered. "It's the very machine I learnt to sew on. Can be quite tricky though. Once you start moving that treadle with your feet, it really moves!"

I had no idea what she meant, but that day I
convinced my parents that we needed to buy the
machine. I promise that I would actually sew
something on it and not just let it collect dust in my
room. Even though I knew that my parents could
afford to pay for it, I insisted that I'd repay the cost
with my own earnings. I had no idea what those
would be. After it was delivered to the ranch house, I
cleaned and polished the wood while father made
small repairs. Later, he disassembled some of it and
oiled the insides, checking and making adjustments
to the mechanical parts. There were drawers full of
buttons, spools of thread and a few extra parts.

A couple of days later, Mrs. Biermann showed
up, for my first sewing lessons. In the beginning, I
was only allowed to watch her sew on it while she
explained how to do it. We talked a lot about sewing,
but she also told great stories from her own family's
history along the great wagon trails westward, those
who fell ill, the skeletons along the way, the pitiful
mud flats upon arrival and how those pioneers made
the best of every situation. She believed, like my
Grandma Kate did, that all the people in her family
who had migrated to Hot Springs were driven to build
a community, no matter how hard it became. Millie
had a simple direct way of telling about things which
I really enjoyed.

When she explained how the old sewing
machine worked, she also taught me about the many
variations of fabrics. There were satins, denims,
velvets, cotton, linen, crepes, polyesters and others.
My head was spinning trying to keep up. She must
have felt my confusion. "You need to learn about
every type of fabric before you learn to sew," she had
said resolutely. "Even if you don't plan to ever use a

particular kind, know its texture, how it's made, how it's cared for, what fibers go into it. That kind of knowledge about textiles is very important to any garment you want to make. I'd never watched anyone sew up until then and seeing her cut yards of fabric, turning them skillfully into curtains for our house or perfectly fitted clothing, was mesmerizing.

When she thought I had observed for long enough, it was decided that I should sew a quilt as my first project. Mrs. Biermann said that at least if I messed it up, I wouldn't have to wear it.

* * *

Our family's general store began to show a financial decline in my father's absence. Initially, the plan was to have the employees and the volunteers manage its daily operations. However; museum hours had grown from the planned half days to full days and he felt the need to personally be there for every tour to answer questions. Father had also recruited Paul to compile the daily cash reports for entering into the bookkeeping. With mother's help, Charles and I did our part too, by devising a calendar of hours that we could cover at the general store after school. Being teenagers though, we were still limited in talent. Charles and I helped stock shelves, take inventories and wait on customers while mother did her best to keep up with the financial requirements of running the businesses which she and father had up to now, always managed themselves.

After I signed up for my first home economics class and, inspired by the sewing semester, I made myself scarce at the general store. The class couldn't compare to Mrs. Bierman's intense tutoring, but it gave me basic skills that I could use. I became obsessed with sewing. I even sewed in the efficiency in the back of the store while Charles covered my usual hours for me. When our mother saw my lack of focus, she hired another employee.

I missed seeing the tourists and the locals while I was so distracted, but the allure of cutting up new fabric pieces and assembling them into a wearable garment was more exciting than anything I could've imagined. Sewing became something that I experienced rather than an accomplishment. The smell of freshly starched and ironed fabrics, the low steady hum of my antique sewing machine, the snipping sound of scissors, the sharp even dots created by a tracing wheel and colored wax papers created another world in which time stood still. Whenever I was fully engrossed in sewing, I felt a hundred miles away from our daily lives. With each piece I created, I pushed the level of difficulty and tried various techniques to find which ones I liked best. Now, with the full wardrobe I had sewed for myself, the lingering desire to travel back to the Minneapolis mall for school clothes had also left me.

In the midst of a busy day at the general store, Old Iron Eyes and his mother stopped by. They wanted to show us a box full of new items that they were selling. Kills Enemy wandered to the office area where I had taken a break from sewing to spend time in the store. I was sitting at the long worktable, putting away the latest shipment of winter clothes.

"I brought you something to read," she said. "I know you're the girl who can't get enough books to read. This is a book I had for a long time. Give it back to me when you finish." She handed me a book called "Black Elk Speaks".

"What's it about," I asked.

"What the title says," she answered.

I thanked her for the book and set it aside. Out in the front of the store, Old Iron Eyes visited with my mother who was waiting on the occasional customer. They were both waiting for my father to return from the museum. It was a perfect opportunity to get Kills Enemy's help. Quickly, I finished putting away the clothes on the stockroom shelves and pulled down my box of beading materials.

"You made something new to show me?" Kills Enemy asked.

"I've only made two things since I saw you because I've mostly been sewing clothes, but here's a medallion necklace and a loomed piece which turned out so terrible. I ended up taking it apart."

"Kills Enemy chuckled critically when she picked up the tangled mess on the loom. "A mess you have to take apart." She studied it for a moment, then put it back onto the table.

"Guess you never do that with your skills," I said.

"Not anymore. No. After fifty pieces or so, you'll never have to take anything apart again," she said, clearly amused.

I unfolded a piece of paper to show her the sketch I had made almost a month earlier. "I've seen these great medallions your people wear. I think they start out with drawn pictures on a piece of leather," I told her. "I want to learn how to do this next. I bought the chamois cloth from a local store, but I don't know where to begin. This is an owl." I put my drawing in front of her.

"I see that. I like how you drew him from an angle and not looking straight at you like a child's cartoon. He looks like he was sitting there and

102

turned his head to you. Very good for a drawing. We can use him for this. He'll work."

"How do I get this drawing onto this thin piece of leather?"

"I can show you," she said. In her usual tedious manner, she sifted through my supplies until she came up with the materials and tools we would need. "This stitch is gonna be one you will like and use often."

She fastened two needles to two strands of thread, doubled over and knotted. Then she punched both sets through from the underside to the topside of the chamois cloth. Beginning in the center of the drawing, she showed me how to fasten down the first set of beads. One step at a time, for about two hours straight, we began the project. The hardest part was holding down the beads already applied, with one hand while adding more beads for the next round. It was doubly awkward for her as a teacher, since she was right handed and I was left handed, but she showed incredible patience.

"Remember colors," she said. "They're very important."

"But, it's an owl," I said. "I can't very well incorporate blue, red or black."

"You can. An owl can be all blue, for example. If I made him, he'd be blue because that is what the spirit of the owl means to me. It depends on what you want him to represent."

"He doesn't represent anything to me. I want to do him in almost real colors. What about white and yellow?"

"Do him in blue," Kills Enemy said.

"Doesn't he need brown too?"

"You make him your owl, Laura. You are the artist and he's your creation. My stubbornness wants everything to be traditional. Like it was before. This is why I see him as blue as the sky."

I detected a resigned sadness in her eyes then. "I know," I said. "It's most important that it's made well, right?"

She spoke slowly with indignity in her voice. "I'm afraid this culture will be lost in the next hundred years. Teaching this to you and my sisters' daughters makes me feel like tradition is being passed on."

"I'm glad for everything you teach me, but can't we blend the old style and my artist vision into pieces--now and then?"

"You finish this piece. Next time I come, I'll look at it for you. Then, we'll really get this, as you like to say, as a form of art. We'll do something made with porcupine quills."

Indians were known to use all kinds of materials for beading; buffalo horn, bone, various metals and stones, but I hadn't heard of beading with porcupine quills yet, and wondered immediately if we would be using them for beading needles or to put into the next piece of beadwork.

She saw my interest pique and added, "And, we'll use horsehair too."

I thought she was fooling around about that part. I carefully pushed the supplies aside, carrying the newly started piece with me. "Let's go visit with Iron Eyes," I suggested.

We walked back down the hall to the front of the store where mother and Old Iron Eyes were having coffee with one of the regular customers, an eccentric older woman, Mrs. Haskell.

Mrs. Haskell wore shorts and a midriff top which didn't quite cover her ever-expanding belly. She frequently talked about random things like the wastefulness of using soap, the flavor of pigeon meat, reading German books at the library and local politicians who she'd like to punch in the nose. Once she began talking, it didn't stop. Charles had made the observation on her first visit into our store, that her over-exposed belly button was unclean and packed with lint. After that, mother and I made it a point to look only at her eyes as she spoke, not wanting to witness this ourselves. Now, Old Iron Eyes was stuck in one of these awkward conversations.

When we walked in, he looked up. "What're you girls doing?" he asked, seeming grateful for the interruption.

"Your mom's teaching me new beadwork techniques," I said, showing them the background I had drawn of the owl.

Mrs. Haskell walked over and looked at it up close. "Where's his big eyes?" she asked.

"They'll be there," I said. "He's not finished."

"She's going to be good at this," Kills Enemy announced edging in closer. "I think she found her talent."

"Thanks for teaching her," my mother said. "I don't have the knowledge or patience for anything like that."

Mrs. Haskell looked down into the items in a display case and continued talking only to herself.

Kills Enemy smirked at me. "I like bright turquoise blue. Blue is a holy color. It's almost the color of the water and it's the true color of the sky." She looked up at the ceiling as if she could see the sky right through the roof. It was in dreamy moments such as these when I caught a glimpse of who she really was.

At last, my father showed up. He immediately avoided Mrs. Haskell and walked over to the boxes. Old Iron Eyes opened each one while father excused himself to grab a cup of coffee as he always did, while Old Iron Eyes waited. At last, he returned to the front office.

"Lookie at this," Old Iron Eyes began excitedly. "This is a new style of hair barrettes our girls on the reservation have made with new designs. Not anything like we sold before." The delicate beaded barrettes looked even more so held in his large hands.

"I dunno..." my father's voice tapered off.

"Try a three dozen batch, maybe? See how they sell. Then, you know how many to order next time. I'll just leave this batch. Pay next time."

My father didn't assign much attention to the things Old Iron Eyes was trying to show him that night. He rummaged through the first box, not taking anything out to look at up close. Instead he asked, "You know anyone who can play the flute?"

Old Iron Eyes stopped unpacking the items and looked at my father. "What for?"

"Because I'm opening our museum on Saturday evening and it would be a nice background."

"Ambiance."

"Something like that, yeah."

"Men like you always think of stuff like that," Old Iron Eyes said.

"What the hell does that mean?" my father returned sharply.

"You think everything has to be staged for special effect. Don't you think the things people are coming to see at your museum--what those things represent--will be enough?"

At that point, Mrs. Haskell walked over and looked into the box. "Hmmm," she murmured. "Pretty, pretty items in there..."

Father cast an uptight glance her way, frowned, then turned back to Old Iron Eyes. "It's how it's done. I'm going to do this properly—with a big bang. So we get good press too."

"Good press is important to open a museum. Uh-hm, right. Sure is," Mrs. Haskell muttered.

Old Iron Eyes walked away from the box and closer to my father. "If you want a big bang and to be authentic, since most of your museum is focused on the white people, why don't you stage a wild-west saloon with a player piano? Maybe a couple prostitutes propped up on it. That's how the west was like back then."

"Dammit!" my father steamed, standing now broad-chested and taking a few steps back from Old

Iron Eyes. "You're purposely riling me. I don't have time to argue this stuff with you. Maybe you've ingrained in my daughter all these great Indian virtues--how your culture is so much greater than ours, but I don't have time for this crap right now!"

Old Iron Eyes appeared unfazed. "I'm only asking why you would take the attention off important things by throwing in a cheap background special effect. It's not necessary. Quiet would be better."

"I didn't ask you to educate me," father said pointing his thumb into his own chest, "or offer your whole take on the opening night. Damn! I just wanted a flute player."

"No, I don't." Old Iron Eyes said calmly, folding in the flaps on the boxes.

"You don't what?" father snapped.

He gazed straight into his eyes and spoke deliberately slow. "Know a flute player, Monroe." With that, Old Iron Eyes lifted the first box back up from the floor. He caught the attention of Kills Enemy from across the room by tilting his head towards the front door in a quick motion.

Pursing her lips seriously, she laid down the leather piece we had worked on and waved a low hidden goodbye to me from behind her long dress. With quick steps she followed Old Iron Eyes out of the building with the boxes. Mrs. Haskell trailed out silently behind them as if she were part of the conflict.

When they were gone, I walked over to my father who was sitting in his chair behind the front counter. I placed my arm around his shoulder to give him a hug. He flipped my arm off and twisted his body away from me without ever looking up.

"Don't be mad," I said. "He means well, right?"

"He needs to not forget who's employing him. Who's buying his merchandise. They don't make nearly enough from that lodge to keep themselves and their families fed. Then, he comes here and acts like he's a grand know-it-all. I can buy my stuff from another Indian real quick." He wasn't talking to me, but rather, yelling. "And, you guys need to corral that loony damn woman out of the store when she comes in! She'll scare off any regular customers."

"Mother says she's got mental disabilities or something--that we should treat her with kindness. It's not like she's causing problems." I couldn't believe that he was getting so angry. I didn't think that Old Iron Eyes had been disrespectful. They just disagreed. "I'm sorry Iron Eyes upset you," I said. "I'm sure he didn't mean it. Maybe you should go to the apartment and rest. You seem tired."

He looked at me with weary eyes. "Don't treat me like that, Laura," he said in a low voice. "That's what you got from your mother." He pointed to where she stood on the other side of the shop. "That's what she does. Treats me like a child when I don't conform to her plan."

I'd never heard him complaining about my mother. Maybe she was noticing these changes in him too. As a teenager, I was hardly capable of understanding how difficult life was becoming for them. Part of me wished that our family had not tried so hard to establish so much in a short period of time. Part of me wished that we could move back to Minneapolis, to our old house, but I was already fully immersed in my interests here too. I returned to the back room to clean up my beading table.

When I thought about family, in my heart, I realized that I was feeling real love for my Lakota friends. I had lived at times, so near to them that I cherished them and they returned my friendship in kind. Although they were perceived during those days to have been otherwise, I found most of their people to be honest, kind, mild mannered, clean and very intelligent. There were no more baddies in their communities than there were in ours. However; over a hundred years of rhetoric was working against them and local sentiment was one massive churn of negative stories over and over again. As a youth, I couldn't do much about it, except try to understand them better myself. Early on, I had noticed that many of the local kids had stopped associating with me. There was no way to be certain if this was because of my friendships; it was just something I felt to be true. For the most part, the ones who seemed to avoid me were people whom I didn't find interesting in the first place, so nothing was lost.

* * *

The county sheriff, Ben Basset, had begun recently to sit with my mother having coffee some mornings on the weekends before making rounds in the community. During these visits, my father always made certain that he'd be away from the ranch. I came to believe that he did this because he didn't like the sheriff much.

"Mr. Basset is an important man here," I once heard my mother say to father.

"In a small town way, you're right," he agreed.

"The small town we're living in now; yes," she said. "He's perfectly willing to help us adjust. Not only that, but he's well-schooled in the arts and history. I find that interesting. He's probably the second or third most well-liked person in Hot Springs."

"By whose measure?" my father asked. "Your assessment of him, a local poll or what?"

"I think if you took the time to get to know him, you might become friends," mother said, giving him one of her disappointed looks.

"You make friends," he had said as he was leaving. "I've got businesses to run. When you're done having coffee-klatch with Lady Basset, come and join me."

On one such morning coffee visit, I decided to try to know Sheriff Basset better myself. I felt in some way that he was casting a shadow on our household, but I didn't know why. He and mother were sitting at the large wooden farm table in the kitchen, the one with the iron legs. I walked right into the middle of their conversation about the history of South Dakota, without asking if they minded.

"Did you know that my great-grandmother used to pray with her Indian friend every morning at sunrise back in the late 1800's?" I said to him quizzically.

"Is that right?" he said only half-interested. He was a thick armed, rather stout man with pale skin. However; his ice blue eyes were framed by dark lashes and brows. In an odd way, he was nice to look at. He claimed to be a Frenchman, but I noticed that he had no accent.

"It's true," I continued. "The other woman's name was Lorena."

"Lorena? Isn't that a Spanish name?"

"No, Silly. I told you. She was an Indian—a Lakota. It was Laura-Helena who gave her that name; it was a combination of both her own names. That woman was called Lorena for her whole life."

He seemed perplexed. "How would you know?"

"Grandmother Kate told me all the family stories every time she came to visit us in Minneapolis about Laura-Helena and her Sioux friend Lorena. She told me how her mother arrived in a covered wagon with her new husband and settled this property, right here, this one we live in. At first, their house was made of hand-hewn logs with sod chinking packed in the crevices and wood plank floors. She even told me how Laura-Helena fought off a bear who invaded that house once using nothing but an iron frying pan."

"Sounds like a tall tale," he said, searching my eyes as he had probably done with many juvenile delinquents, looking for signs of deception.

I left the dining room and walked into my room, opening the old steamer trunk. I fetched a particular scrapbook and returned to the dining table. I opened it in front of him pointing to the photo of Laura-Helena standing outside of the old homestead with Lorena. "See," I said.

He leaned forward and, pulling his glasses out of his pocket, looked at the photograph. "Holy smokes! They're in their gosh-darn bloomers."

"Yes. That's how they prayed--that way."

My mother set a cup of coffee in front of Basset. She smiled seeing the open scrapbook. "Laura loved hearing those stories about my grandmother who left Chicago and traveled west into the unknown way back then."

I couldn't resist relaying a favorite story, exactly as it was told to me by my grandmother Kate. "One day they were out praying in their bloomers," I said. "Like in the photo. They were kneeling beside the water instead of standing as they usually did when this cowboy on horseback showed up unexpectedly in front of them with a delivery of some sort. My grandmother, who was much younger then, realized that her right breast had fallen out of her nightshirt and she stood up quickly fixing herself proper. He handed her the package, gave her the usual rundown on the gossip in town then, as he rode away, laughingly suggested that she 'really must keep abreast of things!' As the story goes, that cowboy always tipped his hat with a smirk when he saw her in town after that."

"Sounds like an interesting life," he droned uncomfortably, quickly folding up the scrapbook and handing it back to me.

My mother set the coffee cup in front of him and motioned with her hand for me to move along.

"By the way," I asked, "what's a prostitute?"

113

"Where did you hear that?" Basset snapped a startled look at my mother.

"Old Iron Eyes said it to father when they were arguing and father seemed to get madder."

"You don't need to know what it means," my mother answered sharply. "It's inappropriate for a teenage girl to say. Go on now."

I returned the scrapbook into the trunk wondering why people didn't show the same interest in the dead as they did the living. I felt a strong connection to my great-grandmother as if I had known her, even though she had passed almost a hundred years earlier. So far, my life had been boring by comparison and I wanted to change that.

Before leaving the house for the day for a hike in the mountains, I passed back near the living room where I heard the sheriff talking again. "You should monitor how close she gets involved with those Indian people and their political affairs. You don't want her to get into trouble. Worse yet, he could harm her."

"I'd be shocked if she got into any trouble with this friendship. She's shown good judgment in choosing her own friends in the past, but of course, that language around my teenage daughter is worrisome. I'll mention to him if he wants to be around children, he needs to rein himself in."

I moved around the edge of the room to watch Basset's face from a distance. He didn't seem to know what to say after that. My grandmother Kate had used that same word in her stories and my mother knew this. The subject of my association with Indians had come up within my parents' circle of friends many times. There was only so far one could be against it, since it was through my parents that I had made friends with Old Iron Eyes and Kills Enemy. I wondered if there were also rumors related to my visits to the millhouse, but it was clear that Basset was making it his business. My parents had allowed me to follow my interests to wherever they led me and for that, I felt lucky. They could have set down rules about my wanderings and my friendships but they didn't. Since they had dealings with several families on the reservation now, maybe it was more understandable. It still seemed weird to me that I didn't know any other kid at school who had an Indian friend. We had only one Indian child enrolled at our public school—a girl who was half Indian and half Spanish. When my school friends talked about their activities outside of school, I gathered that the entire town was like a private enclave which associated only with each other.

CHAPTER NINE

Hot Springs was a town with a population of under a thousand residents. There was no movie theater, no dance classes, no fine restaurants, no golf clubs nor any number of things that were available back in Minneapolis. Our family had discovered an incredible array of things to do since we arrived. In the midst of drastic changes, we constantly found ourselves excited to learn more about our area. When Charles and I headed out together, there was no way of knowing what kind of day it might be.

One day, Charles and I decided to take a hike together out past the city limits, then down by the creek to try our luck panning for gold. We both also hoped to catch a glimpse of a herd of Dall sheep which had been spotted up on the rocky cliffs there. Charles had bought a real antique gold pan at the second hand store in town and was anxious to try it out in the stream. He also brought along his archery set for practicing our aim on trees along the way.

"We've got to ask Mom and Dad first," I cautioned. "They need to know where we're at."

"Come on," he argued. "They won't let us go that far. They'll say we can't go."

"No," I said. "We're asking permission or I'm not going."

"You go ask them and if they say no, I'm going anyway."

I marched away to find my mother who I had seen moments before in the large front room. After I got approval for where we were headed, I grabbed my instant camera in case I needed it too.

Outside the city limits, we found the house of Jiggs Throckmorton. We knew it was his home because of the name on the mail box. "This is fortunate," Charles stated. "Now, we know where he lives."

"What does it matter?" I asked.

"Because, I've about had it with his crap. I might march up to his front door one day...punch him in the nose."

"Please, don't do anything like that, Charles," I pleaded. "He's a grouchy, mean old man. We'll stay away from him. That's what we're gonna' do."

"We can hardly stay away from him when he's everywhere we are. He said to stay out of his store, so we did. Now, he's at every event our parents are at. He's at every school basketball game or play you or I have and he doesn't even have children. Doesn't even like children--far as I can tell. It's like he's purposely antagonizing us."

"He's not," I assured him. "He lives here too. This town's population is only a thousand people. At some point, we're bound to run into him. Let's get down to the creek. Forget that guy."

As we walked past his fence and turned down towards the creek, Charles spotted an enormous tree in the backyard. "Look at that, Laura. A pear tree!" He took off running towards it.

"What's so great about that?" I asked running behind. The wind picked up and shook the leaves on the tree as if it were waving us over to it.

"I love pears," he said, climbing over the fence.

I followed.

"His car's gone," Charles said. "We're in luck."

I ducked down, keeping my head low, in case Charles was wrong. "Uh; I don't think we should be doing this."

"Come on, Laura, you little baby. You never do anything outside the rules. It's a damn pear tree! Look at those rotting pears on the ground. He's not eatin' them." He was already reaching for the lowest branch.

We both climbed high up into the middle of that tree and began eating pears while we sat on the branches talking and looking out at the distant hills. After about an hour, I started to climb back down.

"Wait," Charles said. "I think he just got home. "Can you see the driveway from where you are?"

"I can't. Let's go then." I was almost to the bottom of the tree when my brother saw Jiggs.

"Oh yea-a. He's home alright. Here he comes."

The back door swung open and Jiggs ran towards us at full speed, swinging a large metal wrench. "Get outta my tree you wandering cretins! Pilfering Norskies! Get the hell outta my tree!" He was so angry it seemed as if his hair stood on end.

I quickly peered through my camera's view finder and snapped a picture. "Norskies? Hah!" I said.

"Wait 'til Halloween comes," Charles yelled back.

As we ran away we could see Jiggs still chasing behind us, red-faced and lathered up like a rabid animal. He was fairly agile for a middle-aged man and it took everything we had to outpace him. As we ran, the square photograph rolled out of the slot at the bottom edge of my instant camera.

Stopping at the top of a hill, Charles and I rested against a large boulder and watched the photo develop before our eyes.

"Look at that crazy old man," Charles said, shaking his head. "You think he would've used that wrench on us if he'd have caught us?" he asked me.

"I don't know," I said uncertainly.

As we hiked nearly four miles back home, my thoughts were mired in confusion. What kind of future would I have here? Would Charles and I grow up to be cave explorers, geologists or fossil hunters? It was an intriguing fantasy in our youth, but I wasn't sure that here was where I belonged. I was seeing our hometown as a bridge carrying me on to a future somewhere else, but I had no idea where.

We had been truly scared that day, robbing Jiggs' pear tree, but being scared wouldn't stop us in the future from doing the same thing again every time we passed by that place. He could've easily shared that fruit with everyone, but instead he let them fall on the ground and rot. That caused Charles and I to feel justified in agitating the man. It became a real thrill for us to take hikes up there during pear season to try picking them without getting caught.

***

Charles was visiting a friend on the southwest side of Hot Springs and mother was driving to pick him up. His daily ritual up until then consisted of school and afterwards, meeting up with his own circle of friends until well after dark. Many of Charles' friends had lived hardscrabble lives and their idea of fun often turned to mild criminal mischief or fist-fighting. Sometimes, he came home after dark and my father would reprimand him, reminding that he was to be home before dinner every night. Charles had already rejected the idea of attending college, saying that after he finished twelve years, you couldn't drag him into another school. Even so, my parents marveled at how he managed to get A's and B's on his report card without even trying.

I waited at the ranch house where he and I had planned to go out for a long hike after lunch. While I waited, I drew sketches of the lively prairie dogs which were outside my bedroom window, near the tree line.

When Charles returned with mother, he ran straight down the hallway to my room and flung open the door. "Guess what?" he said, breathlessly.

"I dunno', what Charles?" I said folding up my sketchbook.

"Remember where they're building the new houses?"

"Up by..." I started.

"You know where I mean. The tractor driver was digging to clear the property and they found a whole mammoth site there!" he announced. "At first they found a tooth. Then, a seven foot tusk they found, Laura! Whole town's talking about it."

"Wow!" I said, standing up. "When can we see it?"

Mother showed up in the doorway too. "That's what everyone wonders," she said. "People want to see it, but it's going to take several months to dig it up properly."

"Yeah, Charles said. They've got to carefully take that big guy outta' there. I'm so excited!" he proclaimed. "Just think, Laura. All the times we hiked around. This could've been us finding it."

"How far down was it?" I asked. "How far did they have to dig?"

"We don't know the details," mother said. "We have to wait and see."

It had been a long time since Charles had been that excited over anything. After that day, all he talked about was excavating or fossils. He hung around the site talking to archeologists and followed the story of the mammoth site like a groupie follows rock stars. Soon after, he announced that he was going to college to become a paleontologist. Mother said the mammoth find was a godsend for how it had helped Charles realize that he needed to further his education. Although he was only sixteen, she began establishing a separate college fund for Charles and gathering information on paleontology courses.

Later, after many months of slowly uncovering the site, it was reported that what they had discovered was the 26,000-year-old grave of a mammoth. In the years that followed, additional skeletons would be found there which led the team to conclude that the site had been a steep sinkhole that trapped not only mammoths, but prehistoric bears, camels and rodents.

In the coming years, the volume of tourists coming to Hot Springs increased and, as my parents began buying great quantities of inventory to stock the shelves of their businesses, I regretted even more the Indian's need to sell off their wares. I hoped, in my youthful naivety, that nothing of true heritage was being sold yet I knew instinctively it wasn't true. How can one replace an artifact handed down from a generation ago? How sad it was to me that these great people had to transfer so much of their culture in order to make a living. Perhaps, as they had adjusted to the new world that we gave them, it was easier than the old ways. The positive side was that sharing their culture with outsiders would help fill in gaps of understanding which weighed heavily on the political aspects of their lives.

Our family businesses now employed fourteen people, which was a lot for a town as small as Hot Springs was then. Paul had originally been hired to do any kind of labor that needed to be done. Now, with his eagerness to learn the trades from the older men on the job and willingness to work long hours, day or night, my father had promoted him as manager over all of the businesses. This new position required on-the-job training by my father, but he was certain that Paul was catching on sufficiently. We often heard him saying how much he admired Paul's ambition.

Now that Charles had matured with thoughts of his future, he was beginning to take an active interest in the businesses too. He had begun, quite often, to make spiteful comments about the time and attention our father was putting into Paul.

Mother enlisted my help part time in one of the retail shops. They arranged to pay me the same as our two full time sales clerks even though I would have willingly worked without pay. It was for the benefit of our entire family and besides, I loved it. I saved most of the money I earned, using it only when I needed to buy new fabrics or beading supplies. Every tourist, every customer and even the curious person who would stop in for coffee, was widening my view of the world outside of our little town. I always took the time to find out where they were visiting from and what it was like living there. Our customers came from all over the United States, Canada and other countries. Most had found our shops while on their way to see Mount Rushmore. In anticipation of who I might meet, I rushed to finish my homework each day, so that I could get to my job. My best friend, Berit, thought it was terrible that I had to work so hard. To me, it wasn't work; I was having interesting experiences, every day.

It was difficult for me to learn about the household hardware, fishing supplies, clothing and everything else we carried in our general store. I could only guess what half of the stuff was used for. Harder yet, was giving directions to those drivers passing through the area to other places, since I was only beginning to learn to drive myself.

On the days when I worked in the store, it was much easier. I hoped with every Indian item sold, its new owner would appreciate the great spirits which also transferred within the item and cherish whatever they had purchased as much as I did. These items weren't merely inventory or things to have. The thought of a hand-sewn pair of beaded leather moccasins taken to a vacationer's home and thrown in the back of their closet often led me to offer up a cheap book of postcards or a glass blown animal as a souvenir alternative. I had developed the habit of looking straight into the eyes of any buyer and determining exactly what was best to sell them. Usually the item I chose was something which could be re-stocked in large quantities instead of authentic Sioux items.

Although school and my part-time work occupied the majority of my time, I never missed a sewing lesson. To my surprise, I had conquered the basics rather quickly. Within months of my first sewing lesson, I had sewed three articles of clothing that I actually wore and now Mrs. Biermann had raised the stakes, supervising and inspecting each seam, dart and zipper of garments as I made them. She had a new level of expectation from me and I was challenging myself to not disappoint her. My mother stayed completely out of our sessions, but seemed pleased. I was certain that she also liked me sticking around closer to home.

It wasn't long before I ventured into tearing pages out of high fashion magazines, trying to draw my own patterns based on the pictures. Often, I would alter an existing store-bought pattern, taping on pieces or cutting it out and expanding it, to create a new design. After much trial and error, I discovered that I could make fairly impressive garments for myself. Always, Millie was around to help me plan, shape and size my projects. I became known to the other girls at school for my sewing skills, leading several of them to appeal to me to make one of my own designs for them. I was so flattered that anyone would want to wear what I considered my art that I said yes to anyone who asked.

Instead of my former habit of reading books of local interest and studying pictures of animals, my interests had shifted to fashion magazines and books with photos of far-away places. More precisely, I had developed a distinct interest in finding out what people wore for clothing in every country around the world. That year, father had found at an auction a collection of dolls in native costume from around the world. To me, it was as if the great spirits in the sky had heard my thoughts and brought these beautifully dressed dolls to me. There were nearly forty in all regaled in fanciful embroideries and bright colored trims. Each one had a double-ruffled skirt which I spread out flat from their head to their feet like a circle. Then I hung them up with thumbtacks, spacing them evenly around the upper portion of my bedroom wall at the ranch house. After I had finished hanging them, they completely encircled my room.

Charles said he'd never seen anything like it. "You're different, Laura," he had said. "I'm not sure if that's a compliment, but you're not a normal girl."

He was only saying what was true. I was different from the other members of my family who were content to spend their time on the ranch or in town. They had no burning needs for art or beautiful things like I did. They could be content with necessities. Hot Springs held for me a deep sense of wonder for its unique geographical features and the surrounding nature, without a doubt. My friendships there were important to me. Only, the larger world outside its borders was already calling me. There was a distinct restlessness growing inside me, constantly contemplating my future with anxiety. I felt myself changing, uncertain if the changes were a normal part of becoming a teenager. Life on the ranch and in our new town had been a grand adventure so far, as my Grandmother Kate had planned, I was sure. However; I was dreaming of bigger cities and I had a constant, yearning desire to create beautiful things.

CHAPTER TEN

In 1975 Fall arrived at Hot Springs in a rush of changing leaves and wind-whipped days which hinted that Winter would visit us soon. Great flocks of blackbirds murmured like black tornadoes against the bright turquoise skies. Father had decided to take the family for a drive up to Spearfish Canyon, an area in the Black Hills of sheer granite cliffs up to a thousand feet tall. He and Charles had a laugh earlier in the day, after telling me that we were going to see a kind of mutant Dall sheep. They knew I was always willing to see something new and that I was often gullible. They had me going for hours on the premise that these fluffy white sheep with magnificent scrolled horns, had evolved with legs shorter on one side as a result of walking the sides of mountains. It was mother who finally cleared it up for me.

There were endless creeks in the area and we stopped to fly-fish for a few hours. Fall was the one time of year when the golden leaves of hundreds of aspen and birch trees lit up the forests, stealing the scene from the velvet green spruce and colossal ponderosa pines.

As we were driving home, father said, "There's going to be a harvest dance at your school in a couple of weeks," as if it were big news.

"I heard that," I said from the back seat. At fifteen, this would be my first school dance.

I could see father's face in the rearview mirror as he drove. He had a contemplative look on his face.

127

"What?" I asked, wondering what silliness he and Charles were plotting now.

"Paul said he was going to ask you to go with him," my father blurted out.

"What!" I said. "I'm in ninth grade and he's already a senior."

"What?" mother repeated.

Father knew it wasn't going to fly when he said it. "I wasn't supposed to tell you. He told me he wanted to ask you to this dance coming up. You love to dance don't you? What will you say?"

Charles looked at me straight-faced. I wasn't falling for this one. "I'll say 'no'," I said. "I don't even like him. He's rude to me and ugly besides."

"That's mean, Laura. The boy's not ugly," father said.

"Ugly enough," I returned. Charles and mother were laughing.

Father looked at me in the rearview mirror as he drove. "You might give him a chance. Besides it's not like it's senior prom. He's a hard working boy and has ambition."

He was serious. "Whose side are you on anyway?" I jumped. "You know I don't like him."

Mother added her opinion. "Whatever you decide; it's your decision. The boy did get a rough start in life. Maybe with a chance to do something normal, he'll lighten up. You're too young to call it a date, so go as friends--dance with other people too. Maybe you'll have a lot of fun."

"No," I said. "It's going to be 'no', so one of you might as well tell him and save him the embarrassment."

"Tell him yourself," father returned. "I'm not involved."

I looked at Charles and he shrugged. "I'm not telling him," he said defensively.

I began to think about this more after we returned home. I had been raised to include all people in my circle of friends; even those who didn't deserve it. Grandma Kate had taught me that unkind people were the ones who needed our kindness the most. Several years had passed since then. Now, I didn't feel obligated to be kind towards anyone who offended me, and Paul had offended me many times.

When we had first left our home in Minneapolis, I remembered worrying about what kind of people we might encounter in Hot Springs. My worries had been replaced by relief to know that there were plenty of Christians, like us, as well as other religions. Even the locals who had no religion had a set of rules to live by which included neighbors helping neighbors and kindness. The Lakota spiritual beliefs coincided, and in many ways, exceeded what I had been taught in the Christian church. The Lakota Spirituality was based on the world view that everything is One and that all creation is related. This is what they meant by the phrase--Mitakuye Oyasin or 'all my relations'. They had an innate sense of being part of the greater whole. Therefore they never put themselves higher in status than any other person or part of creation.

It made sense, the more I thought about it: that everything one does to another person they also do to themselves and to the rest of the world. I was torn between trying to follow what I had learned and going with my gut instinct which was telling me to say 'no' if Paul asked me to the dance.

* * *

There was a boys' basketball game at the high school, one of three games that would be played that year between our school and the athletes from the Pine Ridge Indian Reservation. The Indians lost the game and while everyone was inside the gymnasium distracted by celebrating the win, they slipped outside, unnoticed by anyone. When the crowd began to leave and go to their cars in the parking lot, they were shocked to see their four yellow school buses had been haphazardly painted bright red. A fist fight broke out, first between the male basketball players, then other male attendees, followed by the high school girls accompanying both teams, cheerleaders and all. After much confusion, the altercation was extinguished by someone wielding a nearby water hose. The soaking wet and freezing cold Indian team boarded their bus, still angry. Our local team dispersed by car and on foot, to their homes.

The next morning, my mother sent me into town to the local bakery, adjoining the diner where townspeople gathered for coffee and to catch up on the latest gossip. As I walked past the glass picture window, I saw Old Iron Eyes sitting at a table alone reading the morning paper. Squeezing my way through the line that had formed, I took the bench seat across from him. "Did you hear about the fight at the basketball game?" I asked.

"Sounds like it was terrible. A lot of people got hurt, I think. You want coffee and a pastry?" he asked. "They're serving the Chock-Full-O-Nuts coffee again. It's the best--my favorite."

"That'd be great," I said. My parents didn't allow children to drink coffee, even teenagers, so this was a special event for me.

He motioned to the waitress. When she looked at him, he yelled out 'two more please'. She acknowledged him with a glance and disappeared into the kitchen.

"One boy on our team needed stitches in his arm," I continued. "They don't know if it was a knife or what, but they're still questioning everyone. How could someone vandalize school property like that? People in this town are gonna say a lot of bad things about 'those Sioux Indians' again because of it."

"They will, but think about it. Did they do this because they were wild Indians or were they a group of wild teenagers who thought it was going to be a prank and then it went out of control?"

I understood what he was getting at. The waitress set down the cup of coffee in front of me and I began to pour as much sugar into it as I wanted.

Old Iron Eyes grabbed the sugar jar away from me and set it out of my reach. "This is how dangerous things get started. When there are weapons involved, now it's too far. They're going to have to take their punishment...whoever did this. You'd better bet if someone takes a knife to me, they're going to eat it, from their insides, out."

"Holy crap!" I said impulsively. My eyes grew larger. "I didn't know you were so tuff," I said feeling tougher myself by half-swearing and by association.

"Let's just say the bad-asses don't mess with me," he announced. "I don't look for trouble but if it comes to me, I'm going to fix it."

I struggled to settle myself down and think more peaceably. "Hopefully, next time we'll get along better."

"I bet being a teenager, you've done things you knew could for sure get you in trouble but somehow you justified whatever your reason was, that you still were going to do it. Am I right?" He stared at me as if he were seeing right through me. I felt guilty because I was recalling when Charles and I played a rotten prank which could have gone very wrong.

I considered what I was about to tell him, wondering if I were risking a penalty for both my brother and I. "Actually, my brother and I did a pretty rotten prank this last Halloween night. If I tell you, you gotta promise to never tell my parents. They wouldn't like it."

He tilted his head curiously and leaned back. "Chances are your parents probably know what you did. Kids think parents aren't aware, but you must remember, they were kids once too. It's likely they did something similar before, but if that's your condition for telling, go ahead." He lowered his voice and looked around conspiratorially. "You have my word. I won't tell." He folded his arms, waiting.

Leaning in towards the center of the table, I lowered my voice as much as possible. "Well, on last Halloween night Charles and I had already begged candy from just about everyone in town. Our sacks were full and it was time to go home. But, Charles gets the idea that we should venture outside the city limits to Jiggs' place...do something mischievous to get back at him for all the nasty things he's said to us over the past year. At first, I said I can't, then Charles went on saying stuff like, 'Not to mention everyone he's cheated on money deals...You can't be a sissy your whole life, Laura...Let's give him a taste of his own shit...' and on and on, right?"

"Go on..."

"So, we talked it over--agreed to not take it as far as damaging his property or to personally hurt him in any way. Even as we arrived at his house, I didn't know what we were going there to do. As we sneaked up to the backside of the property, the lights were on inside the house. At first, we decided to string toilet paper up into his pear tree. Charles had obviously thought out his plan before telling me--he had three rolls stuffed down in his candy sack. He said by doing this, Jiggs would know for sure it was us who did it, without us having to get caught in the act, in which case he'd tell our parents. Realizing that adults always side with other adults in these types of situations, we couldn't afford for him to catch us in the act. As we're getting ready to toss the toilet paper rolls up into the tree, the back door opens and here Jiggs comes walking down the steps carrying a flashlight. We bent down low in the underbrush and watched him tread out to his old wooden outhouse."

"He still uses that old thing?" Old Iron Eyes cringed and glanced around the diner. "Even *we* have sewer hookup at our house."

"He uses it all right," I answered, suppressing an eruption of laughter now seeing the scene once more in my mind. "So, he comes walking out to this outhouse, which my brother says sits right over top of a big hole of..."

"Yeah. I get it, so get on with it already," Old Iron Eyes was already starting to giggle like a child.

"Charles says to me, 'Let's tip the house over on its door. The only way the mean old bastard can get out then would be crawling out the bottom of the seat while avoiding a fall into the poo-hole.' Well...he didn't have to encourage me any. We sneaked up behind it, with me sniggering like crazy and Charles shushing me the whole way. We waited till we heard him making noises inside like he was settled. Then, we shoved that house right over on its own door while he sat on the wooden seat. I was running way ahead of Charles who had stopped to look back. He told me when he caught up that all he could see was Jiggs' big Halloween moon shining in the dark, scrambling around and then crawling through the open bottom of the outhouse. We ran about a mile, laughing 'til our sides hurt, until we reached the city limits again. Then, we walked the rest of the way home. Charles was so glad that I finally did something outside the rules—that I supported him in his plan."

"Hrrraaahhhhh!" Old Iron Eyes tried talking through his unruly laughter, "I'll never be able to look at that man again without busting out laughing."

I looked around the diner and noticed several people staring over at us. Old Iron Eyes tried to straighten himself out for my sake. "That was mean, you know."

I said defiantly, "I really don't care," and smiled proudly.

* * *

There I was at the high school dance with Paul, looking around a room packed with awkward teenagers like myself wondering who might ask me to dance. He had promptly left me sitting alone while he walked outside with some friends, presumably to smoke. I wondered how I had let myself be guilted into coming. Even in the car on the way to the dance, I had nothing to talk to him about except for my parents' businesses. The turquoise blue wrap dress I wore was much fancier than anything I saw around me. Many of the boys wore jeans and the girls' dresses would have been better suited for a square dance. I fidgeted nervously with my shoes for a moment then headed off to the bathroom. If I passed by the rows of chairs, I thought, maybe one of the boys seated would actually ask me to dance. I made sure I strolled by very slowly and stopped to talk to any girl I knew from school. After reaching the bathroom with no offer to dance, I considered exiting the back door and walking home. It was only three miles. I would tell one of the chaperones where I was going, so they could tell Paul.

Paul returned and told me several of his friends there were bored and were leaving the dance. There was a party at someone's house and the parents weren't going to be home. "We're going to meet them there," he said, taking me by the arm and moving me towards the door.

"I can't do that," I argued. We were standing outside with the music beating in the background. "My mother said I have to be here, not another place. What if something happens, she wouldn't even know where to begin looking for me," I explained. "Besides, I don't think it's a smart idea that we go to this house if the guy's parents aren't home."

Paul pointed to a group of four friends who were pouring out of the entrance doors. "These are friends I've known my whole life," he said, motioning to them. The kids had gathered around. They were all looking at me expectantly.

"I was thinking about walking home, anyway," I said. I stepped out of the group and released myself from his hands. "You go ahead and have fun. I'll just walk home."

"No you won't," he said, pointing at me. "No way Monroe's daughter rides with me to the dance, then walks home and he jumps my ass for it at work the next day."

I was getting angry now and I raised my voice so that he understood me. "My father will have no problem with me walking home alone. I've hiked in the forest for hours alone and he doesn't worry."

Paul's friends were whooping and hollering, saying things like "forget about her" and "are you coming or not?" Suddenly he clenched his jaw and looked into my eyes. "You're a spoiled one-way little bitch," he said. "With no manners. Walk home then. Don't expect me to take your dumb ass anywhere again." Behind him, his friends were looking at me and laughing. The girls cozied into the arms of their boyfriends and one of them repeated "bitch".

I turned around and headed back into the dance until they had cleared the parking lot. After a few minutes, I told one of the chaperones that I was going to walk back to my house. She gave me a telephone number to call when I arrived so they could confirm when I made it home. As I headed out the entrance doors once again, I wondered why I had ever agreed to go with Paul.

As I walked home, I breathed in the fresh clean air which had the crisp unmistakable smell of certain snowfall before morning. Fall was my favorite time of year, not only for the beauty of the aspens and birch trees, but the boldness of color changes before Winter settled upon us. The lamp-lit sidewalk into town was uneven concrete with cobblestone or brick in places. I had never noticed how intricately laid it was or how the bricks were not consistently red, but a mottled red. I wasn't sure if it was my happiness after being released from the dance, or a new ability to see treasure in an evening stroll, but the night had captured me completely. Every brilliant star in the darkened sky, every burgeoning apple tree lining the sidewalk, even the sound of the river moving in the distance turned a simple walk into a thing of beauty. This wasn't the first time I had felt myself more connected to my surroundings, but it was the first time I really drank it in, savoring the affect it had upon me.

Rounding the corner near my parent's general store, I walked up to the massive old double-doored barn which was rumored to be over a hundred years old. The thick grey wooden exterior had open holes which used to be knots. During the day Charles and I had looked into those knots trying to see inside. We could only make out the remains of old farming equipment. Suddenly, I saw crazy Mrs. Haskell bent over and digging around the edges of the structure.

"Mrs. Haskell?" I said. "Is that you?"

"Last time I checked it was me," she answered. She stood up and moved out under the street light. "What's Laura Hansen doing walking around at night?" She carried a hand spade in one hand. The other hand was clutching freshly dug-up flower bulbs.

"I was at the dance at the school and decided to walk home."

She hid the hand holding the bulbs behind her back. "Didn't have a date to drive ya?" she asked, not looking at me directly.

"I went with Paul, but he left with friends."

"Probably smart of ya," she said. "If you were really smart you would notta' gone with him."

"That's true," I said. "I don't really like him anyway." I started to continue on my way. "Have a nice evening, Mrs. Haskell. Feels like snow before morning, doesn't it?"

"That boy is not good," she said as I kept walking past her. "Put his mother in that barn. He's who did it." She saw me slowing my pace to listen to her and looked directly into my eyes in a way that made me very uncomfortable. "Don't dance with him," she said.

She had never given me the creeps before but this time I suddenly had a cold shiver up my spine. I moved away at a quicker pace now, hoping that she wouldn't follow me and chat more. The lights were on at the store in the distance. I hurried up the last stretch of sidewalk and dashed inside. After phoning the chaperone at the school as promised, I quickly explained to my mother why I had left the dance. I also told her about my conversation with Mrs. Haskell.

"Sorry you didn't have fun," was all she said. She didn't seem concerned over what Paul had said to me or that Mrs. Haskell had given me the creeps.

CHAPTER ELEVEN

The day came when I was officially invited to the great Pine Ridge Reservation by Kills Enemy and some of the other women in her family, including her teenaged niece, Mary. It was my first visit there and I was eager to see Mary. They picked me up in the late morning and seven of us girls and women traveled, in one car, over sixty miles to the reservation. That evening, we ended up sitting around a great outdoor bonfire in a circle of a dozen or so people, which consisted of mostly Indians, an elderly tourist couple and me.

"Wey yah, Wei yah, wei yah, wey yah," ....the strong male voices sang out together repeating the same melody over and over again. An Indian I had never met before this night, Teddy Walking Hawk, beat the taut skin drum with a padded stick, his eyes closed.

Closing my eyes too, I absorbed the beauty of their voices better. When the men's voices paused, the women's voices took over with the same "wei yah, wei yah, wei yah," only slower and softer. I could tell this group had sung together many times before. If there is a true definition of musical and societal harmony, this was it.

Mary and I huddled together watching darkness fall deeper and deeper over the mountain. By the end of that night, nearly fifty other people, mostly Indians, sat in clusters around four separate bonfires. The faces in our group, shone with a light illuminated beyond the fires and the moon. We were Mitakuye Oyasin—all one relation.

I whispered to Mary, "Do you have a pocket knife with you?" knowing that she carried a little white handled one in her purse.

"I've got it. Are you thinking the same as me?" She was taking the knife out of her pocket and wiping the blade on the lining of her jacket.

"That's not going to sterilize it," I pointed out. "But, what the hell do we care?" I was feeling free and invincible.

"Right. What the hell do we care?" She giggled at our swearing. "I'll go first." With that, she punched a tiny hole in the palm of her right hand at a spot below the thumb.

I took the pocket knife from her and punched a similar hole in my left palm about a quarter of an inch below my thumb. It stung a bit and the blood rose quickly to the surface.

We pressed our palms together and raised our hands up high into the night sky. "Blood sisters forever," Mary said to no one but me. "Whatever happens in our lives, we're in it together 'til the end."

Keeping the pressure on our palms, I announced, "Blood sisters for life. I'll always be there for you--always, Mary."

A bright thin red line trickled down our coat sleeves as we grasped hands for a while longer. Outside the circle, Kills Enemy walked by. She stopped and peered into the circle. Bending in towards us, she saw our hands pressed together and a slight trail of blood. She whispered, "Silly girls. I hope you don't think this is Lakota tradition. You cut yourself for nothing." She continued on her way with a shake of her head and waving her hands overhead.

"We don't care," Mary said to me. "Do we?"

"No," I answered. "It's as real to us as anything."

That evening, we slept in large white canvas tipis that were painted in traditional Lakota motifs. They were set up in a circle around the churning bonfire. On the inside, there were woven blankets spread out, carpeting the ground underneath. Many mismatched star quilts and down comforters were also inside, around the perimeter, to keep us warm. I propped my head up on the pillow I had brought along and watched the churning flames for hours until the last coals dwindled into complete darkness.

Late the next morning, Old Iron Eyes showed up in his old red Ford truck. Mother had sent him to pick me up and drive me back to our family's ranch. I was still singing the repetitive songs I heard around the campfire the night before. Old Iron Eyes would turn his head toward the driver's window now and then trying to hide that he was laughing. My singing voice had always been off-key, but my heart was really in it. After about thirty minutes of it, I could see that these incessant songs were wearing on him. Still, he never told me to stop.

About twenty miles before we reached Hot Springs, Old Iron Eyes made a stop at a roadside hardware store. He was that kind of person who would go into a store with nothing in mind to buy and come out with several things that he didn't know he needed. My parents called that impulse buying. In fact, they had trained me well to make our store displays in such a way as to capture exactly these kinds of shoppers. Old Iron Eyes was an impulse buyer and that made him happy. I wandered around the store too, looking at merchandise until at last, he was at the check-out counter buying a shovel and a can of Chock-Full-O-Nuts coffee.

"What're you getting that for?" I asked him, pointing at the shovel.

"I'm getting you guys a shovel for your father to keep at the ranch," he said. "Every time we look for one out there, we can't find the right one that I can use. I'll put this nice heavy one where I can find it. If I need to borrow it for my house, I'll come and get it."

It made sense in Old Iron Eyes' world to keep a variety of things he owned at other people's houses. "We have those at our store," I said. "Why don't you buy it there?"

"You don't have this one," he returned. "See this red handle? See the rubber grip?" He handed the shovel to me while he finished paying.

As we neared the car, distracted in our conversation, we encountered a western diamond-back snake! It skipped straight toward us, its rattles quivering with malice. Its head was standing up as it inched dangerously nearer.

Old Iron Eyes yelled out to me in a deep baritone voice I hadn't heard before. "Kill it! Chop its head off!"

Since I was holding the shovel, I did—and with one vicious slice! After my knees stopped going rubbery, I walked a few more steps to the car, opened the door and dropped myself onto the seat. I felt as if I might pass out

Old Iron Eyes said nothing, but looked straight ahead down the road as he turned the key to start up the car. Finally, he let out a long sigh. "That was close," he said, pulling the car back onto the road.

"Close for you? Close for me!" I shrieked. I had my own arms wrapped around myself for comfort.

He said, "When a snake appears in a place where you didn't expect to see him, sometimes it's a sign either of a pending death or significant change."

"I don't want to hear any of that right now," I said. "It was nearly my death back there."

"You weren't going to die, Laura," he laughed as his hand made the motion of a snake striking at me. "I wasn't going to let anything happen to you."

"I can't believe you made me do that," I said, genuinely annoyed. "I'm telling Mrs. Iron Eyes that you really are crazy."

"She already knows," he laughed. He shook his finger towards me as he drove. "You needed to do that."

"No. I didn't," I said. For the rest of the ride home, I stared silently out the window watching the grasses pass by alongside the road. I felt exhausted and little bit proud of myself.

* * *

It was early morning on a Saturday in 1975. Our family had stayed off the ranch at the little apartment behind our commercial property in town. I was awakened first to the sound of the telephone ringing, then to the sound of the television right outside my room. Neither of my parents watched much television, and they had raised us to watch it only for special programs and for nightly newscasts. I wondered why they would be up so early with it on. As I forced myself to wake up, I could also hear cupboards opening and closing, then the sound of coffee gurgling in the tall percolator. My room was dark, so I pulled the curtains open only to realize that it was still dark outside too.

My parents were usually early risers, but recently, I couldn't recall when I had last found them up before daylight. Putting my slippers on and wrapping my robe around me, I trudged down the stairs. "You guys are up early," I noted.

"Quiet!" father snapped. "Go back to bed."

"Monroe," mother said. "Don't get uptight. She doesn't know what's going on."

"What's going on?" I asked then.

Suddenly, Charles was also moving up alongside me. "Whaa..," he started.

Dad cut in. "Everybody shut up and we'll all know."

Charles and I backed up substantially out of my parent's field of vision and watched the television. There was a special news report running about an apparent gunfight at the Pine Ridge Reservation. Two FBI agents were dead and several other people had been injured. For the rest of that day, my parents stayed on the telephone and took visits in town, discussing this happening with everyone we knew.

Two days after the shootings, Old Iron Eyes pulled his truck into the back of the commercial buildings where the museum and general store sat divided by a swath of a lawn. I peered out from the living room window to watch him. He got out of the truck and pulled the thick rubber tarp off the top of the bed. His sense of order had always fascinated me, how even the simple folding of a cloth tarp was done with precision. He dropped the tailgate down and slid several boxes forward to its edge. I heard the back door slam and saw father walk out to him. Old Iron Eyes put his arms out for their usual embrace, but my father didn't put his arms out. Instead, he stood back several feet to talk to Iron Eyes. I couldn't make out what they were saying, but both their bodies had stiffened and gained an inch in height.

After about a minute or two, Old Iron Eyes had repositioned the boxes in the truck bed, slammed the tailgate, fastened the tarp over the top and was driving away. His hand waved goodbye out of the window, but my dad had already turned his back and was walking toward the back entrance to the store.

Knowing Iron Eyes would slow down for the

potholes near the middle of the road, then reach the stop sign shortly thereafter, I thought I might have a chance to catch him. I dashed out the back door, running barefooted through the rough grass, jumping over the corner rhubarb patch and circling around the trash cans which the coyotes had messed up again. My foot caught the edge of one of the lids and it whipped up hitting my leg, tripping me up. I fell face first into the dirt, sliding into some of the trash that had been strewn around. Sprinting again towards a length of fencing where our neighbor, Mr. Haakanson, kept his horse, I looked for the hole. It wasn't big enough for the horse to escape through but I knew it was plenty big enough for me.

Slipping though the fence easily, I ran full speed across the pasture, seeing the truck slowly bumping along the dirt road to my right. It occurred to me that I had no idea what I was going to say. All I knew for certain was that I needed to talk to him. Whatever my father had said, I could explain because he hadn't been himself lately and could be easily angered. The incident at the Pine Ridge Reservation had put the whole town on edge. No matter how the local politics and details of the incident turned out, I knew in my heart that my family's friendships, shared for these few short years, meant everything to us.

At last, I reached the end of the pasture. The stop sign stood on the other side. I grabbed the edge of the large swinging gate and swung myself over it, not wanting to waste a moment with the latch, and waited for Old Iron Eyes' truck to appear around the bend. A moment later, he drove up and smiled seeing me waiting there, sweating, out of breath and dirt covering my clothes.

I spoke first. "Why didn't you stay?"

He shut the motor off. "Monroe is worried about politics right now. It's best we wait for a better time," he said.

"Because someone else shot those government people we shouldn't be seen with you? You agree with him then?"

"I agree and I understand, Laura. Nobody knows for sure what has really happened. We have to wait for the story to come out all the way. I think it might never be known. One thing is certain. It's not over. People are tired of being threatened on these reservations, forgotten by the US government with false promises and then, Indians pushed to desperation. I can't get into that conversation with your father because it's natural for him to only see what happened to his people. But, desperation makes people do things they wouldn't do otherwise."

"How long did he tell you to stay away?" I asked, standing up closer to the window. I had to follow whatever the adults said to do, but my heart was breaking.

"He wants me to stay in contact by telephone for now and that'll be enough. He believes the tourist business is going to drop off, maybe even halfway over this, so he won't buy stuff from us until he sees what will come next."

Tears ran down my face. "That's terrible," I said. "This is breaking my heart, so much." I was both angry and embarrassed that I couldn't stay stronger in my emotions.

Old Iron Eyes took his big thumb and pressed the tears away from my eyes, first on one side of my face, then cradling my chin, again on the other. "Listen to me," he said. "Everything's alright. You and I, or your father haven't done anything. We're only involved in the way that we care about other people who suffer from what happened. I'm safe. My family is safe and your family's safe. We can be grateful."

"Alright," I said bravely, pulling my chin up deliberately. "Please, tell Kills Enemy that I hope to see her after this waiting time is over. Can you bring her to see me the next time you come? If she wants to."

"It's only if she wants to," he repeated smiling. "I couldn't make her do anything and look how big I am." He slapped his bulging waist to make it jiggle for my amusement.

"Quit!" I laughed. Moving closer, pushing my head uncomfortably into the open window, I wrapped an arm around his neck with a half-hug. I lingered purposely in the awkwardness it just to feel again his wonderful long silky black hair that smelled of a perfumed shampoo. "Bye for now, then. Give lots of love to Mrs. Iron Eyes from me, please. I'm gonna say prayers for you and Pine Ridge families," I said, still holding on.

I pried my hands off, folded them together and pushed them to my chest. Without another word, he turned the engine on, pulled down on the gear shift and moved the truck forward. I watched until he reached the end of the road, then I turned back towards the pasture to walk the fence line home. I felt confused and helpless, like I didn't understand anything anymore. It would be many years later before the magnitude of what had happened really sunk in. All I knew on that day was that a deep sadness fell over me like an unwelcome shadow of unfairness. When I got home, I went straight to my room, climbed into bed and stayed there until dinnertime.

When I awoke and walked downstairs; my mother was sitting at the kitchen desk talking to someone on the telephone. After a few minutes, I realized it was Sheriff Basset. He had called to tell her that Charles and another boy had been in a fight. The parents of the other boy insisted that Charles should be arrested, but Sheriff Basset had made him apologize instead. Now, he was delivering Charles back home. Mother hung up the telephone and began to cry.

"I knew I should've been watching him closer," she started. "He's getting into trouble." She was breaking down with every word. "I was already upset about the trouble at Pine Ridge. Now this."

"It's alright," I said, putting my hand on her shoulder. "Boys just like to fight. Pretty soon, he'll realize it's not fun anymore--hopefully before anyone gets hurt. He must be scared thinking of the trouble he's in when father finds out."

Mother looked up into my eyes. She wasn't only upset over Charles. "Your dad is down at the bar again with Paul. I don't know what they're thinking either, honestly."

It seemed that my parents might be having some kind of fighting too and this worried me. "Why don't you tell Paul that he's your employee too and that you don't like him taking father there?"

"Your father's a grown man. He should quit this himself. I shouldn't have to go through this while we struggle to build these businesses. It's my hard work every day, same as anyone." She began to cry uncontrollably. I wrapped my arms around her in a comforting way, but I honestly didn't know what else to do.

Sheriff Basset knocked on the door and I answered it. There Charles stood, dirty and with a ripped shirt. "You'd better go see mother right away," I advised. "She's in the kitchen crying."

"Because I got in a fight?" he asked, grimacing. "I feel double bad now." I could see that he meant it.

"That and other stuff," I hinted.

Charles looked at me for explanation, but I turned to Sheriff Basset instead. "You need to see my mother?" I asked him. I didn't want to say anything about my father and Paul drinking.

"Tell her I'll stop by the store and see her tomorrow morning. It's wasn't really as bad as she imagines. It's just boys being boys."

I saw the dried blood on Charles' face and I knew it hadn't been a trivial fight. As he walked towards the kitchen I said goodbye to the sheriff. At the door, I put in a good word for Charles. "My brother likes to fight," I said. "But, inside he's a good guy. You've been around our family for a long time."

"I know," he said, as he turned and left.

I headed back to my bedroom instead of the kitchen. I wanted to give mother the privacy to talk to Charles alone.

* * *

For my sixteenth birthday my parents asked me what I wanted most as a present. Without even knowing who would take me there or where I would stay, I said I wanted to go to the reservation again, but this time for a whole week.

"We can't let you do that," my mother answered immediately. "It's way too dangerous. Do you realize the high murder rate there is one of the highest in the United States? Not to mention what happened with the government agents, less than a year ago. What about their view of outsiders now? Not all of them are friends."

My father interjected, "I think she'd be okay with the people we know there. Besides, many people think these murders are a result of the corrupt commission set up by the government to handle reservation affairs. It's not every Indian there but rather the head of affairs, Mr. Wilson, who's at the root of this turmoil, for his own financial and political gain. A sort of underground movement's underway now that's helping to keep the peace. I think it's settled down quite a lot."

I had never heard my father say anything even remotely anti-Government, but I sensed now that he was disappointed in what he was hearing from his contacts and in the news. In the past, he used to read newspaper articles aloud to my mother as if they were the gospel truth. Recently, I had watched him take a pencil and outline certain sentences or paragraphs and put a question mark in the column or even mark out what he thought was wrong.

My mother looked at me in a pleading way. "Can't you invite school friends over and have cake and ice cream? We'll play music and dance and have a bunch of good food, whatever you like."

Charles walked in just then. "She's sixteen years old. That's past the cake and ice cream days. Everybody knows the only thing Laura's interested in is the Indian culture and making fancy clothes or jewelry. It's not like she's going to ask for a new doll. Besides, I'll go with her if you guys want. I can keep her safe."

"You're going to keep her safe," mother repeated cynically. "Because you're always thinking about what's safe, right?"

"Sometimes I am," he answered. Then, he added, "More than I have before."

I was gaining ground. "These people are my friends. I had a great time when I got to stay there before. Please?"

She wasn't budging, so I focused on father. "We can celebrate my birthday here when I get back," I pleaded. "You did ask me what it was that *I* really wanted. I need to go there."

"Need?" My mother looked desperately toward my father for support. I could see she had run out of argument against the idea.

153

"It's fine," he said without further discussion. "Besides, we can ask Old Iron Eye's relatives to look after her. He must have fifty aunts, cousins, sisters and so forth down there. They can show her around and include her in whatever they normally do. What better way to learn than by going there and seeing how they're living?"

It didn't take much to arrange my birthday wish and Charles went with me. I spent the most memorable birthday, staying between several houses of Old Iron Eyes' and Kills Enemy's relatives on the Pine Ridge Reservation. There were unmistakable signs of tensions in their community. At one house where I was staying, police came to the door and asked if they had seen a certain man. After talking for a few minutes, he left and we all continued with our visit.

Charles got invited by the teenage boys in the neighborhood to participate in some Indian games. I reminded him that the rules of him being home before dark, applied here same as they did at home. "Our parents are going to be phoning after dinnertime and you'd better be here," I warned him. "Remember that you were coming along to keep me safe, not for me to track you down."

"Gotcha," he said and dashed out the front door. He returned before dark as promised. However; I found out later about the games the Indians had lined up. Charles mentioned one they called 'knife rolling'. The older kids competed in a contest whereby they would be tied to a skinny log at their legs and chest, rolling downhill, knife-in-hand. The competitor who made the most knife marks into the log before it reached the end of the hill was the winner.

I was furious. I could only think of what might have happened. "Are you nuts!?" I yelled. "You're older than me. You're supposed to be thinking; then you went to do this? I should tell father."

"I wanted to participate," he said. "That's why we came; to do what they do."

Charles had become the master of convoluting things back around on anyone's argument to try to make them second-guess their own valid position. "You didn't have to," I stated simply."

"Too late now," he said. He spread his arms out and scanned himself all over for a second. "And look, nothing but a couple bruises. Not a scratch on me."

When I was together with the Lakota family we often prayed several times in a day. They said prayers at sunrise, prayers before eating to give thanks and prayers before going into any sort of battle. That next morning during a community worship service, I prayed extra hard for Charles. The locals were praying mostly for the wisdom to stand up against what that was oppressing them at that time. Watching a Lakota pray at sunrise was the most pure and beautiful thing; their grateful hands held high, almost capturing the sun in their silhouette. Seeing their reverence and wishes for a better life, I had become more grateful for simple things—like food or clothing or my warm bed at night. Even a single beautiful wildflower held more meaning to me now than before.

I returned from my trip to the reservation to find that my New York City uncle, Arne Hansen, was going to be at our house in a matter of hours. He was bringing with him my cousin, Thomas. The contrast between the people I had just visited and the people who were coming to visit us now, couldn't have been greater.

Since we had moved to Hot Springs, every visitor we had ever hosted, wanted to go to see Mount Rushmore. It was 1976, the year of America's bicentennial celebration and the entrance to the monument was decked out in pathways lined with flags. The Fife and Drum Corps was even making scheduled special appearances to play old marching national songs there. I considered myself as true a patriot as any of them, but after the sixth time accompanying our visitors there, I had had enough of seeing the mountain of presidents' heads.

Uncle Arne was delightful. He was American born, but Norwegian by heritage, through and through. Even though he was third generation in this country, he spoke Norwegian fluently. It was always an upbeat atmosphere in the household when he was there. His visit helped us all to slow down a little and enjoy good food and storytelling for hours on end.

Toward the end of his visit, father invited Paul out to the ranch house for a big dinner to be cooked only by the men. Charles was recruited to help too. Mother and I were looking forward to being served whatever it was they were making.

Uncle Arne set the table while the other men manned the grill. Charles ran in and out of the house carrying supplies. A few minutes before dinnertime, Paul showed up carrying a bag of vegetables father had asked him to pick up on his way out to the ranch.

I happened around the corner of the backside of the house while Paul and Charles were chopping vegetables on the heavy outdoor table. There were carrots flying and lettuce being shredded and tossed into a large red plastic bowl. Apparently, they were having a contest to see who could chop through their assigned vegetables the fastest. In the end, Paul won.

Charles set his knife down and said, "If I'd had only lettuce to shred, I could've beat you easily."

"Don't be a poor sport now Charlie Boy," Paul teased. "You know, I've got at least two years knife experience ahead of you."

"Probably sticking it in some poor bastards back," Charles said. "Doesn't prove anything anyway, except that you're a half a slave in the kitchen."

"I'm the slave of no one," Paul said. As he said it he motioned with the knife he was holding towards my brother, as if it were an extension of his finger.

"You might keep that blade pointed away from me if you want to keep your nuts," Charles said. "Didn't your mother ever teach you it isn't polite to point a knife blade at someone?"

Mother was passing by and stopped immediately. "I'm sure she raised him well," she said.

For a moment I wondered why she cut in to their conversation, then I remembered the way that Paul's mother had left them and was later found in a burned out building. No doubt, Charles hadn't thought about that before he spoke.

"Your mother probably took a good look at you when you were born and wondered if she could send you back," Charles laughed.

"I'll send your stupid ass back," Paul said still pointing the knife towards Charles, but now raising it higher. "Don't ever talk about my mother!"

Mother walked up behind him and snatched the knife out of his grip. "You'll not point a knife at my son!" she said fiercely. "And, Charles," she continued, looking at him disappointed. "You should think before you speak. Paul lost his mother tragically. Remember?"

"Oh yeah," Charles said stepping toward Paul conciliatory. "I did forget. Sorry, guy. You accept my apology?"

"Forget it," Paul said, handing him the bowl. "Here; carry the salad out to the table."

Mother and I followed Charles back out to the front of the house and we sat down at the long table. After a while Paul rounded the corner from the back and joined father and Uncle Arne.

We were all in the midst of enjoying the dinner when Paul pulled a gallon jug of whiskey out of a bag. He took up one of the water glasses off the table and poured it half-full. He then passed the whiskey to my father who did the same. Mother tried to glare with disapproval, but my father avoided her gaze. Uncle Arne poured himself one about one-quarter full.

"A toast to the ole Navy boy," Arne said. With that the three of them raised their glasses. "Skål!" Arne shouted.

"Skål," father and Paul repeated in unison.

"Where's mine?" Charles asked.

"Nice try," mother snapped at him. "Not a chance."

"So, tell us about the old Navy days," Paul prompted my father. "What did you do in your time there?"

"It's not something I talk much about. Those memories aren't always pretty," father answered.

Charles spoke up. "My dad saw a lot of bad incidents. Saw a lot of men lose it."

"Is that right?" Paul urged. "Must be tough to live with pictures in your head? I heard some guys come back and keep reliving the sounds and dying 'round them like it was happening all over again. Many go completely bonkers, out of their minds just from memories. Wouldn't catch me thinking 'bout shit like that. I'd do my thing and be over it."

"If a man hasn't been there, he doesn't know that," mother said to Paul. "Try to keep the language clean, if you don't mind," she said to the entire group. "Let's not let the whiskey talk through you guys." She was seriously peeved and I could see it.

Paul continued. "Those memories gotta' be a burden for anyone. Can't imagine things you must've seen. I don't think I could live with myself, knowing a

159

certain number of women and children died too, at my hand. You've got a will of iron. That's for sure."

Father took a deep breath before pouring whisky up to the rim of his glass. He refilled Arne's who was sitting beside him, in the same manner.

"I think you're trying to put me to sleep," Arne said with a laugh that broke the tension. "That business about us Norwegians liking to drink is just a rumor—at least for me. I'm a soft Viking who gets sick easily on the stuff."

"Don't be a puss," Charles said, delighted at including himself in the scene. He lifted his glass of tea and said, "Skål! Drink up. Be real men." Father and Arne toasted one another silently and drank.

"Real men don't have to drink to prove anything," mother chimed in. "Real men aren't so easily steered." Seeing her plate was finished she stood and carried it into the house.

Mrs. Biermann stood taking her plate too.

Paul shoveled in another mouthful of food while reaching for the whiskey. "A feisty wife you got there, Monroe. I see where Laura gets her spunk. Her mother's one of those who goes silent until she's mad types too. They'll get you..."

"Aw," she's not mad, father said waving his hand. "Just not exactly social these days."

"What do you mean?" I said. "Mother's social. She likes being with people as much as anyone. Maybe she's not happy seeing her husband..." Then

Mrs. Biermann took me by the elbow and stood me up away from my chair.

"Us ladies are going inside now," she announced, lifting my plate off the table and forcing it into my hands. "We wanna talk about the finer things in life. Don't we Laura?"

I caught the hint just as quickly as she had removed me from the table and I hurried to keep the pace alongside her. When we reached the walkway, Mrs. Biermann whispered, "You almost got in the soup there, young lady. Your father shouldn't hear corrections from you. Your mother's gonna have plenty to say after the guests have left today, dear. You needn't get involved."

I sat inside with my mother and Mrs. Biermann watching out the large picture window while the men and Charles sat outside. Now and then, we could hear the conversation getting louder. Uncle Arne was the first one to come into the house and head for the guest bedroom. Then, a few hours later, we heard Paul's truck starting up and watched him pull away down the long driveway. When father and Charles walked through the front door, my mother abruptly stood up and escorted Mrs. Biermann back out of it. I retreated to my room.

After a few minutes, Charles poked his head inside my doorway. "Father's mad at Paul."

"He should be," I said. "Mother's mad at him too I think."

"No. I mean he sat there while Paul kept poking at him about Navy days and stuff. Saying things like 'I couldn't live with myself if I saw the stuff you did' and crap like that. It was Uncle Arne who finally told him to shut up."

This made me like Uncle Arne even more. "Cool," I said. "I'm going to sleep now."

"Okay, Sis," Charles said. "Tomorrow we're going to the cave, remember?"

I'd been looking forward to Charles' Cave since the day he showed it to me. We had prepared a duffel bag of supplies that we thought we might need to explore it. I had checked out a couple books from the library at school about the early days of cave exploration which I had been reading aloud to Charles in the evenings. The books in our library were generally outdated, but I was comfortable that we knew more than we did the first time.

The next morning, as soon as our parents' car reached the end of the driveway, Charles and I headed out. They would be gone for the entire day giving us plenty of time to reach the cave, explore it thoroughly and then be home before they returned. The fear I felt on our first short journey inside the cave had now been replaced by an intense excitement. I imagined ancient cave paintings or even diamond, lurking in the channels beyond the first room. Getting past the deep hole was going to be tricky, but Charles and I had decided that the ledge was wide enough. We had both psyched ourselves up in advance to overcome the natural urge we would likely have to look down. Charles told me if I looked down into it, I could become dizzy and fall in.

As we walked up to the first divide between the prairie and the forested hills, a flock of birds scattered from the underbrush. Startled, I jumped to one side and stood still watching them take flight. Charles laughed at me and before he could say it, I said it myself, "I know," I chided myself. "What a puss!"

"I wasn't going to say it, Laura," he said. "Don't be so darn skittish all the time. We're going to have a great exploring of this cave, so stop worrying."

We climbed up to the crest of one hill, then up another and another, then winding down and around the base of a steep incline, we stopped. "It seems longer than before," I said. "Are you sure you remember the way?"

"This is it," Charles assured me.

"I'm following you," was all I could say. I was out of breath and we had another mile to go. At last, we reached the place where Charles' half-moon of rocks marked the entrance to the cave.

Once inside, we took out our flashlights and wrapped sturdy nylon ropes around our shoulders, just like the drawings in the books. We passed the narrow ledge without incident and chose to follow the larger of two passages off to the right. It wound back for about half the length of a football field. There were no diamonds, but the walls were quartz in places and Charles said the dark grey vein running through the rock was actually raw silver. Most of the cave was limestone which we both easily identified from our earth science classes at school.

It was at least ten degrees colder underground that it had been on the outside. The further we traveled, the more cold and damp I felt. Charles moved further away from me and found a second branch off of our passage. From the other side of the cave from where I stood I heard him say, "Don't breathe in too deeply. Looks like bat shit here." I followed his voice into the adjoining space and looked at the black residue on the dusty floor. I looked up expecting to see hanging bats and marveled at the calcite crystals on the upper portion of the walls. "Doesn't calcite form where there used to be dripping water once?" I asked.

"Never heard that," Charles said. "Is that true?"

"Don't know where I heard that. I dunno," I said still staring at them. "It's not exactly diamonds, but they sure are pretty."

"Mrs. Biermann told me that out of seventy or so calcite crystal caves in the world, all but three of them are in the Black Hills," Charles said.

"Can we take some?" I asked him.

"What for?"

"Maybe, I can drill small holes...use them for beads."

"You and your beads. Why don't you try to make bat shit beads?" he said, sneering at me in a goofy way.

"Never mind," I said. "Can we go now? There's nothing else here."

"Okay," he said. "We should only check out a section at a time. Save a little mystery for later."

We headed back out of the winding passageway and stopped at the large hole near the entry. I went first across the ledge and waited on the other side for Charles. "Hey," he said, shining his flashlight down into the hole. "There's something here on this ledge."

"No way," I said. "What does it look like?"

"A black shiny diamond," he said. "About the size of my fist."

Before I could say anything he was inching near the hole and trying to find footing on the irregular pillars rising up out of it. "Don't step down on those," I cautioned. "They could break off and you'll fall down in there." I was getting scared.

He was already wrapped in a tied-off rope and lowering himself down into the hole. Only the top of his head was visible. "It's just about a foot away," he said cautiously. And then I heard him slip and rocks powdered off into the dark hole below.

I laid down on my stomach and pointed my shaking flashlight inside the rim, hoping to see my brother still attached to his rope.

"Did you think I fell down in there?" he said. He was standing on a wide ledge that jutted out over the hole. "It's perfectly stable right here. Look at this." The rough black rock he held up in his hand sparkled even in the faint lighting. "Here's your diamond, Sis."

I said, getting angry at his impudence. "I don't care right now. I want you to get out of there."

He milled around for a few seconds more and then yelled back up to me. "I can't grab onto anything, Laura. The part that held me before is broken off now. I'm stuck on the ledge."

"Don't joke about it," I said. "I'm getting scared. You'd tell me if you were kidding?"

"Look Laura. I'm not kidding. I really mean it. I'd throw you my rope, but you can't pull my weight up. There's too big a chance you'd cause me to fall back down in here, possibly into the hole."

I was trembling now. "Oh, God! What're we gonna do?" I felt tears rushing into my eyes and I was unable to think clearly.

"We're not going to panic," Charles said. "I'm going to stand here perfectly still and you're going to run back down the hill, up and over the next two, just the way we came. Call somebody to help."

"Like our parents?" I asked through my tears, trying not to let him see how upset I was. "What if I can't reach them at the store?"

"Try first to go get Iron Eyes," he said. "He'll be at the lodge. Hurry it up please. It's gonna be dark soon and it's gonna get colder."

"Oh shit, oh shit, oh shit," I said, truly panicking now. "I'm going to get Old Iron Eyes, Charles. I'll be back before an hour is up. Just stay there and I promise I'll get you out. Just don't move."

"Stop babbling and go already, Laura. I'm not scared so you don't be. It will turn out alright."

I turned around and climbed up and out of the small entrance effortlessly. I began running back, taking in the mental landmarks I had noticed on our way up into the mountains. At the halfway point, I had to stop and walk for a while to catch my breath. When I was able, I began to run again.

I arrived at our house where a couple of the ranch helpers were around. They looked at me as I approached, but I continued without saying what was going on since they would immediately tell my father. After phoning Old Iron Eyes and telling a fast version of how Charles ended up trapped on the ledge, he agreed at once to meet me at the edge of the forest. I ran back to the edge of the forest and waited. In a short time, Old Iron Eyes showed up with another friend to help too. I led the way back up through the hills, up into the edge of the mountain and down inside the cave. While I watched and waited, the two men lowered ropes down to Charles which he tied around himself. Then they pulled. It didn't feel like the ordeal was over until we were, all four of us, standing outside—above ground.

Old Iron Eyes simply looked critically at Charles and shook his head. "I'm not even going to say anything to you about this incident," he said. "I think you already have learned everything you need to know about it."

"Which is Indian for 'I hope you learned your lesson, right?'" Charles asked. "I knew it was a bad decision, but I had to. For this." He reached into the pocket of his hooded sweatshirt and held up the black rock like a trophy. "Get a load of this, boys," he said proudly, holding it flat out in his hand. "I'm gonna' remember this day forever."

I was crying, not caring who saw it.

Old Iron Eyes took the rock for a moment and studied it carefully. "Never seen anything like it," he marveled. "It's a beauty—those oily colors—like tiny black mirrors." He gave it back to Charles.

I hugged my brother like never before. "I'm glad you're okay. That's all. I would've been sad forever if I lost you. And now, I'm so tired you may have to carry me home."

The four of us walked slowly back towards the old homestead. My legs felt wobbly like jelly. At the edge of the forest Iron Eyes and his friend got into the truck and drove off. Charles and I managed to get home before our parents, just as we had planned.

* * *

Paul walked into the kitchen as if he lived at our house. He went directly to my mother and put his hand on her arm. "I want to apologize, Mrs. Hansen. I shouldn't have got so carried away with the guys at your house the other night."

She considered his words. Then, she said, "I'm not angry with you, but understand that Monroe doesn't hold liquor very well. His own father was an alcoholic and none in his family had a high tolerance for drinking."

I had never heard her speak about this. I remembered that my grandfather on his side had died young, but they said he had a heart attack. Now, I thought drinking must have been why.

Paul looked down at the floor seeming to absorb the information. "Well, he told me to buy whiskey for them on my way in," he told her.

This was a lie. I had heard father talking on the telephone, asking him to buy vegetables. Not wanting to upset mother again, I said nothing.

As if mother had never said anything to Paul, a few evenings later, he and father returned to the house with a pair of traders from Arizona. I came home from school and my mother informed me that father had invited them to stay at our house overnight. The couple had sold my parents nearly an entire season's inventory of turquoise and silver jewelry for "a very large discount." I had never met these people before and I didn't like them from the outset.

The woman was blond-haired and fairly attractive, but she never looked directly in our eyes when she spoke. When she addressed me or Charles it was as if she were speaking to the floor. Her husband was a loud bragging kind of man who followed my father around, listening to his tales of traveling during his Navy years, asking questions about local things like Indians and gold mining. When the woman spoke, the man would respond very kindly and do whatever she asked of him immediately. My parents fed us early that evening saying that they would be having a special dinner later with their guests. I assumed they would be going out to the new German restaurant a mile down the road. The Williams had a new car and I figured they would want to take a drive in it later.

Around nine o'clock that night, I awoke to find the kitchen lights on. Walking quietly around the corner, I saw the blond lady cooking in our kitchen. That was strange because my mother never let anyone take over her kitchen. Peering around the corner to avoid detection, I watched the lady line up vegetables tidily on the plates which were lined up on the countertop near the stove. Then I saw her stuff two large soup bowls with a bundle of skinny scallions and then place what seemed like a single furry animal in another bowl. *What the hell is she serving them, I thought—rat soup?* I noticed my mother standing back cringing apprehensively.

"This is the most important step," the woman said. "This is how to cook it immediately. And it is so tender." I still could not make out what the things in the bowl were but I thought I saw a round stub tail. I saw her take the creatures to the long-handled deep sauce pan and throw one into the steaming hot soup. Then the next one. There was a muffled screaming, like a teapot whistling but more like a living creature being scalded. I ran straight into the dining room now not caring if anyone saw that I was up and pushed my way up to the stove.

As I neared, my mother nudged me backward. I struggled against her and looked anyway. In the pan I saw two curled up little hedgehogs, red and burning near death. To say I was angry was not even close to the emotion I felt. I wanted to put this woman in a vat of boiling anything and out of our house. "They're burning to death!" I screamed. My parents stood frozen for a moment as if they didn't know what to do.

"Why are you letting these people do this in our house?" I screamed at my father.

"Go back to bed!" he ordered harshly, pointing towards my room.

"No! I won't!" I screamed back at the top of my lungs. I could feel my face getting puffier and every inch of my body tensed. The woman was staring at me angrily. "You're a crazy, evil bitch!" I shrieked at her. "Nobody does anything like that to a little animal." Everyone in the room gasped as if my language was worse than what this woman had done.

My mother quickly took me by the hand and led me out of the kitchen. In the living room, she spoke quietly to me. "I didn't know what she was making, Laura. Your father will take care of this."

"No, he won't," I said. "He never does!"

"I think that was horrible too. Just horrible," she shuddered. "That's nothing I'd eat, ever--but no matter how angry you are, dear, you can't go around using language like that. Especially to adults."

"I don't give a shit about language or adults," I said. If my mother had reprimanded me at that point, it would have been useless. She was changing so much farther away from who my grandparents had raised her to be. Even at my young age I recognized this. She had grown up with literature, music, chaperoned balls and polite conversations.

She must have known my inner thoughts, for she turned and left me standing alone without confronting me further. I went to my room and locked the door. I laid in bed tearfully imagining those poor hedgehogs' pain and picturing that evil blond-headed witch in our kitchen cutting into one with her knife, trying to impress my parents with her culinary ignorance.

The next day I was relieved that my father had arranged for me to go to the reservation with our employee, Mark Paulsen, to pick up some antique red clay pots for the museum. I was to go along to help count and package them for traveling. When I returned, I was relieved to see that our ignorant house guests were gone. Part of me feared that I might rip the woman apart with my bare hands if I saw her again. My father walked out to the truck as we were packing up our supplies for the trip.

He pointed his large-knuckled forefinger straight at my face. "Don't you ever behave like you did last night in this house again," he barked. "Or I will knock sense into you!"

I stood there shocked, not recognizing fully what he was saying, knowing only that he had never threatened me before. I started to walk away. "I guess it's more important you're impressed with that woman throwing hedgehogs in boiling water, those barbaric people, than to care how I feel..."

Suddenly, I felt a slap in the back of my head. I spun around to see my father, hand drawn back, as if he might strike me again.

I put my hand over my throbbing head, walked over to the passenger side of the truck and climbed inside the cab. Mark climbed in too, saying nothing before throwing the truck in reverse and clearing the driveway in a cloud of dust.

"I agree with you," he said, when we were on a long stretch of road. "That woman must be crazy to do that."

"Father doesn't care," I said angrily.

At the reservation, I found Old Iron Eyes standing on his porch pouring himself a glass of tea from an antique pitcher. He looked even larger than I remembered, his round belly pushing out from what he had called his 'leather hippy vest'.

"That's a pretty pitcher," I said as I approached the first step up to the porch.

He walked down the first three steps and gave me a big hug. "You're a pretty picture," he said. It was a wonderful hug, leather fringes on his vest smashed up against my cheeks and the long black unkempt hair floating in the light wind, surrounding me. "What's the matter with you today?" he asked.

"Why do you ask?"

"Your brightness is gone."

"Maybe." The long trip had been tiring and the incidents back at the house were replaying over and over in my mind like a repeating nightmare.

"Wanna' go for a walk to the upper stream?" he asked, smiling.

"Yes. Let's do that. I'll go tell Mark where I'm going and I'll come right back." I ran away to find Mark, feeling grateful again for the chance to see a part of the reservation which was mostly unknown. I had hiked to the stream on my first trip to Pine Ridge and remembered the rushing clear water, the rainbow and brook trout by the hundreds swimming all along its path and beautiful wildflowers of every color. Back then, Old Iron Eyes had shown me some of the plants growing wild there which could be used for medicine--like cohash, chamomilla and sagewort.

We sat at the highest point on the top of the rocky outcropping. As I sat on the edge, I could feel the lightness of the air where my feet dangled.

"This is a place where strong energy lives," Old Iron Eyes told me. "See the giant trees; how green they are and the big chunks of rose quartz all around? You can hear things in the wind up here which help to clear the mind. Many in my family have had their first vision here."

"Like a real vision?" I asked.

"Not like a picture. Like seeing with every part of you. We have different names for this...even the Japanese have it too. They call it a satori."

"How would you know what the Japanese call anything?"

"I can read books," he said, smiling down at me sitting beside him. "Sometimes the Lakota would have these visions unexpectedly. Other times they would make it come after praying or chewing on a peyote button."

"My mother says that's a drug the Indians use."

"My own mom considers it a drug too. I guess you could call it that. I never needed it to have my vision, but it can be helpful to others who have difficulty getting theirs. Anyway, it should only be used in the right way. It's dangerous if you don't get it right."

I thought about Kills Enemy. "Your mother loaned me the book by Black Elk where he wrote about his vision on Harney Peak. He saw then that the center of the earth was on the top of that mountain."

"She had you read that one too?" he said, taken aback. "She's loaned that book to every person in our family. It's like the only book in the world to her. Funny thing she made you read it too."

"Sioux and Plains Indians also went to the Badlands on vision quests or to pray," I said. "How could they travel so many places like that on foot?"

"I couldn't do it. Guess I'm a modern Indian because I'd need to drive my truck to the Badlands if I was going. Don't tell my mother I said that. She might send me out on foot just for the experience. She thinks you learn best when you push yourself beyond what you think you can do. Those Indians went on quests for four, five days and nights. No food or sleep, singing chants and meditating."

"How did they know the vision wasn't caused by being tired? Like when you're overtired and you're not clear headed?"

"They went back home--to their elders--and the elders would find out circumstances of the vision. Very many times, the Indian had picked up an animal spirit this way through the vision. The animal spirit would protect the Indian for the rest of his life; give him good hunting and good life."

"Wish I could have a vision. You know, naturally, to understand what I should."

"It's better to not force a vision to happen or wish for it, Little Star. It'll come to you when God wants it; when he feels it's the best time."

This was a surprising revelation. "You said God and not all the 'Great Spirits'?"

"We're part of God, including the Great Spirits, but oh yes, there are Great Spirits. Can't you see them everywhere--in the birds, in trees, in the rocks even?"

"No. I just believe in Jesus and God like they taught us in church."

"Good enough," he said. "So, why are you so dark-spirited today?"

Tears welled up in my eyes as I blurted out the story of the woman at our house and the hedgehogs. Old Iron Eyes listened and was silent for a long time after I finished. He sat looking out at the mountains in the distance without a response. I was hoping he might have something to say which would make me feel better, but he said nothing. He sat staring vacantly for nearly an hour. I got up and climbed down the rock where we sat to stretch my legs, thinking he would follow when he was ready.

I strode out into the open field which consisted of layers of wild dill weed, sagebrush, various grasses and patches of ragweed. I collected wildflowers, mostly columbine and violets, and a few unknown plants that I wanted to start in my garden and identify later. Placing them in a linen drawstring pouch, I felt the lightness of the breeze and the sun on my face. Withdrawing my binoculars from my pocket, I scanned the open meadow as far as I could see hoping to spot prairie dogs or maybe a coyote, but saw nothing.

Realizing now that we should be getting back to his family's house, I hiked up the steep pathway to the rock where we had been talking earlier. There was Old Iron Eyes sitting by himself still looking outward at the mountains in the distance. I settled in quietly beside him and realized that he had tears in his eyes. He glanced over at me. "That was a sad story," he stated. "Let's go now."

We walked without speaking all the way back to his house. I broke the silence first. "Old Iron Eyes?"

He stopped walking and took my hand in his, pushing a strand of long hair away from my eyes in order to see my face clearly. "What is it?" he asked.

"Today has been really wakan, don't you think?"

"Agreed."

"If you agree, then, it has been."

"Your heart is smiling again," he said. "And now your face follows it."

* * *

Old Iron Eyes had offered to take Charles and
me up into the mountains near the lodge to include
us in the archery lessons he was teaching to some of
the local kids. On our first day there, he showed us a
special bow and quiver set. He handed an old arrow
first to Charles and then one to me.

"Some of the heads are metal, some are stone.
This set has newer arrows, but the rest of it is from
about 1860," he told us.

Charles and I both handled them with greater
care when he said that.

"Notice the metal head is iron, which my
people got by trading with white men. We've been
making trades with white men for many years. It's
attached with sinew, same Laura uses in beading,
only it's woven to be stronger. The flint was carved
for the heads by hand with tools that were also
handmade."

"I'd like to have a set this nice," Charles said.

"Bet Monroe would've liked to have this in his
museum," Old Iron Eyes said. "This quiver and the
case for the bow are deer hide, all laced together and
beaded by my great-great grandmother."

He handed it to me to hold for a moment while
he pointed out the details of the beading. "The
women used traditional colors and geometric
patterns. The design was symmetrical for balance."

The pattern was a geometrical star in deep
turquoise blue, yellow on white background, with

black outline. Even Charles was impressed. I couldn't get over the age of it.

"Beading this piece was a way that my ancestor was honored. Since everyone's work was original, it was easy to recognize who owned a certain set of bow, case and quiver. This shoulder strap is long because it was probably used on horseback, carried across the rider's back."

I want to let you shoot these, but I can't. I'm responsible for these." He handed me the second set he had carried with him. "You two use this one."

After pulling on the bowstrings a couple of times and inspecting the arrows, I felt ready. "I know how to do this," I said, eager to show him. I shot a round of arrows at the target, rather poorly.

"That's the best you can do? What if you had to hunt and gather?" Old Iron Eyes said. Charles was laughing at me.

"It's not like I'm going to get the center every time," I countered. "Let me try again. I want to do this."

"Little Star, you missed the target twice out of six arrows," Old Iron Eyes said. He made a silly gesture as if he were pulling out his hair. "You shoot like...."

"Like what?" I asked, frustrated.

"Like a girl."

"Dammit," I muttered only to myself.

He positioned himself next to me, lifting my elbows up as I pulled the bow back again. "Parallel and tight to the body," he said. "Patience is not your best quality, but think about it like this. Say you were hunting and you didn't hit in the right place. You'd injure the animal instead of killing him. He'd run off in pain for days before dying. Try again."

"Yeah, Laura," Charles offered. "Think of the target as your enemy instead of a hay-stuffed circle with paint. Get pissed off!" he shouted.

"I don't get pissed off," I said. "And, I don't have any enemies."

"How are you going to make it in the world being a flower-child?" Charles teased. "My sister..."

"Leave her alone," Old Iron Eyes said. "She's doing fine. She needs a lot of practice; that's all."

I wasn't ever going to hunt animals. Killing the snake was one thing, but harming an innocent forest creature was another. Everyone there knew that I didn't want to hunt animals. But it made sense that if I were going to improve at archery maybe I needed to start thinking as if I were a hunter. My second try turned out to be not much better than the first. However; with each successive lesson, I felt more confident that I would someday be able to hit the bull's eye at least half the time. It was a challenge I never did meet, but after several months of practice I did gain enough skill at it to end the laughter.

Perhaps the flower-child was a part of me by inheritance. One day shortly after our archery lessons, I told Kills Enemy about how my great-grandmother and her Indian friend, Lorena, used to heal local townspeople with herbs. Less than a week later, Kills Enemy had made arrangements for me to take a walk up into the higher elevations of the mountains near Angostura Lake with a full blooded Lakota medicine man. He had been quiet in the ride up to the lake, but once we began walking in the field, the medicine man talked incessantly about healing with prayer, meditation, sweating and things taken from the earth.

The three of us walked around through several different areas around the lake, collecting a wide sampling of native plants. This medicine man could identify the plants, not by their Latin name, as we had learned in biology class, but in Lakota language. He talked for hours about how each plant could be used and what ailments they would heal. Now that I am older, I wish that I would have written down everything he told us that day, but I do still have my drawings.

On that day, I had also brought along my sketch pad. I drew several of the plants so that I could remember exactly what they looked like. Kills Enemy hovered over me while I drew each picture and would point to certain details to be sure that I had it right.

While feeling this burst of creativity, I sat down on a large flat rock facing Kills Enemy while she sorted the various plants we had gathered into separate pouches. I made a sketch of her, purposely erasing several years of wrinkles from her face. It was a gesture meant to make her feel prettier. After about thirty minutes, I turned the sketch pad around so that she could see my finished work.

"Why would you make me look like such a young woman?" she asked right away.

"I thought it might make you happy." I answered cautiously, knowing by her expression that she didn't like it.

"You should put the years back into my face. Those years are my story. For a girl who likes stories so much, you should understand that."

I didn't fully understand her request, but when Kills Enemy asked, I complied out of respect. After I finished, she again inspected the drawing, this time looking at it pensively for several seconds. At last she spoke, "This....it is so much like me. With your hand and thoughts woven into the picture. It's good. I like it now very much."

With that, I removed the paper gently from the sketch pad and handed it to her.

She took the sketch and rolled it up neatly before tying it with a long blade of wild grass. Clutching it to her heart for a moment, she then tucked it into the lining of the light jacket she wore, giving me a warm smile. "Thank you, Laura-Helena, my Little Star. I really really love this." Then, she added, "With your interest in art, you need to meet another friend of mine." Her warm smile turned into a wide grin. She was holding back something big. I could see it in her face.

"Who is it?" I pried.

"A man who's gonna be famous one day. Not yet, but he will be," she said. "Get permission from your mom. Tell her it's only you on this trip. Not Charles or anyone else. You'll meet this person face-to-face. This is for art. For you only."

When I told mother, even without knowing who it was, she was all for it. Usually, Kills Enemy came to our house 'chauffeured' as she said, by Old Iron Eyes. This time, another woman from her family was driving her.

On the way driving up into the mountains, she began to prepare me for who I was about to meet. "We are going to meet a professional artist, a sculptor. He's Polish, but he lived a long time in the U.S., in the East. He got famous first for a sculpture he made of Paderewski, the Polish president who they say was deeply loved in his country. This man you're gonna meet—he came out west when Mr. Borglum was carving Mount Rushmore--worked on that. Now, he's carving by himself. This is what you will see today."

I figured I was about to see a head-on-a-stick sculpture of a famous foreign president whose name I wouldn't recognize, carved by another man whose name I wouldn't recognize nor probably remember after this day. I didn't ask questions though. If Kills Enemy believed that this man was important, I wouldn't ask his name because I knew she wanted me to wait until we were there.

We arrived at a wooden building that was the visitors' pavilion and I was immediately introduced to a man named Korczak Ziolkowski. He was wearing blue jeans and a dusty work shirt. His face was weathered and heavily bearded. His hands were thick

183

with muscle. He had a full beard and a very pleasant demeanor. Kill's Enemy asked him to tell me the background story about what he was carving.

Around the time Mount Rushmore was being finished, Ziolkowski had become known and respected by the Sioux as someone who was intimately familiar with the Black Hills. He had also been sympathetic towards Indians. Chief Henry Standing Bear of the Lakota had written him a letter that said, in part: "My fellow chiefs and I would like the white man to know the red man has great heroes, too." In this letter, he asked if Ziolkowski would consider carving a monument honoring Native Americans. Shortly after that, Ziolkowski met with the Sioux leaders to begin planning a monument. After volunteering to serve the U.S. Army in World War II, he returned to the Black Hills and set out on a search for a suitable mountain for his sculpture. The mountain he chose was a six-hundred-foot high mountain located in the sacred Black Hills.

I had never heard of Korczak Ziolkowski before that day, but I'll never forget him. His work on the mountain depicting Crazy Horse, the great Sioux warrior, was well underway. The head of Crazy Horse alone would be the size of all four presidents' heads on Mount Rushmore. One arm would point in the direction of his Black Hills homeland. Ironically, the U. S. Government offered millions of dollars in grants to help fund this ambitious effort, but Ziolkowski refused. He raised money for the project by charging admission for tourists to watch the work in progress.

"You like doing this kind of work? I mean, do you ever wish that you chose something else to do?" I asked him, pondering my own future.

He sensed the weight of my question and considered his words carefully before answering. "I was led to this mountain by fate. This is the work I'm supposed to do. I've dedicated my life to finishing this sculpture, because I promised I would," he said.

For a sixteen- year-old girl, it was an unforgettable honor to meet him. I had yet to decide what I was born to do, but seeing his enthusiasm inspired me to reach unfailingly for my own dreams, even if I knew it would be on a much smaller scale.

CHAPTER TWELVE

During the summer of 1977 I turned seventeen. As my senior school year ended, I found myself feeling more aware of not only my own teenage world, but increasingly willing to argue and stand up for who I was becoming. At home, my parents were arguing almost every day, about the businesses and mother's new desire to be away from it more than ever. This added turmoil only increased my ever-quickening irritability. My mother, rightfully so, constantly reminded me of my manners and it seemed most of my teachers, who were confidantes and friends only one year before, were now opposing me at every turn.

Towards the end of that school year, everyone in world history class had to give one final oral report that would greatly affect our final grade. As I felt especially emboldened against most authority figures and somewhat scrappy, I offered this provoking report on the Lakota Indians:

Following Red Cloud's War, in 1868, the Lakota signed the Fort Laramie Treaty with the United States. This treaty set aside a portion of the Lakota Territory as the Great Sioux Reservation, including the Black Hills for their exclusive use and occupation.

However; miners and settlers had already begun descending upon the Dakota Territory, virtually nullifying any protection outlined in the treaty. Territorial officials considered harvesting the rich timber resources of the Black Hills, to be floated down the Cheyenne River to the Missouri, where new plains settlements needed lumber. Further, the geographical uplift of the area suggested there were mineral resources below the surface. When a commission approached the Red Cloud Agency about the possibility of the Lakota's signing away the Black Hills, Colonel John E. Smith wrote that "it would require nothing short of annihilation to get it from them."

When the government dispatched the Custer Expedition to examine the Black Hills, even before Custer's column returned to Fort Abraham Lincoln, news of their having discovered gold was telegraphed nationally. The presence of gold and other valuable mineral resources was confirmed the following year by the Newton-Jenney Geological Expedition. Prospectors by the thousands, motivated by the economic panic of 1873, seeped into the Black Hills from the East, violating the Fort Laramie Treaty.

Attempts to enforce the treaty and keep miners out of the regions were pointless. Miners would be evicted by the United States Army only to return at their first opportunity. This constant policing of the lands kept political pressure on President Grant's Administration to secure the Black Hills from the Lakota. In May 1875, Sioux delegations headed by Spotted Tail, Red Cloud and Lone Horn traveled to Washington, D.C. in an eleventh-hour attempt to persuade President Grant and others in the government to honor existing treaties and keep miners out of their territories. The government leaders offered to pay the tribes $ 25,000 for the land and have them relocated to Indian Territory (present day Oklahoma). The delegates refused to sign a new treaty with these stipulations. Spotted Tail said, "You speak of another country, but it *is not my country; it does not concern me. I want nothing to do with it. I was not born there. If it's such a good country, you ought to send the white men now in our country there and let us alone." Although these chiefs were not successful in finding a peaceful solution, they chose not to join Crazy Horse and Sitting Bull in the warfare that followed.*

Looking out at the classroom of students, many of them my friends, listening, as we had all been taught to do, with interest in the speaker. As I read my report, I had watched bewildered glances passing between the teacher and the students as if someone were waiting for her to put a stop to it. It's hard to fathom now that these truthful words could have been so unacceptable, but during those years, they were.

I read the last two sentences of my report:

"A monument to the final showdown which ended in the slaughter of hundreds of Native people is being carved now, less than ten miles from this very classroom. It is the monument of Crazy Horse."

It wasn't the version of the story we'd been taught in elementary and junior high school, but this was high school. These were the years in which students were being encouraged to search for truths, to begin thinking for ourselves. I was proud to have given this report and had high hopes that our teacher would give me an excellent grade.

Even before I was seated again, the teacher questioned my research. "Where exactly did you come up with your facts?" she said, visibly disturbed.

I answered matter-of-factly. "Mostly from books my uncle in New York City sent to me, but I also have Indian friends who tell this history. And, I have the writings of my great-grandmother, Laura Helena, who I am named after."

"That explains a lot," she said, looking upon the eager faces in the class. "But, you shouldn't assume that because your parents own a museum, that you're the local authority on Indian history. Keep in mind that the East Coast where you're originally from, has often had a different take on our history, but they weren't the people who were here, living it." Within her voice, I sensed my grade lowering.

It was all pissing me off. "And...you were?" I countered.

She moved in closer to my face, her teeth lined up tight behind her lips. "I didn't need to be, Ms. Hansen. My great-grandmother helped to settle this town. She knew as much as anyone the truth about these wars—about the savagery of the Sioux Indians. I think I've heard the history passed through my family about as certain as it gets."

"My great-grandmother was one of the town's original settlers, too." I said as neutrally as I could muster. "She wrote in journals and kept scrapbooks

189

throughout her life. She wrote plenty about the history of this state and this town. We have that in common."

"Show me what she wrote and I'll look at it but, you should've also researched your report at the town archives."

"Her writings aren't ready for everyone to read yet," I said.

"Yet?" she repeated. "Why not? If you used them for reference, they should be."

"Well," I started, unsure if I should continue, "I may use them myself someday. You know—write a book or something based on them."

The teacher laughed aloud. "If your report is any indication of your writing skills, my dear, you've got a long way to go. A great-grandmother and a few Indian friends—whatever their take is on history—doesn't make it so."

I walked back to my desk and sat down in a huff. I threw up one more question for her. "So, you don't agree with my views, or you didn't think the writing was good?" I asked, doubting myself now.

"Afraid it's both," she said looking at me pitifully. "A shame a girl whose parents own a museum can't get history right."

I watched her lay my neatly typed report down atop the stack on the desk. Maybe, a part of me purposely slanted the research in favor of my own feelings, but it was based on facts written and told from person to person, during that time. Those stories carried weight too.

As I walked home that day, my snow boots were heavy with a feeling of failure I hadn't known before. Our home life was evolving into a disjointed, everyone-for-themselves kind of home, not the wide open anything-is-possible air we had lived with just a few years before.

I arrived home, sensing right away that my father was drinking again. For the first, Paul's truck was in the driveway and it was becoming almost ritualistic that whenever he was there past five o'clock the whiskey was opened and the intensity would begin. Secondly, my mother was sitting out on the front porch in the wooden swing. I could see her blanket beside her, ready for nightfall. It was as if sitting out in the open air, cleared away the problem which was growing by the day. As I opened the screen door she raised her head from the book she was reading to acknowledge me.

"What's for dinner?" I asked, putting as much cheer in my voice as I could muster.

"Wasn't sure you when you were going to show, honey. What took you so long to get home?"

"I stayed after school to talk to Mrs. Eriksen about the report I gave on the Indians," I answered. "I was hoping to change her mind about my grade."

"Was it a bad grade?"

"For the work I put into it, Mom, a C is terrible."

"That's not going to affect your overall average, Laura. You've got an A in that class. Don't be so hard on yourself."

"It's not the grade. It's her lack of understanding of how I'm seeing things. Shouldn't we be allowed to put our own views into our writing? I have my own perspective on this Indian history business. They should let us think for ourselves-- don't you agree, Mom?"

Paul walked out onto the porch with my father following close behind. My father sat in his usual chair next to the tree stump he had hauled up onto the porch for an end table. Paul took a place beside my mother on the porch swing. He leaned over to see her open book. "Whatcha readin', lady?" he asked.

She closed her book without answering and looked toward me, "Let's hear this terrible report."

I tried to ignore how much I resented Paul intruding in on our conversation. "Really? You want to hear the whole thing? It's kinda' long."

"I don't care," she said. "I'm all ears."

"Yeah, Laura. Let's hear your li'l report," Paul said, leaning out from the swing so that he was directly in front of me. There was a belligerence in his voice that annoyed me more than his presence.

Straightening up my posture, I stood there holding up my papers and proudly read the entire report from beginning to end in exactly the same way I had read it to the classroom that day. When I finished I waited for her reaction.

"I can see where your teacher might construe that to be arguable, Laura. Sheriff Basset warned us to be careful not to appear like we're part of any political controversy. You understand why."

"I do, but, this is true."

"As you see it," Paul interjected. "What your mama' is trying to point out is that not everyone wants to hear what you see as the truth right about now. With three dead government agents...you gotta' be sensitive." That tone appeared again, only sneakier this time.

I glared at him. "I don't need you to say what my mom means about anything," I said. "And, why're you here after work drinking with my father again?"

He shirked back a few steps and my mother continued. "Laura; what we do know, is that whatever has happened, that the Sioux overall are not criminals. We know that because we've had dealings with them which have gone fine. They've been nothing but honorable with us. The other side of the coin is that your own father was a government man for many years too. It was two FBI agents who were shot probably just doing their job."

"That's what they're telling people, but is it true?" I said. "Who knows what happened out there? Every side to it." Politics were for adults and beyond my understanding, but I knew how much anyone on the reservations trusted anyone from the American government. "I do know that we have great friends from that reservation."

Paul's mouth opened to enter the conversation again. I instantly cut him off. "Who asked you?" I snapped before he could speak.

Paul laughed. "She's got her daddy's spunk and her momma's good looks."

"She does," my father piped in. "And, we do have great friends on Pine Ridge, but..." He hesitated to collect his thoughts. "Laura, they had a saying in the Navy—'Don't stick your neck out too far or you might get it cut off'." He took a deep swig of the remaining amber liquid in his glass.

Paul raised his glass from across the porch toasting my father, who was fading out for the night.
"You said it, Monroe. We're going to sit back. Let the government sort this thing out. Keep our noses clean."

My mother rose dutifully to lift my father from his chair and steered him toward the front door. As they disappeared into the house, Paul turned his head toward me, with a movement which reminded me of a snake.

"None of our feeble minds could sort it out anyway," he said.

"What?" I didn't want to talk to him.

"Sort out those shootings." I could tell he was half-drunk himself. "Plus you aren't anywhere near a real writer. You and I could get together though, and I could help you study English better. If someone tells your great-grandmother's so-called extra special unique story, you gotta' be a better writer than that report."

"Screw you," I seethed and stood up to leave.

"Maybe soon you'll be lucky enough to get that chance," he teased, seating himself in the porch swing as if he owned the place.

"Nasty piece of crap," I said. I kicked the huge bolt on the right edge of the porch swing which I knew would occasionally slip out of the hole. It slid out of the slot and sent his dead weight straight to the floor. Before he could scramble up to his feet, I dashed inside the house and locked the front door.

He could see my parents sitting at the table on the other side of the window and didn't dare think about beating the door down, which I knew intuitively is exactly what he wished he could do. I watched through the slit in the curtains as he limped to his truck and drove away. I was sick of seeing his face around our house after working hours were over, sick of his snide comments to me when no one was listening and sick of the way he was seeping into our personal lives like sewage floating in a pristine well. I made a decision that by the next morning I would come up with a way to discuss the issue with my father without turning it into another argument.

At the end of the year, I would be out of high school and I was still unsure of what I was going to do for occupation. If I stayed in Hot Springs, I could continue to help in the family businesses, but I didn't feel that they were my dream--those were my parents' dreams. I loved beadwork and I loved sewing, so naturally I thought there must be a place for me in the world of design. The collection of dolls from around the world which father had bought me had also been a great source of inspiration. Since the day

I hung them around my bedroom, I had studied the details of the patterns and fabrics. This led me to many books borrowed from the library on one country at a time which was represented by my dolls. Studying costumes and native dress, as well as those of the Sioux, had helped me decide that I wanted to pursue a career in fashion.

However; I tried to be a realist too. I had been advised by a school counselor that the people who were truly successful in fashion, the recognizable names with signature looks, had qualities that I didn't. I had not grown up in trendy circles with unlimited funding for any artful venture I chose to undertake. My life didn't fit the mold. Still the dream was becoming an obsession for me. I knew I had to make it happen.

As a sort of test, I decided to design a few pieces of clothing that I could wear and have my friends wear to promote my work. I'd get the overall reaction to my designs, even though Hot Springs wasn't a big city. The idea was that the outcome of this would help tell me where I needed to go next with my dream. After talking over my plan with Mrs. Biermann, who encouraged me to do it, I went into an intense period of planning and creating.

After school every day for a period of about four months, I cut out patterns and selected fabrics. This undertaking was proving costlier than I had anticipated and I had to ask mother to fund the last four pieces out of ten, which she did. I was grateful for her encouragement and belief in my creative endeavors. This was another time that she came through for me when my plan was coming up short.

I had designed dresses, pants and tailored jackets, with common elements which I hoped would evolve into a signature look. By mixing up fabric textures and colors, I hoped to create clothes for people like me who loved high fashion, but happened to live outside of the big city life. The trick would be to make these clothes also appropriate for local wear.

Berit was the first to wear a pantsuit I sewed to school. At first, nobody said anything about it and I was concerned. "You have to ask for opinions," I coached her. "Don't wait for them to offer their opinions because maybe they won't. If they think it's terrible, they might not say it. Go ahead and ask."

When she wore the pantsuit again, Berit actually wrote down what everyone said about it, so that she could remember word-for-word to tell me. The overall comments were positive, however; I still had more pieces to try. One-by-one between Berit and I, plus a couple other girls willing to model, we showed all of the clothing.

What started with me questioning myself turned overnight into a little business. The first experimental clothing line had gone relatively well, even with some critical opinions that only helped to make them better. Several of the mothers had heard about what I was trying to do, and asked me to sew custom designed pieces for their daughters. Suddenly, I was up to my neck in sewing jobs and I hadn't even graduated from high school. Berit and Mrs. Beirmann helped me with cutting and sewing whenever they could. Seeing that sewing on a larger scale at our house wasn't going to work, mother let us set up an area in the back of the general store.

There we could store our growing bevy of supplies and have plenty of room to work.

Even Charles was becoming inspired by my newfound talent. Whenever he saw someone wearing my clothes, he would immediately point out the fact that he was my brother. The girls he once knew as our school friends were now referring to themselves as 'models'. It felt good to know that my brother was proud of my growing notoriety, even if it was only local fame.

The day came when the college decision had to be made and, all on my own, I applied to a couple of colleges of design in New York City. It was, from the outset, the only place I would consider moving. My cousin Thomas who lived there, had been quite successful and owned a second apartment next to his own which he offered to lease to me until I could get my own place. My parents planned for me all along, to attend the state college; however, I hoped they would support my plan.

CHAPTER THIRTEEN

I was standing outside the high school one day, talking with friends when Charles showed up with Paul. It was unsettling, seeing the two of them together, knowing their history of conflict. As they walked closer to me, I noticed that they both were smoking cigarettes. "What're you doing," I instantly snapped to Charles.

"Aw, cut the act," Paul said. "You're not his mom."

"It's not your business," I said to Paul. Looking again at Charles I repeated myself. "What's this?" I pointed to the cigarette.

"It's not your business either," Charles said defiantly to me.

One of my friends chimed in. "Let him smoke if he wants. Don't be so mean."

"Yeah, meanie," Paul said, crinkling up his nose.

Leaving them standing there, I walked straight home and told my parents just as I said I would. I wasn't going to let Paul get my brother started smoking and I didn't care what anyone thought about it. Father scolded Charles and said later that Charles had only taken a few puffs which had sickened him. "I don't think he's going to do it again," father laughed.

"Don't you see how Paul causes problems in our family?" I asked. "Charles would have never done this on his own."

"You can't know that," my mother said. "A lot of young guys try smoking. It's not a big deal. He probably won't do it again."

"I don't like Paul always being around our house or our businesses," I said, pointing my finger a mile down the road towards the school.

My father had a way of dismissing anything I ever said about Paul. True to form, he offered defense, "Thing is, that Charles is responsible for his own actions. Paul's a good employee. He handles so many things for us now that his minor flaws are easy to overlook. He's nearly doubled our sales in the general store this year. He works his tail off for us, Laura. Try to get over this squabble you have going with him, would you?"

"Well." I said. "I'll be leaving for college soon and then you both will have one less problem with me," I snapped.

Mother looked surprised. "You've decided your plan already?" she asked, trying to sound conciliatory. "You haven't discussed it with me. Do you know where you want to go, even?"

As she asked this, Paul strolled into the store, without Charles.

"Where's my brother?" I asked. "And, what are you doing here?"

Paul smiled broadly. "Your brother is with his girlfriend. If you remember right, I work here. I'm checking in for work, Laura."

I glanced at the clock on the wall and then back at Paul. I wanted to punch him in the nose.

Mother tried to soften the tenseness in the air. "Laura is just telling us that she's decided to go off to college as soon as she graduates."

"Interesting," Paul said, looking almost stunned. "And where will you be going?"

"One thing is certain," I said, "I'll be leaving Hot Springs. There's so many places I've read about and want to visit. I'm likely moving to New York City and staying with my relatives there who offered me a room at their place. I'm going to college for fashion."

"Saying and doin' are two different things," Paul said.

"You should know that for sure," I said. "Because you're such a good guy, right?"

"I am a good guy," he said. "You could always stay here and marry me. I'm going to be a big land owner someday, just like your dad."

"What an odd thing to say," I said, walking out of the room. I'd have no more conversations about my private plans in front of my father's new best friend. I couldn't bear to watch him gloat, knowing that he was driving wedges between all of us. To mention marriage when he knew I couldn't stand him, was insulting. Making me madder yet, was the fact that my parents never said anything in my defense.

I had sent letters to four different schools to see which ones might accept me. I had a new sense of urgency to follow up on their replies. The thought of leaving my home saddened me, but my friends and my family knew I'd be back to visit whenever possible.

They seemed for the most part, supportive of my decision. The further along I progressed into my local design venture, the more daring I became. I had started out with demure, feminine designs which reflected the local definition of appropriate. However; I wanted to attempt something I'd seen in a magazine that my New York City cousin had mailed to me.

For me, New York City was the ultimate city for fashion. I decided to design my own dress, resembling a very trendy dress from the magazine, for my senior prom. It was a chic form fitting and even, yes, a sexy look. The boys were finally beginning to notice me this year, just as Mary had told me they would. I couldn't wait to wear it.

Paul had continued with his self-initiated idea that I might be romantically interested in him. At the café in town one morning, he asked me point blank if I'd let him take me to my senior prom.

As coldly as I knew how, I said, "Right. I'll call you." That should've ended that conversation for good, but it didn't.

On the evening of the dance, I walked out to the outside front entry where the entire senior class and their dates had gathered waiting for a photographer who was coming to take a group photo. As I stood in the crowd, suddenly Paul appeared at my side.

"How'd you get here?" Paul asked, visibly annoyed.

"I'm with Mark Paulsen," I said, moving away through the crowd.

He grabbed my arm at the elbow. "You were supposed to come with me."

"I never agreed to go with you," I said, pulling away.

He still had a grip on me. "Yeah you did. I asked you. You said 'Yes, I'll call you'."

"I didn't call. You should've known. And, I never said 'yes'." I wriggled free of his grasp.

He looked me up and down for a second. "Now that I see you, isn't much to look at anyway. That dress makes you look like trailer-park trash."

At that very moment, Charles had walked up beside us with his date. I could tell by the look on his face that he had heard. "I know you're not talking to my sister, Paul. You just bought yourself an ass-whippin!"

Paul turned his attention to Charles, and I stepped back a few paces.

By then several seniors who had overheard the arguing were also circling us. I thought that at least Paul was enough of a realist to know that he had no chance to win in a fight against my brother, but it wasn't so.

Paul shoved Charles by his shoulder. "Relax, Scrappy. Your sister can deal with her own shit. She created this. Let her deal with it."

"My sister doesn't have to deal with any shit like you," Charles snapped. I could see the storm building up in his eyes.

"You might tell her to stop dressing like trash. Maybe she could get someone better than Mark Paulsen. Maybe..." That was all he got out. Charles had already lunged at him, landing a sharp fist on the side of Paul's head.

Paul whirled back to face Charles and pulled back to punch. Charles was faster though and landed another smack squarely on his jaw before Paul got the chance to see it coming. Paul put his head down and rammed, throwing my brother into the crowd. Charles stumbled but kept on his feet.

I screamed out, "Stop fighting!" I looked around for teachers, but there were none in sight.

The two eyed each other for a split second. I hoped they might leave it at that. Then, I recognized the murderous look in my brother's eyes. He hated Paul. I saw it. He had hated him for a long time. This was about me, but it was also about the two of them. Probably more than I even knew. It wasn't going to go well for Paul. In my heart, I wanted Charles to inflict pain on him too, for his meanness to me and for what he was doing to our family, just by his presence in our lives.

Suddenly, there was a slamming of bodies. Charles caught him with a side kick to the ribs and Paul stumbled. Then a series of punches flew, each clipping the other with furious pounding blows. Then there was blood. Paul staggered backwards and blood was dripping from his mouth. Charles was at his face, cursing, being held back now by a couple of his friends. "Don't do it," someone said. "You'll go to jail. Let it ride."

"It's okay," Paul said, holding up both hands above his head for a moment. Then he pointed at Charles. "You're going to pay for this, Charles Hansen. It ain't over." With that, he walked back out the front entrance to the gymnasium.

I moved past the others and put my arm around Charles' back, the only place on him that wasn't a mess. "Couldn't you let it go?" I pleaded.

"No; and you shouldn't either. That son-of-a-bitch-bastard needed his ass whipped. If he ever talks to you or me like that again; it's gonna' happen again." Charles' regular group of friends laughed. His date stood beside him, looking like she was in shock. I tried to comfort her for a moment with a hug. "By the way," Charles said to me, "don't ever yell out for me to stop when I'm in a fight. It's not going to happen."

Mark showed up at that moment, apparently oblivious to the fighting. "Ready to go in?" he asked.

"We're supposed to be waiting outside for a group photo," I said.

"So, we'll wait here," he said. "By the way, you look fantastic tonight. I love your dress and you should wear your hair up more often." He handed me a corsage and helped me pin it near my shoulder.

That evening was everything high school proms should be, with plenty of laughter and serious dancing until midnight. After that, at my urging, Mark offered for Charles and his date to join us for a late dinner at Wurlitzer's German Restaurant. The restaurant had stayed open to accommodate the prom crowd and we celebrated until the wee hours of the morning.

Even after the prom night dresses were put away, my loyal group of local customers continued to ask for more and more of my clothing. These were mostly the younger girls I knew from school and people who had been referred to me. Now and then, someone's mother would also hire me to sew a garment for a special event--a dress or a skirt usually. A couple of times, the high school drama teacher had let me sew costumes for a play.

All of this added up to valuable experience, but I longed for the formal training which could potentially carry my dream of designing forward to a true profession.

CHAPTER FOURTEEN

In the quiet of my room, I opened up the scrapbook of news articles and thumbed through them trying to recognize any historical buildings which might have still existed. After that, I boxed up the collection of my great-grandmother's journals which I had tucked in neat stacks under my bed. These journals had been like an ongoing adventure for me and I had read most of them, one at a time, beginning at age twelve before we moved from Minneapolis up until now, at the age of seventeen.

As I lined them up in the box, I opened one of the journals I hadn't read yet. There were scripted letters in the lower right hand corner: *'Laura-Helena 1897.'* Propping my pillow up against the headboard, I turned the first pages.

We attended a Women's Suffrage meeting hoping to find out that the rumor of women being able to vote was true. Our women's club (informally assembled to read the Bible) has evolved into a political force. The mayor has agreed to attend our meeting-we think he is only coming to observe what we are doing. Most women in town have arrived from points East, but they are now 'Westerners'. We discovered things about ourselves on our long journeys west that none of us ever counted on.

We learned we could shoot guns and drive wagons pulled by a team of oxen or horses. Our newfound strength has turned women here into a different breed than our sisters in

the East. Most of the men (not my husband)
would like to rein in these once obedient
housewives, but they also are astute enough
to realize they need our help much more in this
new environment. We are adjusting.

It occurred to me that what Grandma Kate said all those years ago about optimism was true. She had said that optimism was what kept people going in the early days when homesteaders headed west. If they had stopped to think about how difficult it might have been or realized the pitfalls they would encounter, perhaps they would have never ventured so far from home. Here I was, fearful of trying to pursue a competitive profession like fashion design, even though it was my dream. I was more afraid though that if I didn't follow this path, I would never be happy. One thing I knew for certain, before I made my final decision, I needed to hike to the top of Harney Peak. Charles had talked about how one could see four states from its highest point. Maybe, like Black Elk, whatever I was struggling to understand would become clearer there.

Even if I failed, it would be better than not trying. Leaving the place I had tried so reverently to understand would be strange, but I could return for visits. Leaving my loved ones so far away and with fresh heartaches to overcome, was something I could hardly fathom. I wondered if every college student struggled with the same dilemmas.

By summertime, the tourists began arriving in cars, tour buses, motorcycles and motorhomes. As they streamed through town on their way to Mount Rushmore or the Badlands or the rowdy saloon town of Deadwood, the unassuming little town of Hot Springs stood ready to divert as much money as possible into its coffers. Most of the townspeople were resourceful, hearty, proud and spirited showing visitors their special brand of western hospitality. Other townspeople were like hawkers out on the street pitching everything in their inventory, dreading a long cold winter without an income. For many, it was a necessary aggressive salesmanship which took hold of them. If the summer didn't bring success, they would inevitably beg and scrape during the winter.

The artist at the end of Main Street had more business than he could handle painting three-minute landscape murals on the sides of vehicles using his own masterful technique. Cars, motorcycles, silver Airstream campers and boxy Winnebagos lined up five or six at a time waiting for adornment. Often, I would show up early in the morning as he was raising the roll-up metal door to the two-car garage that was his studio. He would show me how to mix paints to achieve exactly the right colors of nature. I loved watching him create trees out of a quick slide of a paintbrush loaded with up to three colors at a time. Another twist of the wrist and a running stream would appear. He was a man who had found his talent early in life and had made such a success of it that he didn't have to work at all during the winter.

Summer would generate enough sales for him to live off of for the rest of the year.

While Jiggs had, in summers past, taken to the practice of hawking the wares of his tourist shop out on the street, this summer was particularly lucrative for him too. His sparse one-window shop was now packed with customers who formed a line trailing out the door as they waited to pay. He had a single counter with a hand operated cash register and he only accepted cash for payment which could make the wait seem even longer. My parents had tried to make our stores more modern and we were now able to make an imprint of our customers' credit cards on a sliding device, for which the buyer only needed to sign. Mother was showing me how to take the receipts from these kinds of sales and enter them into the accounting ledgers. This was her way of getting me to become more involved in the business side of things and to begin thinking about my occupation for the future. I was willing to help, but I found the work monotonous. Accounting wouldn't be the core of my future. My heart was set on fashion design and there was no denying that, even if it seemed illogical to my parents.

Although our family's businesses were booming during the summer months, my parents enjoyed catering to our winter customers too. It struck me as interesting how the summer and winter customers were distinctly separate groups. The summertime tourists seemed intent on learning what they could about nature and the history of the wagon trains, outlaws, Indians and gold mining towns. The winter customers seemed to come for hunting and fishing or simply to run up and down the mountains in snowmobiles or skis.

It turned out to be the best summer financially that my parents had so far. Father was leaving his worried state and coming back to life. The years of hard work was paying off. The excitement we felt over our good fortune was injecting energy into our operations like never before. We all pitched in without thought of complaint knowing it was for our mutual benefit. Paul was taking the lead on many tasks that father had previously handled himself. Seeing him do this took a great burden off of my father. I was grateful for this, both for his peace of mind and for his physical well-being.

Paul had come up with the idea of paying Kills Enemy and Old Iron Eyes to sit in chairs outside the front of the museum in their native clothing so that tourists could pay the museum to have their photos taken with them. Normally reserved, they seemed to enjoy doing this for hours at a time for half of the money. To pass the time in between photographs, Charles and I would visit with them.

One day, the four of us were sitting outside the museum talking about the march to Mount Rushmore that had been staged that day, by a group of angry young Lakota Sioux. They were marching up to Mount Rushmore with buckets of red paint threatening to paint the presidents' stone faces bright red in protest. They were protesting not only the ongoing animosity of white people owning land in their sacred Black Hills, but the ever growing mistreatment they felt was being aimed at them by those in authority. The police were on standby and had already sent a warning that if they tried to approach the monument, they would be arrested for trespassing and attempting to damage a government property. The return threat only infuriated the group more, who then said they were also going to pass through the old mining town of Keystone and start scalping the locals.

"What if they come here?" I asked, fearful again.

"They're only saying that for shock value," Old Iron Eyes told us.

"The elders will talk to them and calm them down," Kills Enemy said.

Old Iron Eyes looked at Charles and I. "Right now you are still only children," he said. "But, someday you'll understand better how there are two wolves inside of every man. These are both constantly fighting against each other. One is good. One is bad."

"This goes on all the time?" Charles asked.

"A man's whole life...and, you know which one ends up winning?"

"Which one?" Charles asked.

"The one the man feeds."

Charles stared incredulously at Old Iron Eyes for a long moment. There was a seriousness in his expression which I had never witnessed before this day. "That's exactly how I feel," he said, almost in a whispered tone. "I really don't know which one is going to win with me."

"It's mostly up to you, but sometimes up to fate. Sometimes, it doesn't matter how much I try to stay on the side of the good wolf, some man gives me a test to see if I'm going to push over."

"You mean be a pushover," I corrected.

"That's what I said 'if I'm going to push over'."

"What do you do then?" Charles cut in.

"If he needs to get his ass beat, then it's going to happen," Old Iron Eyes said, hammering his fist down hard into the palm of his hand. "Some guys won't quit until they get it."

Charles busted out laughing. Old Iron Eyes didn't talk much about fighting, but now and then his tougher side showed up. I knew he mostly kept it hidden for my sake.

Kills Enemy, standing next to me, winked one eye in comradery. "Old Iron Eyes is a big fighter?" I asked, wanting her confirmation.

"He's been in a couple real nasty ones," she said. "He was much younger when those happened. He doesn't get so easy angry now. I'm proud of these Indians marching up the mountain of these American leaders. They're walking wakan with dignity for all Indians being treated unfair. They know what's the right thing to do. They do this hike for no other reason than that."

Someday my sister's daughter, Mary, and also you and Charles will learn to walk with your own footsteps when it needs to be done too. You won't care about what might be or what other people think. You'll just walk that way because you must."

This made me think about the real violence which had taken place between men caught up in wars. "I've got a serious question. What was the point of scalping?" I asked.

Old Iron Eyes cringed, before offering an explanation. "That practice went away mostly, a long time ago. The scalp itself would have the skin of the man with the hair still attached."

"Taken while he was alive?" Charles asked, wide-eyed.

"Usually cut from the enemy after he was dead, but if the man were considered extremely evil sometimes they would cut it from him as he was still alive." He gestured as he said it with a large hand grabbing imaginary hair while the other hand made a furious slice.

I shivered. "God! That must've been horrible pain." I was torn between being sorry I had asked and being too curious to stop the conversation.

"When one suffers too much, it's natural to want to hear the one causing that pain to suffer also. Some Indians long ago would be fighting against men who were like vicious animals. It's then when regular men most easily return to the animals living within themselves."

"So...they kept this scalp as a trophy or something?" Charles asked.

"We believe—I say we—because I mean me too...there's great honor in actually making physical contact with an enemy. Think about this. If you shoot someone with a gun from far away, it's not the same as jumping on his back and taking his life with a knife. If you already decided you were justified in killing the man. It would be an important decision, even if it had to be made quickly. So yes, sometimes this scalp would be celebrated because it belonged to a man of evil. They would stretch it around a wooden ring, pulled tight to dry it out. They might attach it to their clothing and wear it. Or attach it to a long stick and carry it in a scalp ceremony, dancing around a great fire with rattles and drums, celebrating the bravery of the tribal member by shouting out exactly what had taken place."

"I could never do that to another human being," I said.

Kills Enemy spoke up immediately. "Depends on circumstances. I would with no problem if I felt that strongly in my heart to do it. If I was that angry and the evil was that great."

I saw Old Iron Eyes turn and look over at his mother, eyebrows raised in shock. "And now, we know why they call her Kills Enemy," he said. "A warrior she is."

"You would too, even today," Kills Enemy countered to him. "So would you," she said, looking straight at me.

"No, I wouldn't," I stated again. "I've always been a puss or a crybaby, exactly like Charles says. I can't even see taxidermied animals without feeling sad."

"Different deal," she said. "Taxidermied animals didn't deserve it, unless they were killed because they were needed for food. Then, hopefully they were killed without unnecessary pain. Different deal."

"I'd kill someone if I had to only. If he was gonna' get me first," Charles said.

Kills Enemy said, "The greatest enemy...the one who can do the greatest harm to us, is not necessarily the one that sneaks up on you. It can be the one you know best."

"And, who would that be?" Old Iron Eyes asked.

"Ourselves," she answered.

When I got home that evening, I told my parents about this conversation. My mother was furious that Old Iron Eyes and Kills Enemy had discussed murdering another human being with her children. Charles and I winced as she picked up the telephone to give them a call. I'm not sure what she said to them then and it didn't matter. They had answered our questions honestly.

* * *

It was around that time that I had walked up to the old millhouse for a visit and arrived at the moment that Little Dennis had been caught in a lie.

216

It wasn't a straightforward lie, but rather the kind of lie which is a trick and only punishable when the perpetrator is caught. He had been caught by his father, Dan. Now that I was there, and since I was considered like their family too, I also was just in time to get involved.

"You can't sell something to people which isn't what you say it is," I heard Dan say. He was holding several small plastic bags in each hand.

Dennis looked up at his father and shrugged his shoulders, nonchalant. "I didn't see harm in it. I only sold them for three dollars a bag."

"Yes. As porcupine eggs." His father looked at me as I stepped up onto the front step. "Porcupine eggs. Cockleburs. Who told you to do such a thing?"

"Nobody told me. I just was lookin' at them and thinking one day that if a porcupine came out of an egg, that's what the egg might look like. So I remembered how Old Iron Eyes said 'tourists are stupid'. I took the typewriter and made paper labels for the inside of the bags, saying 'porcupine eggs'. Then I took them to town and sold them all day long on the main street."

"Wow!" I said, impressed. "How many did you sell?" Dennis gave me a little sideways smile.

"Don't encourage him," his father said, speaking to me. He squatted down to eye-level with his son. "You can't do this anymore. It's not honest or right. You understand?"

"If you tell me not to then I won't, but Laura's daddy sells those jackalopes. Monroe Hansen sells

217

jackalopes in his general store. There's no such thing as that neither. It's nothin' but antelope horns on a stuffed rabbit hide!"

His father put his arm around Dennis's back, carefully guiding him a few feet more away from where I stood. I could hear him when he whispered, "Monroe is wasicu--a white man. He doesn't have to live by our rules. You're Lakota. Think about that." He shifted his glance towards me and winked.

Dennis walked down the front steps and tossed his remaining bags of porcupine eggs into the outdoor trash bin. He looked over at his father who gave him an approving nod.

* * *

There were a few times in town at the diner, when I saw Paul sitting in a booth talking with Jiggs Throckmorton. They seemed like unlikely friends, not only because of Jiggs' dislike of people who weren't just like him, but also because I was certain Paul knew of the friction between he and father.

Our store sales had slowed almost forty percent, according to mother. I had heard her telling Sheriff Basset about it one morning and was surprised to hear her say that she wasn't going to get involved. She told him that in the past she had been too quick to come to father's rescue or stay up late at night discussing new marketing ideas or ways to trim their budgets. She told Basset that she wasn't going to do it anymore. She had said, "It's best to let my husband tend to these things himself."

Before long after that, I opened the door to the business office one day and interrupted an argument my father was having with Paul. Apparently, they had sold some quantity of hunting and fishing licenses on behalf of the state and instead of setting aside the money to be paid at the end of each season it had been spent. From what I could gather, Paul had put forward the extra money as larger-than-normal sales and father had happily used the funds to purchase a lot of extra merchandise for both the museum and the store. Father was ranting loudly at Paul. "I told you to keep that money completely separated from sales!" he yelled.

When he saw me standing there, he stopped arguing, walked over to me and asked calmly, "Do you need something, honey?"

"I wanted to show you this beadwork." I held my hand out to show him my latest piece. "Are we in trouble about money?" I asked.

"Aw, it's a minor thing we have to deal with. Nothing Paul and I can't fix. Let's see this fancy medallion here..." He turned the piece over and over in his hands and checked the stitching carefully. "I can't believe this, Laura. You make these just like a true native. Your friend Kills Enemy taught you well. What a gift." He looked at me deeply as he handed it back. I saw that his eyes were watering.

"Glad you like them. I'm going over to Berit's, if you'll tell mother," I said. Leaving them alone, I bounded out the front door and down the street slowing only when I had traveled a few blocks. I needed to be far away from the store. My mind felt troubled over what I thought I knew, even if father had reassured me. I wasn't going to mention it to anyone yet, but I had to tell Charles.

When I talked to Charles, he told me that he had seen Paul on several occasions taking cash from the cash register. He had once even asked why, and Paul had said that he was making bank deposits. He said he didn't want extra cash in the drawer in case someone tried to rob us or something like that. Now, Charles and I suspected that he might've been putting that extra cash in his own pocket.

Later, Berit told me she had been in Jiggs' shop one afternoon and heard a customer say that Paul had sent him in. It was normal for the shopkeepers in town to send customers to each other if they didn't carry the same products, but Jiggs carried many of the same items sold in our store. I didn't dare bring our suspicions up to father as he was so defensive of Paul's work.

A few months later, Charles and I both helped with a new inventory list. Father compared it to the sales reports and found that a big chunk of the inventory was missing without any sales to account for them. Paul suggested that we might have been robbed and my father changed the locks on the storeroom. The more these things happened, the more father was beginning to strike out against everyone around him, blaming his bad luck, local thieves, the incompetent tellers at the bank and even Charles and I when we were working.

Paul had convinced father that he needed to take out a loan at the bank, putting up the property of the general store as assurance that they would repay it next season when the extra merchandise they purchased was sold. After the loan came through, my father's tension eased, as if all he needed to do was wait. What he didn't know, was that there had already been a flurry of hefty fines mailed by the state over the license funds that had not been fully repaid. He never saw them because Paul had been throwing them away. When father found out about the fines after a visit from a state auditor, which were in the thousands by then, Charles overheard him asking Paul not to tell our mother. What Charles overheard father say exactly was, "Don't tell her because she'll think I'm a failure now for sure." When Charles told me about this, I struggled with not telling. Then, I remembered the day Mrs. Biermann had told me to not interfere in matters between my parents. Charles and I agreed between us that we should stay out of it.

CHAPTER FIFTEEN

My parents had left for their annual three-day trip to a trade show in Denver. They were looking forward to making connections with new suppliers for the latest merchandise for the store. Charles and I were looking forward to being in charge of ourselves while they were away. We made a pact that neither of us were going to break the trust that our parents had placed in us by doing anything we shouldn't while they were gone. Besides that, we were going to keep our eyes on Paul, whom my father had instructed to take his place at the stores while they were away. Mrs. Beirmann had been put in charge of checking up on Charles and me, but we expected that Paul would try to muscle some authority over us too while they were away.

At the general store, early on the second morning after they left, I walked in the front to see Charles confronting Paul. I heard him say, "I'm telling my mother when she gets back."

"Go ahead," Paul said then. "I'm the one Monroe listens to. You don't know anything about this business."

"He put you in charge of running things right. Not robbing us." Charles said. A glazed anger crossed his face. I didn't want them to fight again, so I called out to Charles from around the corner to come to me.

"My car won't start," I improvised. "Can you come look at it? I'm late for school."

Charles left to follow me and started the car with no trouble. "What's going on now with you and Paul?" I asked. "I could hear you all the way outside the store."

"Son-of-a-bitch-bastard has been ripping dad off into the thousands," Charles told me. "Not just dad, all of us. He's a thief, Laura and I'm exposing him to mother. Dad doesn't believe anything if Paul doesn't present it to him. It's like he's an employee of Paul's instead of the other way around."

"Mother's upset most of the time now, Charles. I don't think she can handle another thing. Why don't you and I try to study the records and sort out what we think? I'm no accountant and neither are you, but we're okay at math. You especially. You're a numbers guy. We can do it together. Meantime, I'll call our parents at their hotel—say you and I are gonna work longer hours at the store to move Paul further down the schedule. At least, that'll take him out of the way until we find out something. If we don't get our facts straight, we'll be the ones in trouble."

"We can't talk to mom yet," Charles agreed. "You're right. She was happy to go on this trip with father." Then, he focused intently on me, "Laura, here's what we'll do. I'm going back in there and saying I was wrong. That I was mistaken. Let Paul think it's been a misunderstanding. That way, he's not covering up what he's done. You know, give him enough rope to hang himself, like what Sheriff Basset says."

It was a surprise to me to see Charles have the ability to cool off and think clear-headed for once.

223

"I'm with you, Charles," I said. "However you want to do it." I watched him walk back into the building. I was proud at that moment for his determination to look after our family. It was more concern than our father had been showing lately. Father should have noticed what Charles had noticed, if it was true.

That afternoon when I got off school, it was beginning to snow. I was looking for my brother when I saw Paul emerging from the back cellar of the general store. He was dirty and holding a small black wrench. When he saw me, he stopped at the halfway point up the stairs and immediately told me that father had asked him to fix the furnace. I hadn't heard there was a problem with it, but before I could ask about it, Charles was starting for the stairs talking about bringing up a bag of potatoes for when mother got home.

As Charles stepped down on the first landing of the stairs, Paul took his pack of cigarettes out of his pocket and stuck one in his mouth. Seeing Charles standing there, he handed him a cigarette too. Charles looked at him for a moment, as if he were puzzled, then accepted the cigarette. "So, what's wrong with the furnace?" Charles asked.

"Pilot light was out and I already fixed it. Real simple," Paul said. "But, I can't slide the bolt closed on the tool storage door. It's rusted and stuck. Maybe you can budge it."

Charles flexed his arms backward, stretching his fingers a couple of times. "Gimme that," he said, grabbing the wrench from Paul. "It's a damn bolt. How hard can it be?"

Smiling, Paul withdrew a silver lighter from his pocket, flicked it open and lit his own cigarette. Charles popped the white stick in his mouth and Paul lit the end of it for him. "I owe you one," Paul said.

"What a puss!" Charles said as he clumped down the creaking wooden stairs.

I started in on Paul. "Stop encouraging my brother to smoke," I said angrily. "He's not going to be like y..."

I never got to finish my sentence.

At that very second, the gas furnace exploded blowing Charles out of the basement and onto the first landing at the base of the stairs. Badly burned and knocked out, he laid there motionless. Flames licked at his heels from the adjoining room.

After a second, the shock wore off of what had happened. I screamed out loudly and started to run down to my brother, but Paul held me back. Paul himself ran down with the water hose to fight the fire and to see to Charles. He began pulling him back up the stairs. At the same time, I decided I should get someone to help. Running as fast as I could, I pushed open the front door leading into the general store and called the fire department and ambulance.

When I returned, there were neighbors and shopkeepers at the stairwell who had come from many directions, trying to assist. I heard Paul shout, "Someone better call the ambulance, ladies and don't look at him 'til they get here."

"The ambulance is coming. They're called," I yelled. I ran up to the edge of the stairs again, but my feet wouldn't let me go down. Mrs. Olsen appeared from the old house on the back lot, took me in her arms and turned my face toward her shoulders, hugging me closely to her so that I couldn't look when they brought Charles out into the open air.

Paul came up to Mrs. Olsen and said, "He's burned really bad. We don't want to make it worse by handling him wrong."

"To hell with that," said Mrs. Olsen. "I'm a nurse. I'm treating him as best I can right here." She moved towards my brother and I heard her gasp loudly. She tried talking to Charles with no response.

"It should've been me," Paul said carefully, hanging his head down. He turned to face me. "What are we gonna do? This is so bad. This is terrible." He dropped his head low into his hands and kept it there for a long minute.

I couldn't even look at him for the rage and pain that was building up inside me. I had to pull it together if I were going to be of any help to Charles. I ran down to the end of the driveway to help direct the ambulance when it arrived. There were more people now, gathered around the entrance to the stairway and I saw a group emerge carrying Charles wrapped in a blanket.

The waning sound of the ambulance as it drove away that day has stayed with me, even now. I can't explain why it's the most outstanding memory of that day. I have blocked out much of what happened after that--the days that followed seemed to blur together. I hear that ambulance still sometimes like a mournful sound announcing more about the seriousness of life and death than I was prepared to face at that time.

Charles' accident and the circumstances surrounding it were unbearable to me. Our parents immediately focused blame on Paul. I blamed him too. Mother insisted that Sheriff Basset interrogate Paul at length. I struggled daily trying to grasp what had happened. Given all the dangerous things Charles had dared and survived, it was incomprehensible to me that this simple task of opening a stuck bolt could have ended as it did.

My parents spent most of that November of 1977, at Charles' bedside in the intensive care of a special burns unit at the hospital where he had been flown to in Minneapolis. Mrs. Biermann came to stay with me at our house, cooking meals and answering both the door and the telephone, fielding endless inquiries after Charles' condition. It was a great help to me not to have to talk with visitors and callers.

When mother and father were home, a few short hours at a time, they updated me on my brother's condition which never improved and only declined. We cried separately in our own rooms and at times, together. Just before Thanksgiving, Charles died. None of us knew how to deal with the grief we felt. Our parents clung desperately to each other at times and, at other times, they navigated as far apart from one another as possible. The confusion I felt ran around inside me and wouldn't let me go. There were days when I made excuses not to leave my room so that I could look through all the things that reminded me of Charles. Often, I wanted to leave the house

227

and sit with a friend and talk about anything besides what had happened to my brother.

After the funeral, which was attended by people who I had never even met, I kept replaying the cruel accident over again in my mind. I missed Charles more than I could have ever imagined. *"If we could just go for one more hike in the forest,"* I would think. *"What a great day that would be..."*

Some weeks later, Sheriff Basset stopped by the house and advised my parents that he had finished his inquiries over what happened the day my brother died. "What I believe is that Paul didn't harm Charles with malice," he told my parents and me as we sat in the living room together. "If anything, I've concluded that Paul is guilty of stupidity. Repairing a gas furnace without the proper training was plain stupid."

"I had asked him to check on it," I heard my father say, nearly whispering. His face paled. "It's my fault."

Mother pulled away from his embrace then and look at him a bit disoriented, blinking back tears. "We can't blame anyone for this, dear. We've got to be strong for each other." I rushed over to hold her hand before the tears came rushing back.

"I'm getting away from this house," my father said, his hands fumbling and searching his pockets and then the kitchen counter for his keys. From across the room, he waved goodbye. He slammed the front door on his way out.

"You want me to go after him?" Sheriff Basset asked.

"Let him go," mother said. "I've got no more energy in me for any other battle. Let him go." Sheriff Basset walked into the kitchen and quietly fished through the cupboards collecting a teacup and some tea. He boiled the water and steeped the tea bag, slowly and carefully, then sat if before my mother.

"Drink this and warm up inside," he said to her. "You don't realize it, but I think you've got about a half a cold." He took a wool blanket off the side table and fluffed it for a moment before placing it around mother's shoulders. "Take care. You're needed and loved more than you know, I'm sure." He turned to me and gave me a hug.

As he walked away, I struggled to contain my emotions. I didn't even see him to the front door. Instead, I stayed seated as close beside mother as I could get and didn't leave her side for many hours until we both retired to our rooms for the night. Well into the night, I heard my father return and quietly find his way to bed. There were many nights wherein he didn't return and Basset came to visit or to check on us.

* * *

One day in December, about a month after Charles died, when I went up to the lodge looking for Old Iron Eyes, I found him outside chopping firewood and stacking it. I had brought along my grandmother's journal.

"What you got there?" he said as I walked up with it tucked under my arm.

"My great-grandmother's journal, again," I answered. "You have time to listen to me read a little? I need to stay away from the house for a while. My parents are pretty sad."

"They will be for a long time. You too, Laura. You need to go into mourning for your brother for a long period of time. It's good to cry about it."

"I don't want to," I said. "It makes me feel angry when I start crying."

He chiseled the heavy axe down so that it stuck in a log. We both moved to the outdoor benches and sat down. He folded his arms, waiting. "Then, let's read this journal," he said.

I opened the journal to a page I had marked before leaving the house. I read the passage from my great-grandmother, Laura Helena's journal to Old Iron Eyes:

'A fat bumblebee darts from flower to flower, buzzing around the insides of the buttercup. Limestone cliffs lined the valley where I sat, cradling me in. It was one of those days when I could lay in the field for hours looking up at the clouds, but I had to continue home. Here and there I could see cave entrances. Made a mental note to go back someday to take a closer look.

The Lakota walked out of the edge of the thick trees carrying an already skinned animal of some sort over his shoulder. He noticed me watching and without even a nod, he continued on his way. Later that evening I could see a spiral of smoke rise up from the hills. I pictured him eating his prey, enjoying the result of his kill distinctly more than we, who had our food prepared by someone else.'

"She happened upon on a Lakota hunter that day," I said. "That's the part I wanted to read to you."

"Sounds like a very strong woman. By that time, if she was helping to settle the new town—they were all hard-working women in those days."

"Are you hunting this year?" I asked.

"Sure am. You want to go along?"

"Actually, I do. I want to see you hunting. I want to understand how you do it."

"It's not for a normal girl, Laura. You sure your little ballerina heart can take it?"

"Charles always said I wasn't normal anyway. He said I needed to toughen up," I said. "But, I don't know. I guess I wanna' find out."

By mid-winter hunting season, it was discussed and settled with my parents that I would go on a hunting trip with Old Iron Eyes and one of his younger male cousins. All the way up into the mountains, I thought about how thrilled Charles would have been if he could have gone with us. I was also dreading the actual killing of an animal, as I knew my little ballerina heart probably would be crying. However; knowing that Iron Eyes hunted for food and not for trophy, made me much more accepting of it.

After a successful hunt, I watched Old Iron Eyes begin to skin the deer. After I got over the squeamishness of seeing what the insides of an animal really looked like with the glossy white fatty layer and then the redness of the meat underneath, I admired his skill. I watched as he meticulously dragged the knife into the space between the hide and the outer layer of animal fat while he peeled back the hide turning it wrong-side-out. The meat was carved up with great precision too, wrapped first in wax paper and then in aluminum foil before being labeled with masking tape and marked with names to be distributed among several of his family members for their freezers.

When his relative had left with the meat, Old Iron Eyes stretched the hide out on a board and tacked it, hair side down, with nails. Then he scraped at the remaining flesh from the backside of it. I watched for a while, then he handed me the knife and relinquished his chair without saying anything.

"Seems gross," I said as I reached out with the knife quietly pacing, cutting, pulling and peeling off the flesh. I found a rhythm in the work which relaxed me and carried my heavy thoughts far away.

"Isn't gross when you're eating dinner or using this leather for your beadwork, is it?" Old Iron Eyes asked.

I didn't say anything then for a long time.

"It's important to not waste animals," he said, breaking the silence while I continued to clean off the hide. "We don't want to waste any food. Even vegetables. Think of people who labored in the field to grow the crop. It passes today through many hands before it gets to the grocery and to your table at home. That doesn't even take into account your parents had to work their tails off making money to pay for that food. Food is not just something you eat. Me...I'm guilty of eating too much. I shouldn't eat more than my share, if I were a good Lakota. My mom reminds me of this. In her day even, food wasn't easy to get. Usually, her people grew their food and hunted I guess more than half of it."

I had wondered if I could survive if I had to hunt my food. I certainly didn't consider hunting to be a sport. After all a sport is two fairly equal opponents—give the deer a gun and then it might be a sport. Still, I understood why the hunters continued to live off the land. In some way, I learned to respect the old ways as well as the life of the animal.

CHAPTER SIXTEEN

I was hiking through the forest going up to the lodge to see Old Iron Eyes when a large feather fell from the sky and landed right at my feet. The importance of eagles and eagle feathers to Native peoples is undisputed. I wasn't clear on exactly why that was so, but I thought it was beautiful. Since Charles died I had been having a hard time seeing the beauty in anything, so I picked it up and carried it with me to show to Iron Eyes.

As soon as he saw it, he spread open his arms and gave me a great big hug. "This has chosen you," he said joyfully.

I didn't feel like talking about anything spiritual or mysterious. My heart was questioning my beliefs. "I'm going to have to side with my father on this," I said. "A feather can't choose a person. It just fell off of the bird as I was walking below."

"Oh, no. Doesn't happen that way," he said as he took it and looked at it closely. "It could just as easily fall off in Lake Angostura."

I stood there saying nothing.

"Laura, my little one," he said more excitedly this time. "If you were a warrior back in old times, you would be given an eagle feather after some brave act. Then it is given only with serious preparing ceremonies and fasting. You usually get it from a relative. They can only be earned."

"How did I earn mine just then?" I played along to see where it was going.

"It chose you," he repeated. "What I'm saying is that it's a great gift. You should pray to the Creator and also say a prayer to thank the bird for the gift."

"I tend to go along with whatever you tell me," I said. "But, I'm not saying prayers of thanks to an eagle for his feather. I'm just not going to do that. It's too weird." Then, more seriously, I said, "I haven't really prayed to God for a long time anyway. I don't remember how—or even what to say."

"Doesn't matter what you say. It matters that you must pray, every day, Laura. No wonder..."

"No wonder what?"

"Nothing."

I could see that I had knocked holes in his amazement over the feather, so I pretended to be interested. "What else should I know about eagle feathers?" I asked, resigned to learn something from him again.

"They're also tied together to create a fan for burning sage. You can use the fan for ceremonies to bless people or to give thanks to the Creator. People have lost their way now. They don't know much about how to pray to the Creator. You must pray to the Creator to stay strong in your faith."

"I've heard some Indian bird stories like in parables, teaching how we should behave and such," I offered.

"The most important reason to have a special eagle feather is for the talking feather ceremony. Where it's passed from person to person while the one holding it is required to share his deepest thoughts. To speak from the heart."

As with every lesson he had ever taught me, I offered up my newly acquired eagle feather to participate in Lakota tradition. Old Iron Eyes and I passed the feather back and forth, until he finally demanded that I go first:

"Father barely talks to me anymore," I started. "And, he has started taking hikes up into the mountains alone--something he never did before." I quickly passed the feather to him.

"Why does this make you concerned?" he asked, seeing that I was on the right track, urging that I should continue. He passed the feather back to me.

"I think he wants to go where Charles used to go. I think he holds on to Charles by going there."

"You worry he's not safe?"

"Oh, my father can manage in the woods. It's like he's running away from us at the same time." We were passing the feather between us very quickly. A lot was being said that had not come out before.

"Did you ever try to go with him?" Old Iron Eyes asked.

"He doesn't want me to be there," I said. "If he did, he'd ask me. Besides, why doesn't he see that

236

Mother and I are sad about Charles too? It's like he's the only one who is sad."

"Everyone feels pain a different way, Laura. Even physical pain is tolerated by some better than others. Let him have his pain in his way. I think what you're afraid of is losing your father too." Old Iron Eyes kept the feather with that statement, walking away and putting it up in a cupboard. "I'll give this back to you next time you come up to see me," he said. I took that as a signal that I was supposed to leave then and think about all that we had discussed.

I walked home and found my father sitting up. It was after dark and I was supposed to have been home before nightfall. I settled into the chair next to him and apologized for being late.

"It's alright," he said. "Can't blame you for not wanting to be around here so much. If you didn't have Mary and Old Iron Eyes to keep you interested in their stories and such I don't know what you'd do for excitement in this piss-ant town."

"We could tell stories too, if you want," I offered.

"Nah. Go on to bed," he said, waving me away.

Mother walked into the room and, giving me a half-smile and motioning with her head towards the hallway. I took the hint and left the room. Before I reached my room I could hear them arguing. She said he was 'drunk again' and he was mumbling about worries over the museum. "That mammoth museum is going to pull away people from ours—don't you see?" he was saying.

"I don't care," she shouted. "You're going to bed and we're going to talk about it tomorrow. Not another word, Monroe or, I swear, you'll be sleeping on the couch."

"Okay," I heard him say before I closed the door to my room.

The next morning, I asked her if father was really drunk. I explained that I hadn't realized it when I was talking to him.

"It's not something you should have to realize," she said, still visibly annoyed. "I'm going to an auction today with Mr. Basset, she explained. Please, try to help your father with whatever comes up here at the house. Let Paul handle the business side of things. That's what he gets paid for."

Sheriff Basset showed up and mother and he left without saying anything to anyone.

When he dropped mother off on the front step, father and I were sitting on the porch nearby.

"Now, you have the furniture, all you need is a wife to take over that house of yours."

"That's not as easy to find as you might think," he assured her. "The good ones seem to be already taken."

"Get out there and date once in a while. You'll find someone special. A big handsome guy like yourself, must be in demand," Mother said, laughing at the same time.

Father shot a glance at me like something was wrong. I was laughing at the idea of Basset being a 'big handsome guy' myself. "I always thought of him as a sort of a frog," I whispered covertly to father. But, he didn't seem amused at it.

"Yeah, I've dated one or two, but I don't find the right person for me," Basset said. "Thanks for going with me and keeping me company, dear heart," he said to mother.

"Goodnight," she said opening the door.

No sooner had the car lights flickered and dimmed away from our driveway than father erupted in angry accusations. "Dear heart?" he repeated using Basset's words. "Dear heart? What the hell? He's a poet now?"

"He's being friendly," she explained. "Why are you getting angry?"

"Why am I angry? My wife's having a date with the local sheriff and you ask why I'm angry?"

"A date?" mother retorted. "For God's sake! We went to an antique auction. If you had come too, you might've enjoyed it."

"Someone had to stay home and look after the businesses, didn't I?"

"What do you pay Paul to do? Can't he cover for you once in a while?"

I couldn't listen to more so I walked quickly back to my room. There was less arguing in the days after that, but a new quiet fell over our house which was unsettling.

As usual, I tried to stay away from the house. When Old Iron Eyes' wife became ill he asked me to sit with her while he worked. I jumped at the chance to do it. She preferred to stay at the reservation more than the lodge, so I rarely saw her.

* * *

I felt Cecilia's forehead for fever and it was still hot. As I sat in the chair beside her bed, I was concerned that I wasn't capable of doing this. "Does Old Iron Eyes ever get jealous of you?" I asked out of the blue.

"It's a strange question," she answered. Her eyes were closed, but I could tell that she was listening all the same.

"Why is it strange?"

"Because, he'd have no need to be jealous. We chose each other out of love and under the eye of the Great Spirit. Neither of us have thoughts to be jealous of the other one. We wouldn't choose each other if we ever wanted to be romantic with any other person."

I sat there thinking to myself about what she had told me.

She opened her eyes and turned her head on the pillow to look at me. "What has you thinking about things like that?"

"I think Paul is jealous of me and I'm not even dating him. I got stuck going to one dance with him and now he acts like he's somehow involved with me."

"Well, Paul; he is a mean person. Why do you care what he thinks?"

"Don't know," I answered pensively. "My father keeps trying to get me to see something good in him and I don't. Paul manipulates my father into thinking that he's nice to me; when nobody's listening, he's so hateful to me. I guess it's wrong, but I blame him for sending Charles down those steps that day."

She sat up and took a long sip of her tea. Then, looking up from the cup she said, "Forgiveness is difficult. I doubt anyone wants to be with Paul because Paul doesn't underneath, like himself."

"Paul isn't the only one jealous these days. My father's furious at my mother for time she spends with Sheriff Basset. They've gone to antique auctions together. She wanted to get away from the heaviness of the store and thinking about Charles. I understand why, but father was so mad that she went with Basset."

"You can't tell the one you're married to, who they should have for a friend. If your father really knew her heart, he could have taken her to see those antiques himself."

"I don't know why we've had such problems in our family," I said sadly.

"Every family has problems, Laura. You have to deal with it. Just deal with it. In a few months, things will change again. You don't know if it's for better or worse, but you keep trying to make things better anyway."

"For now, we need to get you well again. What would Old Iron Eyes do without you? What would those school kids do without you?"

She pointed up to the wall behind me. "Look over there. Twenty-eight of them."

On the wall were twenty-eight handmade note cards with colored drawings by the children in her classroom.

"That's true love," she said. "There's no human beings more accepting and willing to understand the meaning of love than school children. Nobody has taken away their natural instinct to love yet. Wouldn't the world be different if we all thought like these children?"

Individually, those cards would have been simply thoughtful, but together they told a story about a devoted school teacher and how much the students cared about her.

"Do you know how happy it makes me to be around you and Old Iron Eyes?" I asked her. "When I see you two so right together, I hope a man will love me like that someday. Don't think I'm being mushy, but I've grown to love you and Iron Eyes. I feel safer when I get to be with him than anywhere on earth. You're his wife, you get what I mean."

"Never be afraid to tell people that you love them, Laura. We have a short time here on this planet, so it's important to say that when you feel it. Old Iron Eyes keeps everybody safe in his care. How he was raised. His mother has been a great caretaker of people too in our family. With friends too. She's the one who reminds us to take care of each other."

I remembered Charles then, and felt his absence heavily in my heart. "Charles, was always trying to build me up or look after me or defend me. He was the best brother, really. It took some time to realize it. We had our share of disagreements, but I wouldn't have traded Charles for any other brother." I began to cry uncontrollably and she left me alone so I could get it all out.

* * *

It was April 1978 and the first dinner our family had hosted in nearly a year. Mother had called six or seven close friends to join us, including Sheriff Basset and Mrs. Biermann.

From the outset, a tension surfaced between my parents that had no definition putting an air of discomfort on everyone there. Usually, it was mother who ruled the cheering section of our previous dinner parties, but now it was the guests who intentionally lifted our spirits. Surely, everyone who had been to her dinners before was thinking about how different it was without Charles there.

Mrs. Biermann was the first to acknowledge his absence. "We surely miss Charles at times like these," she said. Her son Michael and Berit quickly offered condolences of their own.

Then, Sheriff Basset commented on how relieved he was to hear that mother and father were forgiving of Paul's mistake in not shutting the gas off properly. "A young man like that can carry a heavy burden on his back after such an accident," he said. "The guy's had a difficult upbringing to begin with. I sure wanted to punish someone over it myself, but I'm afraid what happened was just a tragedy."

"I don't want to relive the accident over dinner," father said. "You're right that we don't hold Paul responsible, but further than that, we don't need to discuss it. We've been mourning for months now and this is an evening for relaxing with friends."

Basset looked at the faces around the table and said, "My apologies, Monroe. "Sorry if I brought this up at the wrong time."

"You've been like a rock," mother said to him. "We appreciate the support you gave to us along the way, and it's especially nice to have you for dinner. As it is for all of you." I saw her look diagonally across the table at me for a split second. There was an expectancy in her eyes. It was a signal to chime in agreement as Mrs. Biermann's children had done.

I took the chance to say what I thought. "Of course, he's responsible either way," I added. "Deliberate or not; he's the one sent my brother down those stairs." Usually, my parents would correct statements like these since they were trying to steer the conversations into lighter subjects, but they both let it go, knowing the depth of my loss too.

Mrs. Biermann had grown close enough to me that she didn't feel out of line by correcting me. "It's not healthy to hold a grudge, Laura dear. I think that's what your mom means by forgiveness. It's not the same as forgetting."

Father straightened up in his chair. "Well, Paul will be coming back to work for us again, soon. He's truly needed. We haven't been giving our businesses the attention they used to get while we've been struggling to get back on track," father revealed. "We can't sink in despair. Best to pull ourselves up and keep trudging on."

From where she sat next to him, mother placed a reassuring hand on his arm. "Our businesses have been a blessing. Helped keep us getting up every day when we might have rather chosen to mope about."

Old Iron Eyes sat at the opposite end of the table from my father. He understood my point of view, better than anyone there. "Maybe we should all smoke the peace pipe together with Paul?" he said, not meaning it. Everyone stared at him at the same time.

"Yeah--that helped a lot with the U.S. Government didn't it?" father said looking down the table at Old Iron Eyes.

Mother rolled her eyes and looked over at Basset. "Here we go," she said. "It always starts like this."

"Not every pipe smoked between people is a peace pipe," father continued. "I remember reading that somewhere."

Old Iron Eyes knew my father would persist until he got an answer. "There's no such thing as a peace pipe. That's why I said that. The United States government thought that when their representatives smoked together with the Indians that they could make land deals without bargaining. They knew that Lakota used these pipes in ceremonies where truths were sent up to the heavens. So, that's where that came from," he explained.

"But, wasn't the government taking their land?" Berit's brother Michael asked innocently.

"They were making a deal on it yes," father said. He lifted his glass of scotch and raised it towards Old Iron Eyes.

Old Iron Eyes toasted him in return with a glass of milk. "Let's just say that it wasn't the Lakota telling lies around those pipe smoking sessions."

"It's all bullshit anyway," father said quickly. "You don't need to have a ceremony to look into the eyes of another and tell when he's putting one over on you."

"Monroe!" mother said, gesturing towards Millie's children. "Children?"

"Sorry," he said. "Not like they never heard the word before. I'm sure Millie here can swear with the best of them in the privacy of her own home. Am I right?" he asked Mrs. Biermann.

Putting on a jovial smile, she said. "I can for sure."

CHAPTER SEVENTEEN

Berit and I had made a pact to meet up at the museum late one night and poke around it in the dark. I had heard that Father hired two new men to set up the latest section of the museum. Whatever they were doing was top secret and only he and Paul were in on the plans. I was anxious to get a glimpse at the new exhibit before anyone else. Charles had always been my ready companion for such ventures, but now he was gone forever. Although Berit was neither as sure-footed nor daring as he had been, she had become my accomplice in everything.

The back door to the large new wing of the museum was open. All sorts of construction materials laid about the place and we wandered down a great hall that had doors on both sides. There was a section at the far end where three large and rugged wooden doors as tall as a barn door were closed. Someone had placed iron hinges on them and a drop-bar closing mechanism on the outside. We could see a light underneath the door and we heard male voices inside.

"God, would you look at the size of him," I heard one man say. "He's gonna' be mad as hell, Samuel. Don't do it."

"Doesn't matter how mad he gets. His days are numbered."

It sounded like they were nearing the door so we quickly hied ourselves completely out of the building. Whatever they were doing, they didn't need us getting in the way. As we stood in the cold night air waiting for the men to leave the building, Berit and I stared up at the stars pointing out the constellations that we knew. She had a great interest in astronomy and it was wonderful to hear her go on about the names of stars and nebulas and galaxies. Just as space went on forever, so did Berit's talk about space. All at once, we saw a shooting star and she suggested we should make our wishes on it. I wished to be a great fashion designer and she wished to be an astronaut one day. "Jesus! You do dream big," I said.

"But, even as far as we travel in life," she said, giving me a hug, "you and I will be friends forever."

"This is true," I said. "Me and you are never losing sight of each other."

Soon the men left the building and as quickly as their taillights disappeared from view, Berit and I took the key out of the secret hiding place behind the building and let ourselves inside again.

Returning to the large wooden door at the end of the large hall, we both grappled the heavy iron bar and slid it open. The door creaked under its own weight. I fumbled to find the light switch on the inside wall.

"Did you hear that?" Berit asked, the alarm raising in her voice.

"Don't be a puss," I heard myself say. "We're going to find out what's in here before anyone."

I was still running my hand along the dark wall when I heard a breathing sound. I found the switch and threw it upwards. An angry snarl rang out and Berit and I turned towards the sound. We stood frozen, face-to-face with two caged black bears. We grappled onto each other like teenage girls do when faced with fear, as if together we might create one strong force. Truth was we were terrified and awed.

The bears grumbled a bit, eyeing us curiously as they staggered from one foot to the other.

"They're drugged or something," Berit said.

"They are?" I asked. "How do you know that?"

"Just look at 'em. They can barely stand up."

"Why in hell would my father have black bears in here, alive?" I asked out loud. "We're not running a zoo."

"Remember the guy said 'his days are numbered? Maybe they're taking them somewhere else, to a zoo somewhere else," Berit surmised. "Either way, we're not supposed to see them here. I'll bet they're not allowed to have these here. What if the game warden finds out your father has these?"

"My father does stupid stuff these days," I said. "I doubt my mom knows about this either. I don't think she'd like it much."

"We're not even supposed to be here at night, so we're not going to tell her."

"But, it's dangerous Berit," I said. "Maybe we should tell."

"It's going to make trouble for your father and us," she warned.

"Doesn't matter about that," I said. "Worse yet—what if they get loose and kill somebody?"

"They look very secure."

"We're telling," I said decisively. "That's it and I don't care what happens."

Berit and I took the long hike back to the house, tapped on mbedroom door and called her out into the kitchen. She was surprised to find us up so late at night and to find out that we had been down to the museum. Before she could admonish us for that, we launched into telling her what we had discovered. Immediately, she sent us both to my room for the night. After that, the house erupted in argument as mother woke my father. At once, it seemed every light in the house was on and father was on the telephone calling someone. He slammed the front door and we could hear his truck throwing gravel all the way down the driveway. In a second, the house was quiet again.

In my room, lit only by the moonlight outside, Berit and I looked at each other expectantly. She spoke first. "That was a great idea," she whispered sarcastically.

"I think we screwed up," I whispered back. "Let's ask my mom what's going on now."

"No. We'd better stay in here. Sounds like she's mad. Let her forget for a night that we weren't supposed to be there either."

"Yeah, right. I hope father wasn't leaving us," I said. I felt tears welling up.

"Don't be stupid. He's never going to leave you and your mom. For sure though, she didn't know about this before. Why would he keep something as big as two bears and not even tell her?"

"That's how he is now," I said.

We went to bed that night and the next morning mother made us breakfast without mentioning the upheaval in the house from the previous night. Father came into the kitchen and, without speaking to any of us, poured himself a cup of coffee before heading out the front door.

After some time passed, Berit spoke up and asked, "Did Mr. Hansen let the bears go?"

Mother stood at the kitchen sink rinsing dishes and answered without turning to face us. "He said he's taken care of them. The danger is over now and I would appreciate if you girls would keep this to yourselves. We could have been in big trouble with the game warden for having those. You did the right thing by telling me, but forget it now."

"Okay," I said. Berit and I looked at each other puzzled, while mother's back was turned away from us. "We're sorry for being there when we shouldn't."

"You both could have been hurt," mother said. "And that was the most upsetting thought of all."

Two weeks later, the new wing of the museum opened up and many locals bought a ticket to see the much anticipated exhibits. There had been ads in the local paper and even printed banners posted around town. It had gained an unintentional circus feel and Paul stood at the center of it like a ringmaster. The three employees at the museum began the tours, opening one door at a time down the hallway, trailing spectators in and out of each room as they made their way to the large wooden doors at the end. Berit and I followed our mothers, the same as every other patron, taking in great paintings and talking dioramas that explained the natural environments and biological diversity of the Black Hills. Now and then a stuffed coyote or bobcat stood open-mouthed under the glaring lights. At last, father had made use of many items he had purchased at auction that were laying up in storage until now. It had come together fantastically.

"It's wonderful," Berit commented.

Mrs. Biermann nodded. "I agree," she said, smiling.

"Monroe and the crew have worked so hard to get it opened on time," my mother explained. "But it's been well worth the extra hours."

At last, we reached the end of the hallway and three groups of the inaugural tour had merged into one. After a short speech by father, the attendants removed the iron bar from its slot on the heavy wooden doors and swung open the doors to the largest room in the building. In the center of the floor, on concrete mountings that were painted to resemble rocks stood two taxidermied black bears.

My own gasps were drowned out by the collective gasp that went up in the crowd. I struggled against myself not to turn and run away, until at last,

I couldn't be contained any longer. Shoving my way out of the tightly packed crowd, I moved quickly toward the hallway. Before I reached the double doors at the end of the hallway, I had already burst out in tears. I could hear Berit's footsteps behind me trying to keep up, but I ran faster than her so she couldn't catch up. Outside, I ran far ahead and turned to see her stop at the open doors before going back inside the building.

I ran to the edge of the forest, unsure of where to go. By instinct, I gradually arrived at our house, but I didn't go inside. Instead, I walked past it, down into the field on the backside of our property. The grass there was taller, unkempt more than the rest. The further away I went, the more the wild state of this field was noticeable. Last summer had been different. Last summer, Charles and I had lived leisurely here on this enchanted patch of grassland. Charles had kept up on tasks like mowing automatically while I tended to the small vegetable gardens that I had started on my own. Then, almost as a reward to ourselves, we always escaped in the afternoons, taking in the surrounding mountains like they were life itself.

The prior summer, Charles and I had both been full of life and all sorts of activity. Now, he was gone and I felt more alone than I ever dreamt possible. I thought about the black bears, once alive and trapped in a cage, now stuffed for tourists to see. Warm tears dampened my cheeks as I noticed myself, subconsciously scanning the forest hoping to catch a glimpse of Charles wandering about. Nearing the steep incline of the hill that we had climbed so many times together, I deliberately searched out the place where he had set a half-moon of rocks to mark the entrance to the cave that he had discovered.

On the way home, I felt a new inspiration to sew for the rest of the week. Sewing took a focus and patience that I needed then. It also provided a joyful escape from my heavy thoughts. Dreaming of designing beautiful clothing transported me to a different realm. For days at a time, I began to draw new patterns and plan whole collections of clothing, doing little of anything else.

After several days of planning what I was going to do and imagining every detail of the finished garments I wanted to sew, I went to the large office behind the store. I dragged down several bolts of fabric from the high shelves, unrolling and examining each one. My new Elna machine sat waiting on the worktable, its miniature light bulb glowing like a faithful friend. Around the top of the worktable was my pin cushion, some thick colored thread for embroidery and various wide-mouthed jars of scissors and other tools. Just as I had chosen my patterns and began cutting out the pieces, making adjustments for sizing, Kills Enemy showed up at the store, unexpectedly.

She saw the work I had spread out in the back office and started to leave. "I'll return later," she said.

"No." I said quickly. "Please stay. I can get to these later."

"Where have you been?" I asked.

"Been staying home more," she said. "But, Old Iron Eyes says 'you'd better come to see Laura today

254

because she asked about you'. So, here I am." I was so happy that I had already wrapped her in a hug.

"Mother made some strawberry-rhubarb pie," I said. "Let's have some." I led the way to the efficiency apartment and warmed a couple slices in the oven.

As we sat down to enjoy the warm pie, Kills Enemy saw one of my grandmother's journals open on the table.

"Looks like an old book," she said, picking it up and feeling the soft yellowed pages.

"Those are my great-grandmother's journals from the 1800's," I said. "You can read them if you'd like. It's okay."

"Why don't you read me a few pages while we have pie," Kills Enemy suggested. "What did she write about? Nothing too personal I hope."

"Some thoughts were personal about her husband and their journey from Chicago. Mostly, she wrote about her life once they got here and starting building their house. I've been reading a section about a bear incident because I'm thinking about those bears father has in his museum."

"What has you thinking about those?" she asked.

"I dunno," I said, not wanting to talk about it. I set the strawberry-rhubarb pie on the table and watched Kills Enemy study the flaky layers of its crust with a fork before slicing off a bite. She lifted the piece to her lips and rolled the warm dessert in her tongue before closing her mouth over it. "This is like heaven," she said. "Best ever pie."

I settled in a chair beside her with my own slice of pie and began to read.

Home alone early evening and an unexpected visitor arrives. A young black bear who smelled dinner on my stove. I battled his outstretched paws waving hungrily through my open window with a hot poker from the pot belly stove. At last, I grabbed two oranges off the pantry top that we were gifted by travelers and tossed them out the window. As they rolled onto the grass, the curious bear followed. He took both in his mouth and lumbered back into the forest. I didn't mean to feed him and worry that now he'll return for more.

"That was some luck from your grandmother," Kills Enemy commented. "The wood and mud houses they built back then weren't much protection from a bear if he wanted to get inside."

"I'd be scared out of my mind," I said. "Now listen to an entry she wrote later....here's where she has another encounter with a bear." I flipped forward a few pages and began to read again.

An outdoor pit dug by four men who captured a bear. After a week a great iron and wood cage constructed in a circle overhead. People paying to come have a look at him. Barbaric to say the least as the poor creature has already developed sores on him and constantly trods in a circle out of boredom. Sometimes spectators spit or throw things down upon him. Tonight I'm sneaking up to the pit to lower some planks that will help him escape.

"Did she actually do it?" Kills Enemy said tapping the pages of the journal excitedly, for me to read quicker.

"Yes, she did." I announced. "She did for sure. She writes about it here..."

I've told my husband my plan. He thinks I've gone mad. When I told him the cruelty of it was more than I could 'bear' he laughed at my choice of words. Still, he supports me 100% and offered to go with me. At night, we lowered the planks without being seen, then broke down a section of the structure. Standing back a distance, we witnessed the skinny bear climb out of what would be his grave if we hadn't intervened. A proud moment if ever I had one—for my husband too.

Of all the stories my grandmother Kate told me when I was younger about my great-grandmother Laura Helena, she never told this one. Perhaps, she didn't want me to do anything so dangerous.

"It was dangerous for sure," Kills Enemy said. "I wouldn't do it."

"I guess I wouldn't either," I said. Emotion suddenly caught me from nowhere and I struggled to remain composed.

"What's wrong?" she asked.

"I'm just tired," I answered. Even though I knew it would have been impossibly dangerous, I wished I could be as brave as my great grandmother.

CHAPTER EIGHTEEN

I had prepared a backpack the previous night for a long walk up to the lodge to see David and Mary. They had invited me the week before to stay with them for three days while the oblate minister visited their family. They told me he was a special visitor and they were excited for me to meet him.

Now, it was morning. Inside my pack I had rolled up my hand-beaded dress and the velvet lined box of my beaded jewelry. I wanted to show Mary the dress and get her opinion on it. If Kills Enemy happened to stop by I could also show my beadwork to her.

Rounding the corner into our kitchen, I ran straight into Paul standing at the counter pouring himself a cup of coffee.

"What're you doing in our kitchen this early in the morning?" I asked.

"Waiting for Monroe, little girl," he answered. "What are you doing?" he smiled and stepped closer.

I opened the refrigerator and took out the food I had packed for my hike. "I'm going up to the lodge to see my friends," I answered. I used to let Paul's presence get to me in the past but I was determined to do as Mrs. Biermann had said and 'take the high road'. Whatever he was doing there waiting for father didn't concern me. I hurried to get my backpack in order and sat down in a chair to lace up my short-ankled hiking boots.

"You look pretty this morning for a girl who likes to be out in the wilderness," Paul noted.

"Thank you," I said. "It's nice of you to say it."

"When you grow up, you and I are going to go on another date. You'll see that I've changed and I want to be a better person. I appreciate that you're willing to give me another chance."

"You're saying that. I didn't say that. I'm just trying to be civil," I stated flatly.

"That's good enough for me, Laura. That you and me can be friends again. You'll see I'm not the bad guy you think. Your parents see it and maybe you will too."

My jaw tensed. I knew that I was failing with the high road. "I'm not for you," I reminded him. "Besides, I'm going to be going off to college very soon, for four years at least."

"I'll wait for you."

"I don't want you to," I said looking directly at him.

"I hope you have a good visit with your friends," he said. "And as I said, you sure look pretty."

Grabbing my backpack and my hat, I turned and left the kitchen without looking back.

As I passed through the front hall, my mother stopped me, "Not so fast," she said. "I haven't seen you all day and now you're leaving again? Laura, it's as if you don't want to be here, ever." I could see a twinge of hurt in her eyes.

"You've let Paul back into our lives. Even when he tries to be agreeable, he brings unhappy times to our house," I reminded her coldly. Hiring him back wasn't exactly her decision, but my father's. "Why doesn't it bother you like it bothers me to see him around here?"

She put her arm around my shoulder and walked with me to the door. "We've got to forgive. There's no sense in multiplying guilt which he already must feel by withholding our forgiveness." She steered me gently so that I was facing her. "You do understand fairness. What's right. Surely, you don't expect us to let ourselves be eaten up with hate."

"You forgive him," I said. "I don't feel this way only because of Charles. It's no secret that I've despised Paul for a long time." For me, avoiding him seemed like the most sensible thing to do.

"It's not that I don't want to be around," I said. "But, you're busy anyway. I'm going to the millhouse to show Mary my dress. Get her opinion on it." I hugged her to show that I did love her.

She sat down on the bench with her elbows propped on the table next to it. Dragging her hands up both sides of her face, she pressed her fingers deep into her hair. After resting her head in her hands for a brief moment, she looked up at me again. "It's hard for moms to let their children go, Laura. I know you're learning and growing into a very capable young woman and I'm proud of that. I want time with my daughter before you run off to the big city."

I pulled my backpack up onto my shoulders. "I not leaving just yet," I reminded her.

At the millhouse, the oblate elder from the reservation had already arrived. He would be there for an entire week, living with the family and offering them help with the rhythm of daily prayer. It was important in Lakota tradition that families didn't fall into the habit of stopping and starting their prayers inconsistently. It was also this full-blooded Sioux minister's specialty to help families outline specific plans, designating each family member's work schedule. He helped them establish specific times for silence and personal time, as these were needed to keep up a person's strength and awareness. Even without living on the reservation they respected and followed his guidance. I was lucky to be there while he was offering help and I naturally asked for his guidance for myself too.

When it was my turn to speak with him, I talked about what mother said about forgiving Paul and how it was so hard for me to do it. I told him about father's drinking and how I worried about leaving mother alone while I went off to college. There were other things too, that I poured out in one long string of anxiety-ridden teenaged concerns until at last, I was finished.

He took both my hands in his and closed his eyes. He breathed in and then opened his eyes again and stared directly into mine. His gaze was strong and piercing. "Go sit in nature for some time. You are weighted down with your thoughts. Climb up into the mountains where the air is lighter," he advised.

"Don't think about these things while you are there. Don't think about anything. Only sit and be still."

"I've been hiking in the forest for many years now," I said. "How's that going to help?"

Clearly he wasn't going to debate his own advice. He looked at me expressionless. "You want the answer or not? It is not a hike I am suggesting. Sitting still and not thinking is the hardest thing for any human to do, but that is the answer for you today." With that, he moved away from me and on to the next family member.

I left the millhouse and hiked up to the place I knew the best--the place where I had recently seen the female bobcat and her newborn kittens. My mind was muddled with unrelated bits of thought. I couldn't seem to stop turning these bits over and over. What I wanted was to rid myself of them, but they clung to me like ghosts.

The cold hadn't quite left me and I felt weakened by it. My breathing was heavier that day, but I knew that walking in the forest gave me energy, so I forced each footstep with hope.

Climbing up on the rocky outcropping, I moved with careful footing knowing that a fall would injure, or possibly even kill me. Settling myself securely on the precipice jutting out over the edge of the mountain, many thoughts again rushed at me, all at once. After some time sitting there, I decided to forget about finding answers. The town below sat quiet, although there was so much turmoil there. It was convenient at a distance to be a removed observer. *"What a perfect postcard scene," I thought.*

262

As I stared blankly at the scene, uneventful and unmoving, it seemed frozen in time. I did what the minister had advised me to do. I merely sat there doing nothing, thinking nothing for what seemed like hours. After some time had passed, I noticed that everything around me had become still and frozen. Nothing moved, not clouds, not blades of grass, not a single animal or bird. Color saturated the blue sky more than normal, glowing with a light beyond the afternoon sun. The light pulsed outward until the outline of the village blurred under its cover.

Above it all, I stared deep into the sky and saw it opening. I'd never even imagined an opening in the sky and it should have frightened me. Instead, I calmly stared, not moving. There was no end to it. Even though nothing appeared within this opening, I could see everything I ever wanted to know. I took it in, not hungrily for myself, but sparingly. It was as if my soul itself took away only what it needed.

The vision lingered as long as I looked directly at it. It was like a visual bridge to another place, only I couldn't travel there. I could only view it from a distance. When I shifted my focus to my surroundings and became aware again of where I sat, the sky returned to normal. At once, I was overwhelmed with emotion. For some time afterward, I sat perfectly still thinking that I might collapse if I tried to stand. Gradually, I inched away from the ledge and slid while still in a sitting position, off the backside of the precipice, tightly gripping the rocks with my fingertips. It wasn't until I was on flat land again that I finally stood up.

I didn't know when or how, but finally I felt that something wondrous laid ahead in my future. Whatever steps I needed to take in the beginning to get to this future, were unclear, but it was clearly there. I had to let myself be guided to it. Now, I had no concern about the unknown details.

* * *

Kills Enemy searched through the drawers of the velvet lined jewelry box examining all the beadwork that I had completed. She spread each item out on the table and picked them up one at a time. She didn't say anything for a long time as she inspected every stitch and every bead. "This has become very good," she said. "You do beadwork well now—just like a true Lakota."

"I only know how because of you," I said. "I've decided that I'm going to take this skill and turn it into my career. I'm going to sew high fashion clothes and they'll have beautiful beading on them. Even though I don't have an exact plan yet, I know that's what I'm going to do. I'm so grateful to you for teaching me this. Because of you I found my talent. Even my own mom has never shown me how to do anything like this."

She smiled and playfully put her forehead on my forehead until we were looking eye-to-eye. "Your mom doesn't make anything, except tasty strawberry rhubarb pies," she said. "That--she does very, very well." Pulling away from me, she looked up and closed her eyes. I sensed that she was imagining the long ago flavor of one of my mother's strawberry-rhubarb pies. When she returned to the present she said, "In our family, all my sister's children are my children too, you know? That's why I've taken care to show you things. Teach things. Like you were my child too. You don't have to be a natural daughter to have another mom. Girls should have many mothers and boys, many fathers. But, that's all I have to say tonight believe it or not," her face lit up with a satisfied smile. "I am tired and I'm going to sleep. I hope you know how much I love you. Knowing that you'll carry this talent of yours on to the next part of your life gives me great pride for my part of it. This has been one of the happiest nights of my life."

Sometime during that night, Kills Enemy moved from this world to the next one. Her lifeless body laid motionless in the bed, while several members of her family clutched her to them, pleading with her to awaken. Finally, they stopped holding her and allowed death's cold grip to claim the body. I telephoned my mother to tell her what had happened. Mary was sitting beside me at the kitchen table while I dialed the phone. She placed her chair next to mine and I wrapped my free arm around her shoulders. As she leaned into me, I began to tell her something I could not even fathom myself.

"Kills Enemy is gone," I said carefully, unsure if Mary was ready to hear the words spoken so finitely. "I'm staying here with Mary for a while—to be with her."

Mother's voice was one of shock and grief. "I'll tell your father," she said. "Tell little Mary that we are so sorry and we'll see you at home later."

As I hung up the phone, I felt Mary embrace me tighter. We both sat in the chairs at the kitchen table, clinging to each other and crying for the better part of an hour. An ambulance came and went, taking Kills Enemy's body away while Mary and I tried to comfort one another.

Old Iron Eyes sat down with us, presenting in each hand a cup of freshly brewed coffee. "Chock-Full-O-Nuts," he announced as he sat the mugs down. "Best coffee in the world. Drink up and we will say some prayers to wish my mom a good journey into the next life."

By the time Mary and I had added the cream and sugar to our coffees three more family members had joined us at the table. Immediately, Old Iron Eyes set about serving them the best coffee in the world too. "We must remember," he said to all of us, as he bustled about the kitchen. "To feel a love as great as we felt for my mother, Kills Enemy, does not end with death. Even the memory of love cannot be changed. Not ever. It stays with us just like the flavor and the smell of this coffee. When I drink this coffee, I can remember a certain café where I used to meet my wife when we were dating. The memory is so close I can almost touch it or taste it or smell it, even though that time is gone. Kills Enemy is gone but her memory will be so close to us we will feel her with us always."

He began to cry then and the assemblage of mourners listened attentively as he struggled to hold his composure. His voice was taut yet certain as he spoke again. "Remember that every breath we take contains the dust of our ancestors. The same air we breathe contains tiny wandering pieces of everyone who came before us. You cannot see it, but it is there. Even the dust we walk on is part of our ancestors."

Looking around the table we silently eyed one another taking in what he was saying. "Love remains." Old Iron Eyes added. "It remains." There were nods of agreement all around.

CHAPTER NINETEEN

On a beautiful fall morning in the Black Hills, a group of nearly one hundred people hiked for an hour and a half to reach the top of Kills Enemy's favorite mountain. I trudged along beside my parents, amazed at their endurance and touched by their respectful reverence within the group. At the top everyone assembled in a layered semi-circle and faced the half-risen sun.

Old Iron Eyes stepped up in front of the assemblage and withdrew a folded paper from his jacket pocket. He spoke loud and clear. "This is a prayer originally translated by the great Lakota Sioux Chief named Yellow Lark back in 1887," he said. He held it up and shook it out flat for everyone to see. "You can see from the paper that it's very worn down. This is the prayer my mother said every morning of her life for as long as I can recall. This was her morning prayer. So, I think it's the prayer she wants me to say now."

Measured and serious, he read the words, his deep voice wavering in places with immense grief:

"Oh, Great Spirit, whose voice I hear in the winds, and whose breath gives life to all the world. Hear me; I am small and weak.

Let me walk in beauty, and make my eyes ever behold the red and purple sunset. Make my hands respect the things you have made, and my ears sharp to hear your voice.

Make me wise so that I may understand the things you have taught my people. Let me learn the lessons you have hidden in every leaf and rock.

I seek strength, not to be greater than my brother, but to fight my greatest enemy–myself. Make me always ready to come to you with clean hands and straight eyes.

So when life fades, as the fading sunset, my Spirit may come to you without shame."

With that, he motioned for the family members to come up to the podium. In the early morning, with the brilliant sunlight barely brushing the backs of the rolling mountains in the background, they placed their hands together to support the weight of the large natural clay urn. They stepped back away from the podium in unison, still holding the urn, and turned toward the mountains. Then, they lifted it high and tipped it, dispersing the ashes out into the ever-shifting winds.

I strolled slowly back down the hillside that day alone, lagging far behind my parents and lingering purposely behind the crowd. I watched Kills Enemy's immediate family walk in a group together. Even though they had always treated me like their family too, I wanted to let them have their privacy. My emotions were running like wild horses all through my being. Losing her brought back painful memories of the unexpected death of my Grandma Kate and the more recent memory of Charles' accident.

My feelings for both Grandma Kate and Kills Enemy, the kinship beyond familial relationships, had been the same. These two women, above anyone else, had effectively shaped the character of the woman I wanted to become. I looked forward to the day when I might walk boldly with my own footsteps, to be able to meet life head-on with dignity, with discernment and without fear as they had taught me to do.

* * *

It was an unhurried beginning to Winter. Father sauntered around the museum with Old Iron Eyes, proudly showing off the latest improvements to the building and its exhibits. He was talking a lot about value and profit and his big plans for the next tourist season.

"But, aren't you satisfied with everything you have?" Old Iron Eyes asked suddenly. "It is enough."

"I want to make it bigger," father said. "We're getting more traffic every year, so expansion is justifiable. Even my right-hand man agrees."

"Who's that?" Iron Eyes said unimpressed. "Paul? He's a help to you, but, you're capable of deciding for yourself if expanding is a good idea."

My father opened an accounting journal of handwritten entries. "See here," he pointed. "Here's what we did season before last and here's the final numbers for this past season."

I watched Old Iron Eyes take a closer interest at what my father was showing him. "Quite an increase; yes, Monroe." He looked puzzled for a moment and then seemed to dismiss whatever thought had struck him. "Better be careful. The city might re-evaluate your businesses and properties. Might raise your taxes."

"That's always a possibility," father said, standing at the far end of the new bar. "Care for a drink?"

"I'll have a beer," Old Iron Eyes said. He seated himself in one of the new wooden swivel stools and twisted back and forth in it for a moment testing its boundaries, seeming amused. Father busied himself behind the counter and produced two large porcelain steins of beer.

"Where'd you get these?" Old Iron Eyes asked running his finger across the raised painted scenes on them.

"Germany," father answered. He tilted his stein so that Old Iron Eyes could see the front. "See that inscription?"

Old Iron Eyes scrutinized the steins and the figures painted on them. "How'd you get the state to license you for alcohol and firearms, Monroe? I thought you weren't allowed to have both."

"Wasn't a problem, but I see your point. Doesn't seem like a wise mixture to give to one man does it?" After a moment of no conversation, father sat his beer down quickly. "Hey; stay here. I got something I want you to hear."

"I'm waiting," Old Iron Eyes said. He looked at me and shrugged his shoulders questioningly.

I have no idea this time," I whispered, climbing up on one of the stools next to him.

A minute later my father returned, arms loaded with a plug-in record turntable with a big square speaker. After fumbling around setting it up, he placed a record underneath the cover. "It's the speech of George Patton. From the movie, you know?"

Old Iron Eyes sat up straighter. "No kidding? I like this guy. Let's hear it."

They both sat captivated while the entire speech played. Father and Old Iron Eyes listened intently only interrupting during two parts. The first part was where Patton said..."the Nazis are the enemy....." Old Iron Eyes blurted out then, "Damn right they were!"

During another section of the speech, father cut in to recite the part that he liked best in unison with the recording. I had heard this speech more than a few times before and he had always chimed in at the very same parts.

At several times during the speech, they knocked their beer steins together and toasted one another and drank. At the end, Old Iron Eyes said excitedly, "Now, that's one guy that was a true warrior. A great American for any time."

Father placed the player on a shelf under the counter. "He believed he was born to lead men in wartime. Did you know that?"

"Like a premonition?"

"Something like that."

"So, you *do* believe in it when it comes to your general," Old Iron Eyes said victoriously.

"He was right about it." father stated. "And, he was in some way, your general too. If we'd been invaded, the war would've come here too."

"True. Well, he was wrong about only one thing in that whole speech, Monroe. That's the part where he said, 'America has never lost a war...'. America did lose a war. The Sioux defeated the United States in war and forced it to sign a peace treaty."

"Nobody 'forced' them to sign it."

"Oh, yes. They lost that war."

"We're gonna' respectfully disagree about this one," father said.

"No. I'm right," Old Iron Eyes said decisively. "Check your history, Monroe. It's there."

About that time, mother drove up and parked her car just outside the window. My father suddenly grabbed both steins by the handles. "Get these beers off the counter," he said. "She's becoming a damned nag about this lately." He wiped the telltale water rings off the bar top.

Old Iron Eyes shot him a serious look. "You've got a special wife, Monroe. Her nagging is a blessing. Don't forget that." He followed me to the far side of the room, leaving my father scrambling to hide the steins before mother walked in.

* * *

Many uneventful days ran together in the months leading up to my graduation and subsequent departure for college. Strange, how once the decision was made to leave, I hardly had any feeling or attention to things that were happening in between. My heart was so fixated on getting to the beginning of my fashion design education and the career that would follow that in my mind I'd already left.

One thing that did stand out to me was that whatever harmony once existed between my father and Old Iron Eyes had begun deteriorating into long tense beer or whiskey drinking sessions and loud arguments. It occurred to me that I was leaving home at the perfect time. As far as I could tell, my father was doing most of the drinking and most of the arguing. I often heard him boasting to Iron Eyes about the property he owned, the pieces he had in the museum that belonged directly to him and even how much money he had in the bank at one time.

Once, I heard Old Iron Eyes tell my father in a very angry way that he was getting too big for himself—that he was too focused on possessions. When he said that, I remembered how Kills Enemy had taught me the importance of sharing. In the Lakota community, they didn't allow social classes. If one person had too many possessions or money, he was obligated to share with family members and even those outside their own family. In this way, everyone remained equal. Iron Eyes wanted us to follow the same ideals, but my father was having none of his friend's well-intended advice.

Paul sometimes joined Father and Old Iron Eyes. During those evenings, Iron Eyes grew cautious and distant, knowing that the one-on-one conversations he valued with my father would not happen. He would leave for home earlier than usual so that Paul and father could stay up discussing grand business plans.

"You're worth whatever I'm paying you now," I heard father say to Paul once. "And, how much *is* that again?" It was shocking not only to see how far gone he seemed, but to hear Paul's reply.

"It's the best hundred grand you ever spent, Monroe. Just wait til next year. You're gonna be beggin' to pay me double when you see the books next year."

"I'm countin' on it," my father answered.

I didn't consider how much money our businesses were making, but to think that Paul had made himself so indispensable to father's dream, the thing that he and mother had built from nothing, was unsettling. Even when Paul tried to be cordial and even flirt with me, I couldn't appreciate his efforts the way my parents did.

After my high school graduation, mother, along with Mrs. Biermann, planned an elaborate outdoor party for about fifty people at the ranch house to launch me off to college. The day began as a luncheon that would run into a full-fledged party on through the evening hours.

There were tables set up outside on the long expanse of grass overlooking the forest where Charles and I used to escape. It was bittersweet to think about reaching this milestone in my life without him by my side. He would have been proud of me. The thought of leaving mother weighed heavily on my thoughts too. I knew she had my father, but now that I was the only child she had left, I could feel a certain loneliness showing in her eyes. Still, she donned a buoyant smile for the guests and shuttled from table to table, with me in tow, making sure that everyone knew where I was headed, what my college plan was and how long it might take me to reach my dream of becoming a real fashion designer.

Berit had made a collage on an oversized poster board--photos of all the garments I had sewed for her to model for me. I promised to hang it on the wall of my new apartment in New York City. Mary, David and Old Iron Eyes arrived, packed into the front of the pickup truck, bearing all sorts of food items and school supplies. It occurred to me that even upon my entry into an unknown world, I had no fear. The excitement of making my dream come true had overshadowed any thought of failure or possible misfortune. I was determined that the only outcome of my college venture would be success.

Mother had set up a sound system where everyone could go up and pick out CD's to play for me. It was great to hear music from every generation represented there. I heard country music, jazz and rock-n-roll, enlivened here and there by the elder's insistence upon some gospel and classical music. We had never had so many people on our property at one time. For a moment, I saw a glimpse of my Grandmother Kate's convivial personality in my mother. I remembered from my childhood that Kate had loved any kind of celebration, but my mother rarely found time to socialize in the years since we moved to Hot Springs. Always, the businesses came first.

Several friends of my parents and my school pals went up to the standing microphone and spoke about their best wishes for me. Mrs. Biermann felt especially responsible for shaping my path towards fashion design since she was the one who taught me how to sew. She gave an emotional speech about how I had been like a daughter to her and like a sister to Berit. I knew I would miss Berit terribly and hoped I might make friends in New York City who shared at least some of my interests.

Father took his turn and spoke at length about watching me struggle to find my talent. He respectfully noted too that Kills Enemy had been a tremendous influence on me. He told Old Iron Eyes that he would forever be grateful for the day when he led his mother into our general store, not knowing the deep friendship that would develop between her and me. He spoke of her patience in teaching me something as tedious as the traditional Lakota beadwork and her dedication to ensuring I understood the meaning behind Lakota traditions. Old Iron Eyes listened intently and was visibly honored that father acknowledged his mother's role in shaping my future.

Then, Paul stood up and walked to the microphone. "Laura Helena Hansen," he began. "We got off to a rocky start on our friendship, but me and you go back a long time now. I can remember you barefooted and planting corn in your little garden. I walked up and thought to myself 'those are the prettiest little knees I've ever seen'. It's no secret that through the years I've grown to love you."

People in the crowd clapped or smiled and looked at me, clearly enjoying the romantic words at that moment. Mother stood beside me and quickly took hold of and gripped my hand in hers for support. Putting my hand over my mouth, I was frozen with embarrassment and disbelief.

"I love you Laura, and someday you'll realize that," Paul continued. "Consider this a standing offer to marry you when you get this college thing done. I'll be here waiting." He looked around at all of guests triumphantly. With that, he walked back to the table where he was seated with some of Charles' former school friends, who were now working for him and my father.

I looked at mother who was just as stunned as me. I didn't know whether to be angry or embarrassed. She spoke first, "He has thoroughly humiliated himself," she whispered quietly. "There isn't a single person here who believes that you're romantically interested in him. What an arrogant thing to say at a gathering like this."

"He's an idiot," I said, making no attempt to hide my irritation. "Well, this is a day you've put your efforts into and we're going to continue to celebrate until the last guest leaves."

"Right," mother said.

As night fell, father lit up several strings of outdoor lights and encouraged everyone to step out onto the large raised platform he had built for a dance floor. After a few cocktails, even he and my mother danced together. Seeing them together, enjoying each other, without any thought to our family's past troubles or business worries, made me incredibly happy.

* * *

I wasted no time getting myself packed a few days later, and at last I was on an airplane headed for New York City. When I looked out my airborne porthole I marveled at the fluffiness of the clouds from a vantage point I hadn't seen before. This was my first flight anywhere and I was absolutely thrilled the entire way. Withdrawing my pocket-sized journal from my backpack, I wrote down my first impression of flying to send to Old Iron Eyes later. He had been apprehensive about me leaving, worrying about every detail from the flight to my city apartment living to the college environment. Despite his apprehension, he wished me well and I promised to write with the details soon as I got settled. Old Iron Eyes said he might try to drive to New York City one day, but said under no conditions would he every dream of flying. That, he had repeated again and again, was unnatural.

For the next three years, I studied religiously and focused entirely on completing design school. The day came when I first held my degree in my hands. I could hardly breathe. The long-held dream of actually being a fashion designer was realistically now within my reach. One of my instructors arranged for me to take an internship with a reputable designer for the following year, so that I could gain experience in the business.

It wasn't until after I graduated that I began to look closer at my environment. Three years of school had isolated me from a real social life, but I was beginning to feel a bit lonely. Having lived in both Minnesota and South Dakota I thought I had experienced every kind of cold there was, but now the New York City winter felt bitterly cold. Possibly, it was due to the isolation I felt not having been acclimated to city life enough to know what to do with myself after school.

After some time, I met a group of friends who had also migrated from other states and we became constant companions for one another. I began to experience that side of New York City which I had hoped to find. The city was vibrant and alive with music, theater and the arts which I loved. There were restaurants of every flavor so one never had to go hungry. It was a much faster paced life than what I had known growing up, but I was adjusting to it. In the mountains I knew I could explore forever and only glimpse a fraction of their mysteries. The same was true in New York City--I could live the rest of my life in this city and still not see everything there is to see.

The first dress I designed for my internship was based on a traditional Lakota jingle dress, a dress worn in the days of tipis on the prairie in everyday life but also for dancing. I knew from the outset that it was a risky attempt in the fashion world. Buyers had already seen years of imitation native designs which unfortunately had little resemblance to authentic Indian textiles. It was a challenge to incorporate the required elements with precisely the right balance to make it interesting.

Instead of leather and deer teeth, I used modern materials—namely a linen/flannel mix fabric and large opaque white glass beads sewn on with a brown jute cord. The cut of the dress was strictly modern high fashion, not a historical throwback to the mountains and prairies of South Dakota. I fringed the bottom with freehand cuts and lightly burned the angular hem with a hand-held cooking torch to give it a sense of mystery.

As part of our debut project, we had to model the finished garment ourselves. The faces of the five person panel selected to offer ongoing critiques of my project seemed puzzled at first. They each asked a great deal of questions about my inspiration and material selection process, but once they understood the background of the piece, they unanimously agreed it was the most unique design they had seen from someone of my young age and limited experience. They were so enamored with the design that they put it into production for that season.

I had done it. My excitement for my chosen career simply multiplied after that. Knowing that real people out in the world somewhere were going to wear my clothes, my creations, filled me with a joy beyond anything I had expected. I kept reminding myself that this was only the beginning. I wore that special dress quite often in the small space of my tiny apartment, snuggled up on my living room sofa watching television or reading until I fell asleep.

After finishing the apprenticeship, I set up my own design studio a few blocks from my apartment building. At first it was a solo venture, but eventually I hired an assistant who, although she was close to the same age as me, already had a couple years' experience in the fashion industry. When I had first interviewed her, I looked at her frail frame. *"A woman like that wouldn't last five minutes hiking in the mountains."* I thought. In a short time, I found out that her modest stature had no bearing on her talent. Not only was she a great organizer, problem solver and fabric buying expert, but she was also a talented seamstress. Her work ethic mirrored mine—whatever it took to get the job done, we'd do it.

Deborah had instantly admired my detailed business plans and I looked to her to help me hire talent for my new company, LHH Designs Limited. Most days we worked in the studio, until it was dark outside. We'd eat dinner at the restaurant next door and then share a taxi ride to each of our apartments.

She and I had been cutting, pinning and sewing one day for five hours straight. I looked up from my machine and said, "It's two o'clock and we haven't even had lunch. Let's go get some food."

"Your back is to the clock. How did you know it was two?"

I pointed to the sun outside our window. "The sun," I said.

"Weird," she said. "Exactly two o'clock."

I laid the garment I had been working on up onto the table. "Really," I said. "I've gotta' eat." The drive to finish the collection in time for the spring show was proving exhausting.

Reluctantly, in the days that followed, we hired four additional people to help sew my first complete collection. I was understandably overly anxious to any problem which might detract from making it happen.

One day however; I walked into my workroom and instantly felt like I was on a kindergarten playground. It was important to me to cast a dignified image of all our employees and the casual atmosphere had gone too far. An ultra-thin older man was laughing hysterically, standing on top of the table and draping fabric around his waist.

"Get down," I said sharply. "You're all supposed to be working."

"We are," he said coyly as the others scattered back to their workstations.

I turned to Deborah. "Why is he acting like that?" I asked.

"Like what?"

"He's waving his hands and talking in a voice like a lady. A couple of guys in my design class were the same," I said. "Is he acting?"

"He's gay."

"What do you mean?" I asked.

"Haven't you ever met a gay?" Deborah whispered to only me. She looked at me quizzically. "You know--a man who prefers to be in love with men instead of women?"

"Gosh, that's weird," I said. "I've heard about them, but no. They didn't have those where I lived."

She looked at me like I had landed there from another planet. "Surely, you knew one or two? They're everywhere."

"I don't think so."

"Don't say that in front of the others," she advised.

"Whatever you suggest," I said, not knowing why.

She hovered over me for a moment. "What *is* that beaded thing on your shirt?" she asked.

"It's an antique," I answered, not caring to explain. "It's an Indian heirloom."

"Like from India?" she asked.

"Like from Sioux Indians. Lakota actually."

She twisted her head to look at it from another angle. "Odd. It doesn't seem to resemble anything," she said.

"It's not really for anyone but me," I said, moving away to the opposite end of the long work table. I had a talent, I knew. Now, I had to get my team to work together for the benefit of all of us. I had to set down rules.

That evening, I called my mother for advice.

"Do you remember how long we tolerated incompetent employees and what a detriment it was to our businesses?" I quickly asked, explaining my dilemma.

There was a decisive tone in her voice that I hadn't heard before. "Cut them loose," she advised. "Start over with new staff. You can't afford to carry them when they're not doing what you hired them to do. You have more experience in business than most people your age, Laura. Put it to use. Be the leader."

For the whole weekend I thought about leadership and not much of anything else. I knew I had to snap my staff to attention or LHH Designs Limited would never be anything more than a lackluster clothing manufacturer.

First, instead of a long rectangular table I decided to change it to round, remembering from my childhood that in a circle everyone becomes equally important. To ensure that each person in my company understood the inspiration behind the collection we were designing, they were all sent on a weekend trip to Hot Springs. I didn't go with them, as I wanted their individual discoveries, their raw ideas instead of only mine, to be translated into a fresh new line of clothing. I gave them instructions to photograph the nature there and return to New York prepared to discuss how it translated to our clothing collection.

When they returned from the trip, at our first meeting I let them know my stance on how we were going to approach the LHH 'Star' collection.

"No one is going to put their drama ahead of the work that needs to be done," I said. I didn't care if they liked me for saying it. I didn't care if it might offend them that I didn't say it nicely. "This is my company, my dream, on the line," I lectured, placing my hand over my heart. "When you are here," I continued, "you are focused on only your talents and skills. It's not playtime, not social hour."

In the end, nearly half of the staff couldn't comply with my expectations. I followed my mom's advice and cut them loose. The next round of staff was hand-picked by me after long grueling question-and-answer interviews. With the second staff we were able to build upon my initial inspiration and design beautiful and unusual couture garments in natural fabrics. The orders were coming in steadily for our original designs as well. The new staff managed to keep up the workflow and meet the established deadlines for both lines of clothing. Finally, we had assembled a cohesive team that I affectionately dubbed, "the tribe". My employees preferred to call themselves "the village". Whatever we were, LHH Design's 'Star Collection' was finally off to a roaring start.

As the Star Collection took shape, I mailed home more and more photos to my mother. She immediately passed on the specifics of my pending notoriety to the media back home. Proud of hearing that a local girl had gained recognition in the big city of New York, the newspaper in Hot Springs phoned me for a telephone interview, asked for a few printable photos of my previous work, and then wrote a full-page news story in the life section of the newspaper. Within two days of its publication, I received a letter with a clipping of the article from mother. "You're gonna' be famous!" she quipped in the outer margins.

Perhaps prompted by that article, I received a letter from Old Iron Eyes. In it, he had tucked a postcard listing ten rules for Indians. It read:

TEN RULES FOR INDIANS:

Treat the Earth and all that dwell therein with respect

Remain close to the Great Spirit

Show great respect for your fellow beings

Work together for the benefit of all Mankind

Give assistance and kindness wherever needed

Do what you know to be right

Look after the well-being of Mind and Body

Dedicate a share of your efforts to the greater Good

Be truthful and honest at all times

Take full responsibility for your actions

I had seen the list before, posted at the lodge. At the bottom of the card, around the border Old Iron Eyes had penned in, *"Rule # 11: Consult your tribal elders."* After that, in red ink he penned, *"Please write back soon. We worry about you out there in a big city by yourself. Etc. O.I.E."*

After five years away, I had not forgotten the importance of showing gratitude for even something as meager as a postcard. When I had written to him last, I asked Old Iron Eyes how they were getting along financially. In his reply, he wrote, *"Money is not important."*

This time, I placed four one-hundred-dollar bills in an envelope and mailed my letter to him. I wrapped a note around the bills—*"You're right. Money isn't important. So, take this and pay bills with it so you and Mrs. Iron Eyes can relax a little. Now that's important!"* It was a fantastic feeling to be able to do it, but even though I was happy with the professional progress I was making in my life, I had begun to feel inside, lonely and wanting. I walked home from the studio one afternoon, looking down at the sidewalk as I went. At once, I noticed the ants were on the move and therefore; I knew it was going to rain. It made me think of Kill's Enemy who had taught me how to watch the animals for specific signs. If only there were something more significant to do with my spare time, maybe the answer to cure my loneliness would come.

As if God had heard my thoughts, I met Gregory, a guy with a great disposition who right from the outset adored me. He was an ambitious new stockbroker who worked in the building across the street from my studio. To get my attention he had flown a paper airplane out of his upstairs window which landed on the curb outside my studio. I saw him waving to me to pick it up from behind a third floor window and when I walked out and retrieved it there was a note inside: *Day # 9 since I first saw you. Airplane # 9. Lunch? With me? Followed by his telephone number.*

Apparently Gregory had thrown eight paper airplanes down towards me before I finally responded to one. He didn't have any of those awkward jitters one gets on a first date while getting to know someone and from the outset, it seemed as if we had known each other forever. For this easy connection alone, I was grateful. My dating experiences up until this time had left me feeling weary and anxious. I was beginning to think that I might never find a romantic interest.

We met up at a festive restaurant at Midtown where the west side of the block is crowded with inexpensive East Indian restaurants adorned with blinking Christmas lights. I had never been to a place where the restaurateurs actually shouted out to passers-by vying for their business. We ate nan, banana fritters, Saag Paneer and Aloo Gobi Matar. He had brought his own bottle of wine which we shared together until the wee hours of the morning. As we rode towards my apartment in the taxi we ended up kissing all the way home. It was quite a struggle to remember my Midwestern good-girl upbringing and not invite him in, but that changed a few dates later.

Gregory and I became inseparable. Without fail, from the day I had agreed to that first dinner, we met up every chance we had. My life became a flurry of lunches, movies, shopping sprees and dinners. The moments we spent together were gaining in importance as the weeks and months passed. Eventually, we began staying at each other's apartments on the weekends. I often called home and told my mother what a great time I was having with Gregory. She seemed delighted that I had found a guy who was becoming a serious love interest. At the same time, she often countered her excitement with ominous advice. "Be sure to know what you're getting into," she'd say. Or, "You never really know someone completely." It wasn't like her to put anyone in a negative light, especially someone she hadn't even met.

"How's Dad?" I asked one evening.

"The same," she answered. "Doing his bit, you know."

"What's that?" I asked. "Drinking?"

There was a long pause. "More than before," she stated quietly.

"Is everything alright?" I urged.

"No. It's not going to be alright like it used to be, Laura," she answered. "I stay at home most days now and let Monroe run the businesses himself. Less fussing that way. Don't worry yourself about these things though. You have your whole life ahead. Us old married folk have to lie in the bed that we made. Part of life, Dear—just a part of it."

CHAPTER TWENTY

The workday was almost over. Even if I was exhausted, I had a few more hours left to finish the piece that I was working on, so I decided to get some coffee to help ward off fatigue. I walked outside the office and ducked into the coffee shop next door. There were nearly four people ahead of me and all the tables were taken. While I waited, I flipped through a short stack of photos of my collection, studying the details. Someone bumped my shoulder, but I had grown so used to it after five years in the big city that I didn't look up from my photos.

Suddenly there he was standing next to me, bumping my shoulder again. "Hey, punk," Paul said grinning in that mean way that I remembered too well.

"Paul?!" My voice raised a couple of octaves all by itself. "What're you doing in New York?" Inside, I tried to reason that it might be coincidence.

He folded his arms high upon his chest and straddled his legs apart, planting his feet firmly. "Thought I'd come check out this big city I heard so much about. Not so much to be impressed over if you ask me."

"I hope you don't think I'm going to suggest that you and I should meet up, Paul." I said, quickly drawing my boundaries.

An angry look flash over his face. "You're saying you don't want to be friends," he stated flatly.

He was the last person on earth I'd ever expected to see in New York City. "We're not friends," I said, as I inched up in the line. "Not here. Not anywhere. Period. Enjoy the big city, but it's not going to be with me." I turned my back to him.

The guy behind the counter interrupted, pointing to me. "What'll it be?" I took a short step up to the counter.

When the other clerk, a young girl, asked Paul, "You next?" he moved away from me to place his order.

"Cafe latte, medium, no sugar," I said. Pulling cash from my pocket, I handed it to the guy.

Three dollars," said the guy behind the counter, as he took my money. He handed me the latte.

"You're good to go," he said, handing over the change.

"Thanks," I said and skirted outside the line of customers. Gripping my coffee while I put my change in my pocket, I kicked open the door with my foot. Reaching the sidewalk I moved in almost a half-skip, not looking back. I felt Paul could be following along beside me but I didn't dare look. An ugly feeling clawed the insides of my stomach. I gripped the handle of our studio's door and gave it a pull.

A large hand emerged beside me and pushed the door closed. "Wasn't very gracious of you back there," Paul said mere inches away from my face. "You could've taken two minutes of your precious time to see why I came here. Even a rattle-brain like you has got to figure out I didn't come here for the scenery. As I said, there's not much here I'd wanna' see anyway."

I looked him squarely in the eyes. "You came here to look me up? What's the point in that?"

"You left me lookin' like a fool back in Hot Springs, Laura. You had an obligation to continue working for me when your father lost it all. I'm the one who worked to put it back together for you and your mom."

"You harmed my family," I defended. "You stole from my father—I don't care what you told him. I know and Charles knew that you did!"

He pointed his finger in my face as if it were a weapon. "You owed me and your family some consideration. I was even willing to marry you, girl."

My mind flashed ubiquitously through all that had happened with my family. "I owe you, you drunken moron! I owe you nothing." I shoved his hand off of the door. He grappled toward my jacket trying to grab ahold of me, but I twisted away. "I have no reason whatsoever to speak to you...and, have never thought for a second to marry you." I said as I squeezed between him and the door. "I hate you!" I shrieked, purposely raising my voice as loud as possible, hoping someone from upstairs might come to help.

He must have thought someone was coming too because he stepped back as if I had hit him with a hammer between the eyes. When he did I pulled the door open and stepped inside. I pressed the security button locking the door behind me. Through the closed door I cried, "Leave me alone!" My heart was thumping in my throat and my breath came in short gasps as I raced up the stairs.

* * *

It was a new day that same week and I had put the creepy encounter with Paul behind me. I pulled my best dress out of the closet and wriggled it on over my head. Taking a few turns in the mirror, I enjoyed the unique bliss that comes from a designer's own perfectly fitted garment. This particular piece had been my first silk and jersey combination. I had struggled tediously with the design and with paring the two types of fabric into something that was elegant in its details and at the same time, slightly casual. The buyers at the most recent show had placed orders for twice as many garments as we intended to make. On this day, we would decide as a company if we would keep the originally intended limited selection or try to produce more quantity to match the demand. Either way, the dress had become a symbol of my achievement and on both days that I had worn it, I felt my confidence soar.

The workday couldn't end soon enough for me that day. I had already phoned my mother and gushed about how wonderful my boyfriend, Gregory, was. We were meeting for dinner that evening at our favorite restaurant. I had never been there but the girls at work said it would definitely be the kind of place I would adore. We had been dating for about four months and I was beginning to think that maybe he would be 'the' guy for me. He never seemed to want to go home anymore without inviting me to stay with him. It had been so important for me to establish my career that I hadn't ventured into anything more than casual dating until I met him. Fortunately for me, our relationship had evolved naturally, without time to think about where it was headed, until we were already in love.

Mother had advised that I had all the time in the world to let whatever it would ultimately be, develop at its own pace. My design team wished me a good evening as I headed downstairs throwing open the door, breathing in the darkening sky.

I waved toward an approaching taxi. Then again, Paul stepped out onto my path. "You're the same smart mouth little twig of a dirty barefooted girl I knew in Hot Springs," he said a few inches from my face, moving his head back and forth with each word. "You aren't ever going to be anything more. And...you're dressed like a hooker." He had a hold on my arm now and was waiting for me to respond.

The taxi slid by and the throng of moving people pushed their way around them. I struggled to not say a word. Freeing myself, turning away into the thick crowd and walking quickly, I thought I had lost him in the crowd. I waved down yet another taxi. It stopped and I jumped my body sideways into the seat. When the car started to pull out into the steady stream of traffic, my tension eased. I was safe again. Closing my eyes, I took a deep breath and tried not to cry. Opening my bag, I took out my face powder compact and flipped it open. As I stared into the mirror, I noticed a sadness in my eyes. I could hear Charles' voice from so long ago, "Stop being a sissy," he had always said.

"I can't help it. I am and I wish I weren't, but I don't know what to do," I said aloud as if Charles were sitting there in the cab next to me. He would have fought for me. He would have laid Paul out right on the New York City street. In his younger days, my father would have done the same. I don't know what hurt worse at that moment—the ever-present memory of losing my brother so tragically or knowing that my father was wasting away his years in a pity-filled alcoholic state.

When I entered the front foyer to the restaurant, Gregory was there. He immediately asked me what was wrong. I relayed what had happened. Wrapping his arms around me tightly, he escorted me into the restaurant. The waiter seated us opposite each other in a booth. After the waiter left us, Gregory reseated himself in the booth beside me. "I won't let this guy intimidate you, Laura," he said. "Believe me. We're going to the police tomorrow and we'll get an order of some sort put on him, so he can't bother you anymore. We don't know what his intention is in this visit, but no one travels to another city to harass a woman like that."

"That's just it," I said. "He's that kind of guy. A real jerk. You have no idea, but I don't want to spend our night talking about him. I won't let him ruin our dinner."

"No; let's don't," he said.

It was a perfect evening. We decided to stay the night together at his flat. Early the next morning, even before sunrise, Gregory called a taxi for me, so that I could get home in time to prepare for work that day. The taxi dropped me off outside my apartment and I walked happily up to the front step of my apartment.

Suddenly Paul was standing in front of me. "Where ya' been?" he asked. "Stayed out the whole night did ya'? Got a man in the city?"

"It's nothing to you, creep." I said. He was standing between me and the remaining steps to the entrance door. He walked up to me within a few inches of my face, his jaw tightening in a way that I recognized all too well. There was no way his bullying of me was going to stand. I yelled out as loud as I could. "Help!" I shouted. "Somebody help me!"

In no less than two seconds, my old neighbor from downstairs, a former boxer, stepped out onto the stairs. "Better get your ass away from her now!" he shouted to Paul. He darted antagonistically at him raising his fists, getting ready to right.

Quickly, Paul raised both hands in front of his face in surrender. "No problem," he said politely. "Just a misunderstanding." Without looking at my neighbor or me, he turned on his heel and walked down the sidewalk.

"If you ever come back, I'll beat the hell outta you!" my neighbor yelled after him.

When Paul was completely out of sight, I thanked the neighbor profusely. He simply waved me away before returning to his apartment without further discussion.

The next day, Gregory and I visited the police station nearest my apartment. The officer they assigned to speak with us said that my 'unexplained visitor who spoke harshly to me' wasn't enough to file charges. "Until he actually physically puts his hands on and harms you," the officer said, "the guy can say things all day long. People are here from many places. Verbal threats get exchanged every day. If we put everyone who's angry up on charges we'd be buried in paperwork."

"You won't help due to paperwork?" I asked.

"Call the police if he turns up where you live. Otherwise, ignore him. Stay away from him."

I walked out of the station feeling completely frazzled and vulnerable.

***

1983 was the year I would put my company and my clothing line on the map of the fashion world. Our regular line was selling much better than we had anticipated and my brand now had an unmistakable look which needed no introduction. I planned to take that look and put it through an evolution which would be a nod to all things earthy and spiritual while maintaining the excellence of high fashion. It would be a difficult combination.

I phoned my mother more often than normal during those days. She was almost as excited as me and talked about possibly flying to see the show. I had not told her about Paul because she worried enough about me anyway. I described every detail of my clothing line over and over, knowingly repeating myself and she listened patiently and intently. When she got the chance, she would interrupt the conversation to inject a bit of local gossip or to update me on some Hot Springs news.

"Did you know they found an enormous Tyrannosaurus Rex about ten miles from the ranch?" she told me. "It's a girl Rex, too. They say it's the largest one ever found. Lots of fighting over where it will end up, don't you know."

"That's awesome," I said. "I miss the old days hiking around, digging up amazing stuff. We lived in a perfect place for exploring for sure. Was it found by kids?"

"A lady, I think," she said. "They call the fossil 'Sue' after the lady who found it.

"Send me a news article, would you?" I asked. "I gotta go now. Love you lots," I said.

"I'm proud of you, honey. Keep up the great work and I know you're going to be a great success. Grandma Kate would have been enormously proud of you too. She loved you so much, you know?"

"I remember. She was a great lady. As you are too. Bye now." I hung up feeling elated. If not for Grandma Kate leaving the old homestead ranch to our family, I would not have found my true talent. I probably would have gone on to college for something sensible, like accounting or legal or medical, but certainly not fashion. What an unforeseen and meandering road I had taken.

I spent many months churning out hundreds of drawings to narrow the line down to only those which my team felt were the best to represent the LHH Star Collection. It was important to me that each piece we showed was heavily infused with an ethnic look without being identifiable with my inspiration. Rather than the fashion writers saying afterwards that the line looked specifically 'this or that' I wanted them to admit that they really couldn't put their finger on the look—that it wasn't like anything else they had ever seen.

It was a stark challenge, not only to me but to my entire team. We had hand selected each person, ensuring that we all shared the same precise vision. For inspiration, I had printed the text from the oversized postcard of the ten rules for Indians that Old Iron Eyes had sent me and tacked it, poster-sized onto the wall.

I had collected fabrics from multiple sources, not letting anything into the collection that I had not personally handled. Each original design sketch, down to the last detail, had been drawn by me. For a period of six months, we had marked off each day of the calendar ceremoniously—these small square paper days which were once blank opportunities to leave our mark were confirmed as deadlines successfully met.

Our sewing crew worked every weekend in that last push for fashion perfection. A few days before the show they were still finishing alterations to make the models perfect. In the large open space of our warehouse, we did a complete rehearsal of our show, only for our staff and design team, two days before hitting the real runway to work out any blemishes in our plan. It went splendid. Afterward, we held a preplanned dinner party to celebrate. It was one of the happiest nights of my life. At last I could relax and look forward to seeing and hearing the reactions to our hard work.

Then the unthinkable happened: a fire. A raging fire broke out in the warehouse adjoining our offices and workrooms. My stomach cramped with sadness. I tried to maintain control of my thoughts and tell myself that I could overcome this setback, but reality was that overnight, everything we had been reduced to melted metal and ash on the concrete floor. There wasn't a single garment or fabric left. The collection was gone. My staff and I stood around that morning uncomprehendingly in stunned silence, hugging each other for comfort, not knowing what to do.

Before the day was over, the fire inspector came to the diner across the street where we had all been waiting that day and informed me that he thought it was probably arson. Our entire team was miserably stunned. The fashion world could be very cut-throat, very competitive, but I couldn't imagine who would want to destroy our entire line. I had expected the same honorable conduct from my competition as I had shown to them. I couldn't understand why any fashion designer would be so worried about my growing popularity that they would do this. I stood there looking at the blackened mess that was once a place of joyful creativity, my eyes stinging from the wet smoky scent. New York was a tough environment that I was ill-equipped to understand. I had been warned that it was a different world, and now I knew why. Even the tears running freely down my face couldn't wash clean the scourge that faced me.

The inspector walked over to me. "We're finished here for now, but you'll hear from us again when our report is finished. You'll need to send this temporary form on to your insurance company too, you know?"

"I'll take care of it," I said, taking the papers. "Thank you," I said. "You'll track down the people who did this?" I asked.

"I'll do my best," he said. "You'll be the first to know when we catch them."

"I'll wait to hear. I can only hope that it's soon," I said. My staff had dispersed to the parking lot in the back of the building, so I left to find them. I sent them home, promising that we would find a temporary workspace where we could remake the entire collection. I was determined and I knew that was enough to make it happen. I had braced myself for the resistance from my staff, but to my surprise, not a single person said it wasn't possible.

Upon my return home that evening, I sat up in my bed and cried as I have never cried before. For my entire life I had been passive, choosing to let things go rather than deal with them head-on. The pure elation I had felt just one day before, seeing the beautiful garments created by my team as a whole original collection, had ceased abruptly. My New York City warehouse studio was now only ash and I wanted to go home to Hot Springs, where I belonged. I felt lost in the wilderness of a dream which had taken me the whole of the past year to achieve.

* * *

The telephone rang once and I saw on the ID that it was my mother calling. How ironic I thought. I wished to curl up next to her in front of a raging fire and pour out the emotions smoldering inside me, but I couldn't bear to explain to her that my dream had been ruined. From the very beginning of my plan to design clothing, mother had been an unsure yet steady supporter. Even if she didn't think I'd be as successful as I had ultimately been, she never pulled in the reins on me. Perhaps she had more of Grandmother Kate than I had realized. We had spent the past nine months talking endlessly about the upcoming show. She was genuinely proud of me and ever anxious to read the ensuing reviews. When the telephone stopped ringing at last, I made my way to my room and crawled into bed.

The anger and hurt was so extreme that evening that at some point I stopped feeling anything. Finally, I couldn't cry anymore nor did I have energy to rant or rave, not even in the privacy of my own space. There was only this empty ugliness gnawing inside me, and I knew instinctively that it wasn't going to leave. When I awoke the next morning, instead of prodding myself to pull out of this miasma, I methodically phoned everyone I knew who was expecting to be a part of the event and recited a prepared statement about the fire. There was no extended conversation and I left no time for condolences before hanging up the telephone.

After I finished this task which had to be taken care of, I set about making flight reservations to travel back home to Hot Springs. I cancelled every appointment or obligation I had for the rest of that week. There was so much anxiety in my life that I was hardly functioning anyway.

* * *

Pulling up to my father's house, I noticed straight away the neglected yard, the leaves up on the porch, the windows blurred with dust. Inside the house wasn't much better. Boxes of his belongings where he had packed them in the move away from mother, sat randomly where he had dropped them.

It was a few minutes before noon and he was in the kitchen trying to make something for us to eat. Seemingly, the task of making sandwiches was a struggle for him. I stood at the kitchen counter with him while he made our lunch and talked about my life in New York. I had brought along some photos to show him of my latest clothing designs. I mulled over in my mind if I would tell him how they had been lost. We moved to the living room and settled in around the coffee table. He shuffled through the photos slowly, taking in the details.

"Who would have known you could do this?" he said. "They're fantastic, Laura." He set the photos down and turned away, walking back into the kitchen. "Something to drink?" he yelled from the other room.

"Tea for me," I called back.

He returned with a cup of hot tea for me and a scotch and water over ice for himself. "Been over to see your mom yet?" he asked.

"No. I came here first."

"We don't see one another, Laura. But, I guess that's how divorce is--real final. Like a knife in my heart to see that Basset bastard living in my house-- the house that I put my sweat and money and years into building."

I could have let it slip, but it needed to be said. "Grandma Kate left mother that house and the ranch," I corrected. "Sorry father, but you know that she had every right to the house?"

"Of course, in that sense. I'm talking about my feelings here, Laura. How I feel about it. Doesn't matter about rights. It's Basset that pisses me off in it all. He stole my wife and now he's living in my house, what was my home. Where you and Charles were raised. But that's how life goes sometimes."

"I've never been fond of Basset. And, of course, I never tried to get to know him, but she seems happy, so what can I say?"

"She's fooled by him. Do you know he bought a Mercedes to drive her around town now? Like he's parading the fact that he stole my wife. He pretends to be on her level and he's not. Isn't ever going to be good enough to be with her. Put the fancy trimmings on the guy if you want--he's still a boring dolt."

"You know I'm not going to defend him. I do wish you and mother could have stayed together. It's sad for us." I restrained from pointing out his role in it. Surely, he'd had enough of those conversations between them before they decided to divorce.

We were nearly finished with our lunch when father started on his second cocktail. "The world is arranged as a deceiver," he said, gazing wistfully into the amber liquid in his glass. "Know how the Lakota think it's tied back into the natural world? Well, I think they're on to something. It's pure and simple natural deception. Every living creature deceives out of the need to eat, or survive or find itself a mate."

"Humans are supposed to be different," I said. "There's discernment in us to know when to show compassion. I'd hate to think we're all animals." Even as I said it, I only halfway believed it. I wanted to tell my father everything that happened recently, but sensing his despair, it was hard to add my burdens to it.

"Humans want to think we're separate from the animals. Then, we disguise ourselves, camouflage ourselves like animals do, so our religion, our political motivations or our own personal relationships bend to our will." His hands were wrenching and his teeth were gritting as he spoke. I noticed for the first time, that he had aged considerably since I saw him last.

"Don't think that way," I said. "You still have a chance to rebuild a life. You could meet someone too. Father, I just lost everything I've worked for and I have to rebuild it now when I go home. If I can do it, with my limitations, I know a strong guy like you can do it." I began to gather up my things to leave.

"Someone stole your beautiful designs?" he asked alarmed. In five years, he had aged nearly ten. For the first time, I acknowledged that he was becoming an old man.

"Yeah; they're gone," I said pensively without explaining. "I'm sorry, but I have to go. I've got to get over to mother's house now.

When he realized I was leaving, he became visibly emotional. "Take care of yourself out there," he said, following me. "You're all I have left." We hugged and then I headed out the door.

"You'd better take care too," I called back to him. "When I come back next time, I'm expecting to find you very happy. Don't stop trying, father."

As I drove away, I noticed he had moved inside to the picture window where he stood steadfast, waving goodbye.

The visit with my mother went much easier. I was surprised to see her wearing a new dress and with her hair restyled in the latest trendy cut. She almost seemed out of place in Hot Springs, South Dakota. Clearly, she had found contentment in her new relationship with Basset and I couldn't help but to be relieved. She questioned briefly why I stayed at the inn instead of with her and I made the best excuses I could to avoid saying I felt awkward with Basset there in our family home.

I returned to my hotel feeling relieved after having the visits with my parents. When I left home, they were together and now they were living in separate houses. That was sad for me, yet I had managed to handle it better emotionally than I anticipated. I took my shoes off and sat down in the overstuffed wing-backed chair near the window. From the second floor I could look out over the dimly lit street. The streets were quiet and still. Now and then, a car would pass slowly by and I'd watch the tail lights fade from view. As I relaxed in the chair, a movement outside caught my eye. There was a man on the street below looking up at my window, then he suddenly walked away as if he noticed me watching. I peered down to the quiet street below briefly again and saw nothing. I picked up the telephone on the side table and called Old Iron Eyes at the lodge. After letting him know I would be up to visit them the next morning, I hung up the handset and went off to my room to sleep.

Then, in the early hours of the next morning, as I was walking outside my hotel, I saw the same man again. This time, he was jumping ever-so-slightly around the corner of the hotel. When I looked around to find the source, I saw Paul standing within the dark shadow of two buildings. I walked across the street to confront him.

"Are you spying on me?" I yelled out even before I reached him.

As he turned to run I saw that he was carrying a gun! A million thoughts raced through my mind and rushed together in one realization. Then, it dawned on me, with unbearable weight. It was as if I had been standing on a glass bridge which suddenly shattered leaving me to fall into an open chasm. Anger snarled inside my guts, wildly chasing my suspicion into speech. With no way to prove it, I knew completely what he was capable of doing.

I ducked down and ran inside the nearest open door which just happened to be the old downtown diner where the locals met up for breakfast. I asked to use the telephone and as calmly as I could, called the police. After telling the police that Paul was following me and carrying a gun, they promised to go to his house and question him. Oddly enough, they found him there.

His explanation was that I had been in a relationship with him a long time ago which turned sour. He told the police that I was jealous of his new girlfriend, so I had been harassing him. He claimed that I was the one who had been following him ever since he had visited New York for a vacation. In fact, he said that I had come back not to visit my family, but that I had been harassing him since I got back into town. The gun he had been carrying, he said, was for a hunting trip that he planned to take that morning—all perfectly legal.

The police phoned me back at the inn that morning and said that my story didn't hold water. They told me to stay away from Paul. The thought of calling Basset to help crossed my mind. Then, I thought about how he had been so naively certain of Paul's innocence after Charles' accident. Basset was no help then and he'd be even less capable now that he was retired. What happened to Charles had always nagged at me begging for answers and accountability. Mother and father had ingrained the need for our family's healing so much that they had overlooked what my heart knew. Paul had somehow caused that gas furnace to explode. I knew it now as certainly as I knew my own name. Furthermore, he had pilfered money from our family's businesses, running them into the ground for his own gain. I used to try to figure out why he would've done anything to harm my family, but the reason why didn't matter to me anymore.

CHAPTER TWENTY-ONE

Driving up to the lodge, I gazed out of the window at the mountain crevices, long gashing splits formed long ago from volcanic activity. They looked like painful wounds. Even a few short years away had dulled my senses to the strong connection to the mountains that I once knew. I had forgotten the joy of hiking in vast fields and brooding forests; how even the delicate yellow wildflowers, blooming by the hundreds and winding their way up the mountainside used to distract me with their beauty. I longed to hike over the hills and up the long gravel road again to the lodge. I wanted to rekindle my kinship with this land again. I knew too, that I was in danger.

My youthful environment had given me sensory perceptions that had ultimately guided my soul precisely in the right direction. This land had defined me. In the overwhelming noise of city life, I had unconsciously chosen to forget from where I drew my original source of strength. Leaving home to study for and work in my chosen profession in a new city had not replaced what lived here, but it had pushed these important memories too far away from my daily thoughts. Now, as I drove slowly through the sacred mountains, those memories were alive and dancing before me all at once like ancestors vying for remembrance.

Despite my current successes, there was nothing more precious than what I had gained here. These were the natural elements which had formed me. This absolute knowing of who I was came not from a passing fancy, or intrigue, but rather from those prior years of hiking in mountains, exploring caves, digging for fossils, listening to elders. It's not knowledge anyone could buy in a bookstore, the way people search for happiness or answers to life in the latest book. One doesn't gain real awareness that way. Reading my great grandmother's collection of journals and plenty of books certainly started me on my path. However; only the events I invited into my life had opened my heart and mind.

There was a peace here, in nature's perfection, indescribable and waiting with open arms for discovery. Within that peace on this day, there also lurked a threatening presence. Part of me still searched for hope that someone would lock Paul up and throw away the key, but I kept remembering what the police in New York told me—nobody was going to do anything until after he harmed me. What he'd already done, I had no way of proving. Part of me fed the wolf that wanted to be a person who knew only goodness. Another part was feeding the wolf that wanted revenge.

It had been five years since I'd seen Old Iron Eyes. The first thing he did when he saw me was chastise me for leaving. He spoke with great emotion behind his words, as if he had been hurting a long time. "You moved a thousand miles away and forgot about us here," he said, trying to sound like he only half meant the words. "We got some letters, but you haven't been to visit for five years now."

I should have known that he was going to say something like that. "I had no idea what would happen in such a short period of time," I said as we walked up the steps and into the lodge. "I was hanging on, trying to see where life was taking me. When I got the chance to come back now, I couldn't wait to see you guys."

"We miss you, Laura. You were the bright light in our lives. When you left, we grieved like when a child is lost. You may not be Indian by blood, but you're still our family."

"I never forgot any of you. Honestly, I carried all of you with me. Life just changes. I followed my dream."

He shifted to another subject. "There's been changes here, but we keep the same laid-back life as before. More tourists now than ever. That's a plus and a minus, you know."

"I understand what you mean," I said.

"We've kept the town pretty much the same though. It's no wonder people want to see it. The mammoth site is still digging, the hot springs are still great for swimming and down the road from here, your favorite mountain is still being carved after all these years."

"Crazy Horse!"

"Yep. Ziolkowski dedicated the rest of his life to carving that mountain, recruiting many in his family along the way. He kept working on it right up until he died at the site in 1982. They buried him in a tomb at the base of the mountain. Today his wife and seven of his children carry on the project, but I don't know when they'll ever finish it."

I repeated what I remembered. "The world's largest sculpture. Right here in the Black Hills. Because the Indian people have heroes too."

"You remember that? Very good," he said smiling now. "My mother was so proud that day she introduced you to him."

"What a day for me and Kills Enemy," I said wistfully. "How could anyone forget a day like that? New York City might have captured my attention and my career, but this place is my home."

"I miss the old days," he said and tears formed in his eyes. He pulled me into him for a strong hug.

"Don't cry or I will too," I said, holding on and crying already. I tried to compose myself. "Tell me how things are with you. Let's talk about your family."

"Good and bad as it's always been. As it'll always be, Laura," he answered.

"No; I mean tell me how things are really," I said. There was so much going on with me that I wanted to tell him, but out of respect, I wanted to let him speak first.

"Our good and our bad is regular life working itself out. Okay, overall, my closest family is doing pretty good, but on Pine Ridge Reservation; it's another story. Alcoholics, kids on drugs who used to be obedient to their parents and no money to be found, no work to be found that pays enough to make a decent living. Same as before, about half of Pine Ridge people live below America's poverty level--

313

according to their calculations, not ours. I happen to think it's higher. Yeah, yet what do I know?"

"But, they're a modern culture right? They have jobs?"

"About ten percent of them. Many have a curse of alcoholism and some are trying to get better education so they get out of this life. People are overweight from the handout government food. I can't talk because I'm a big guy too, but I mean really too fat for the heart. It makes problems--diabetes and such are normal. Me and my family are okay, so I shouldn't let it bother me so much, right? Except these are my people."

"They are, Iron Eyes," I said. "Doesn't anyone from the state try to get more federal people to help?"

"You don't understand," he said. "Nobody cares about these people. Maybe some churches here and there come out to the reservation for a week or so. It's like this country wants to kill us off, one generation at a time. When a man in Europe kills off a bunch of Jewish people, everyone in the world wants to tell the story for generations, even teach it in school. A hundred books written on the subject. But, let my people be eliminated from their homeland and you can't get this country to listen.

I'd like my son to be more involved with his heritage, but he's spent his young years in public school here. Now, he refuses to stay with relatives on that reservation, as you did a couple times when you were growing up. There's houses there with no clean running water, no electricity, windows boarded up to keep out the cold wind. He doesn't want to see that despair—where many children don't even have coats in winter. He won't attend the school there and why should I send him somewhere to get a knife in his back while he tries to get an education? It's a rough, fight-for-survival existence that only gets worse."

I clenched a hand over my mouth and held back tears. "I hadn't realized," I said quietly.

"My oldest nephew lives now in government housing at Pine Ridge. In his house is his parents, a couple more uncles and the children of his sister. They got twelve people living in a three bedroom house. This house was built in the seventies with no upkeep. Moldy walls from leaking roof and walls, but they can't leave public housing with no money. Plus, classrooms are overcrowded and can't attract the best teachers, across the board, they're uneducated. In every way, they're unprepared to step outside of the borders of that reservation and make any kind of life for themselves. So, they don't."

He talked more about the increased problems of drugs and family violence on the reservation; how reliance on government support was stronger than many individual's desire to work. The internet, in his view, was both another outlet for commerce as well as another distraction from participation in the old ceremonies or learning to speak their language.

Knowing how important these things were to Old Iron Eyes, I was deeply saddened. I thought back to my girlhood, realizing how blessed I was to have been able to climb the mountains, drink from the natural springs and get to know the history of all that had happened. We were living in a new world no longer isolated by local history and local concerns—

we were connected to the holy as well as the wicked. The concerns of every being on the planet would affect us whether we chose to be a part of them or not. People were growing more disconnected from caring for one another. For Old Iron Eyes it was clearly becoming too much to bear.

I didn't know how to tell what I needed to confide in him, but I valued his wisdom. There was no one else I trusted more. "Remember when we used to hold the talking feather ceremonies?" I asked cautiously.

He considered the expression on my face and knew right away that I had asked for a reason. "You want to have one again I think."

"How do you still know everything before I say it?" I tried to muster up a smile, but it died before my next thought. "It's just that I don't trust anyone anymore. You and your mother never changed who you were, even when everything around you changed. That, for me, means so much."

He paused for a second as if he had realized something. "This is a serious matter you want to talk about?"

I looked deep into his eyes. "Very serious."

"Let's get the eagle feather which we will pass only between ourselves. First, we smudge a bundle of sage for clear answers."

I had forgotten the importance of ceremony. Having lived a fast paced life wherein there was no real time for stopping to consider if something is completely clear before delivering answers, I had learned to move on New York City time. As soon as Old Iron Eyes passed the feather to me, I began to tell about how Paul had been stalking me, how he had showed up in New York at my job and then followed me to my apartment. I told about my neighbor threatening to beat him up if he ever returned. I explained how, in my first night at the hotel, I saw Paul looking up at my window and carrying a gun.

He looked startled and grabbed the feather quickly from me. "What did you do?" then quickly, he passed it back again.

"I started to confront him until I saw the gun, then he ran," I said, nearly breathless from the anxiety of reliving everything. "I called the police who went over to his house and questioned him. He told the police that I had been in a long relationship with him which turned sour...that I was trying to get even over him having a new girlfriend. He told them that it was I who had been harassing him after he visited New York for a vacation. The police said my story didn't hold water. They told me to stay away from him."

"What the hell...?" he stammered.

"I'm disappointed in myself for not dealing with this further. I keep hearing Charles' voice, telling me that I'm a sissy." Mentioning Charles' name brought a lump in my throat. I had more to say, but I sensed that Old Iron Eyes needed to speak, so I handed him the feather.

"Paul is evil. This I've seen for many years. He never stopped harming you. He stole from your family's business and has much responsibility for your parent's divorce, even if Monroe made his own mistakes. Beyond that, what he did to Charles is...I always thought that Charles' accident was caused by Paul. What I didn't let myself believe was that Paul caused that accident on purpose. I couldn't prove this to legal courts in the way your people like to do it, but it's clear to many people now, that Paul sent Charles into an accident to cover up his stealing money from your family. I just heard recently that Paul was talking out of alcohol one night when a fight was starting...he said the last guy he fought with ended up burned to death. If that's not admission." Fat tears fell from his cheeks and he wiped them away. "Even I wanted to believe he was just lying to make himself tough to the other guys. But now, he's got the intention in his evil heart to harm you too." He passed the feather back to me.

I was crying too, struggling to speak. "I overheard mother telling Basset around the time of Charles' accident that the financial books for the business showed profit was down almost halfway from other seasons. Charles believed Paul was stealing from the businesses, but he worried he could never convince my father to listen. At that time, father was insisting something must be wrong with mother's numbers. I knew that Charles, on the day he died, was going to confront Paul about this. I heard him say it. Now, I believe the same as you, but it doesn't mean we can prove it far enough to have Paul arrested."

The two of us sat in silence together as if neither one wanted to digest the truth. The pain that my brother went through with his burns had been excruciating. He always had the loyalty to defend his family, me especially. I felt ashamed that our parents hadn't pressed someone to investigate my brother's accident further. Someone should have fought for justice for Charles. Now, my family was fragmented, wounded and would be forever marked by Paul's vindictive and jealous actions.

"I'm going to confront him," I said decisively. There was an intense fire inside of me for which I had no control.

"No, you're not," Old Iron Eyes jumped. "You're not. Not no way."

"I need to look at his face--tell him I know up close. So, he knows that I know."

Old Iron Eyes stood and open-handedly slapped the feather down hard upon the table. "You don't have the strength or experience to deal with this guy. Look what he did in New York. Here in Hot Springs he's in his own element. As I said, he's evil completely through himself. You cannot do it."

I picked the feather up and tried to calm my voice. "This is my element too," I reminded him, grappling for a plan in my mind. "I'll bring a recorder with me. I'll get him to talk. Then, I'll have proof. I can make him pay for what he's done to us."

"He's not going to confess."

"He will." I clenched my teeth stubbornly. The anger in me was a sheer madness which I had never felt in my lifetime. I couldn't control it and I didn't want to. "Dammit!" I yelled out. "My family never should've moved here. If we didn't, Charles would be alive."

319

Old Iron Eyes stood up abruptly and released a burst of breath, heavy and disturbed, the way a buffalo does upon seeing a rattlesnake. He was mad, but rather sure-footed and rock solid. I could see that clearly. "If you had not moved here, both our families would never meet. That would be the greatest tragedy, wouldn't it? Let's be finished with this talking feather ceremony," he said.

I wanted him to understand that I wasn't going to run from this situation. "You were supposed to be listening, not talking." I held the feather up. "I had it. It was my turn." I laid it back down on the table.

Pausing for effect and studying my face for a moment he said, "You're right. It was your turn." He had dulled his voice down. "Sorry; but I did listen. I heard you, Laura. We heard each other clearly."

He walked around the corner into the adjoining room and I could hear him rustling around in the hall closet. When he returned he had his hair tied back into a ponytail and he was wearing his dark brown leather jacket. "My advice to you is to go back to New York and put this out of your mind just for a while. This man is here now and I don't think he's going to fly back to New York soon. Whatever he went there to do, in his rotten head, he carried back here with him." Iron Eyes looked deep into my eyes and I felt the weight of a thousand ancient stars when I looked into his. He spoke with deliberate resolve. "I knew much of what we have talked about tonight," he said. "There were pieces of the story that were only hanging in my own imagination telling me they were true. He's not going to stop trying to get to you. You did right telling me these other things. Drive back to the inn and I'll come by tonight to check on things—make sure you're safe. If it would help you to sleep before your flight tomorrow, I'll rent the room next door to you--if you're scared. I can stay awake and listen all through the night."

It was like old times. Always Old Iron Eyes or Charles had looked after me, kept me safe. I should be able to handle my own affairs and yet, I felt extremely grateful that I could talk with such a steady friend from my innermost self. Part of me wished that my father was as protective of me. "I'm not scared anything will happen at the inn. It's when I'm out in the open I feel scared. I keep looking around me, scanning every tree or alleyway expecting him to jump out and slash me up or shoot me or set me on fire. I don't want to feel scared anymore, even when I'm a thousand miles away in my apartment."

"That's exactly what he wanted, Laura-Helena. To make you feel scared and helpless. We have waited for fate to take up this problem and as a result, more pain." His voice drifted off as he mumbled only to himself. Then, taking a deep breath, he changed the subject. "Hey.....you remember the day I made you chop the head off that snake?"

"Do I? I was scared out of my mind that day! I can't believe you made me do it. I was only a young girl then."

"If one sees a snake, he should kill it, not have a bunch of meetings over it, and wait for it to bite, then say I wish I would have killed that snake. You chopped its head off with that shovel like it was nothing. You were stronger for it later weren't you?"

321

"I was. You're not suggesting that I should kill anyone in this situation, are you?"

"Not at all. I advised you to go home, remember?"

"You're saying Charles was right. That I should stop being a sissy and stand up for myself. To fight harder."

"Go home, Laura," Old Iron Eyes said. "You got a ticket for the plane to fly inside in the morning. You must go back, rebuild your company and tend to your work. That's exciting stuff." He attempted a half-smile for my sake.

I purposely lightened my mood. "It could be exciting for you too," I said, not missing a chance to try to convince him to fly to New York City while knowing it wasn't ever going to happen.

"Not me in a plane. Nope. Not me. It's too strange." He held both my shoulders firmly, looking deep into my eyes as if he were reading the history of my entire life. "It was a fortunate thing that your family moved here. Don't ever say that it wasn't again. My family--we love you like you're inside our family, Laura. Decide how you're going to walk in this life. There's no way around it. You must walk wakan. No other way."

Old Iron Eyes handed me my car keys off the table. He led me to the front door and we paused for a moment in a long hug. "I might stop by tomorrow on my way to the airport and try to catch David," I said. Then, I noticed a strange object on his shelf by the door; a poorly executed figurine of a bird with scant white downy feathers, bent wire legs and a brown tapered body. "What in the world is that?" I asked.

He pulled the object down and held it up in the flat palm of his hand like a treasure. "This," he said, pointing to the printed label on the front of its wooden base, "is a 'Turd Bird'. And yes, before you ask, it really is made of precisely what it says. Dried and shellacked, of course."

"Eeew!" I shuddered. "That's disgusting. Where'd you get it?"

"It's the latest thing they're selling in some tourist shops now. Everybody loves the South Dakota Turd Bird. Can't make 'em fast enough to keep up with the demand." He laughed and shook his head as he placed it back on the shelf. "Tourists are stupid."

"We should know," I said, staring at the little bird sculpture once more. It was a moment of lightness within my seriously burdensome thoughts. I gave him a final hug and left.

I drove my rental car back into town, in the old section, to visit my favorite places. The wonderful authentic sandstone buildings were just as quaint and welcoming as I had remembered them. It was a relief to see that Hot Springs had not fallen into the trap that resembled the movie set like so many other western towns. Walking along the paved pathway which winds along the swift moving Fall River, I absorbed the gift of fresh clean air and cleared my head while at the same time keeping a weary and watchful eye around me.

That night, back at my hotel, I had a fitful sleep. I dreamed intermittently of Indian children crying in the streets while snow poured down from an angry lightning-filled sky. Still in a sleep-state, I pulled on my jacket, fearfully slipped a knife into my pocket and left the inn. Out on the streets the heavy snowflakes fell, illuminated by lamplights.

As I headed into the forest, the apparitions of children had reverted to a half-wild state and when I approached them with my hands outstretched, they ran away frightened. I dreamed that Paul was tracking me. I saw myself doubling back behind him, sneaking up on him, while he was in the process of hunting me. I followed him, walking softly further into the black woods on the well-worn trail that I knew so well from hiking up to the lodge. I walked in the exact manner that Charles and I used to, taking care not to crunch even a single leaf and without compressing the heavy snowdrifts. Deftly and swiftly, I approached my enemy. I blindsided him with my knife and fought violently until he was dead. Walking through a dimly lit forest, I came upon a beautiful glowing stream that was bubbling with rainbow trout. I knelt beside the stream frantically washing my hands and face. After a moment, I waded into the water and dipped myself below the surface, immune to its icy temperature. For a long time, I swam around in circles, diving effortlessly under the water. Everything under the water was glowing. As the dream ended, I retraced my steps through the forest, feeling its thick towering evergreen trees comforting me.

When I awoke in the predawn hours, I realized that it was freezing cold. I felt overwhelmingly frazzled and alone, but entirely protected from harm. The heater was turned up full-blast and my clothes were wet from where I had been sweating profusely during the nightmare. After dragging myself up to shower, I walked around the room a few paces before sitting down and thumbing through a magazine, trying to take my mind off of a list of so many horrible things. I longed to get back to sleep, dreading the morning which would come all too soon. I had a flight to take in the late afternoon and sleeping on a plane never seemed to work for me.

The vivid nightmare haunted my thoughts, darting in and out of my mind like nervous bees. Making direct deadly contact with my enemy physically, even if only in a dream, had left me feeling undeniably vindicated and proud of my inner strength. The Sioux believed that this method was more honorable than shooting a person from a distance and so did I.

CHAPTER TWENTY-TWO

With the mist still hanging over the quiet town, I pulled myself together and drove my rental car up to the lodge. Along the way, I spotted certain landmarks and places where I used to hike, retracing the footsteps of my unfettered youth. From the car, I picked out certain rocky outcroppings in the landscape where I had sat years ago taking in a particular view, remembering a certain day or happening when I was there before. Memories echoed across the vast open sky and settled on landmarks which might have meant nothing to an ordinary soul, but they now meant everything in the world to me.

I remembered that first day when Charles and I came to the lodge in the midst of a winter blizzard, on horseback with our Lakota friends, having all the faith in the world that we were safe. For a few moments, my heart felt heavy and remorseful for ever leaving Hot Springs. There was a mixture of the unbearable memory of my brother's accident and a yearning for long lost friends running through me. It hadn't been a lack of caring that kept me away, only a normal human desire to follow one's dream.

At the small picket gate, I reached on the other side and pulled up the string to release the latch which served only as symbolic security. Not much had changed; maybe a few more trinkets hanging around the front entrance and new flowers in the flowerbed beside the front gate.

Old Iron Eyes must have been out hunting with his younger male cousin again, for there was a bucket of bloody knives, hammer and gloves to be cleaned sitting out of the side porch near the screened door. The practicality of hunting for survival, as well as understanding the importance of passing the skill along to future generations, left no harsh or uncivilized impression on me now. The lives of my Indian friends were as civilized as any society on the planet. I wondered if they had gone out in search of deer meat or to take the hide of the three coyotes that had attacked and killed their orange tabby housecat. Either way, I knew from the mess that they had found success. Old Iron Eyes had seemed to grow stronger with age instead of weaker, much like an old bear and his disposition was as confident as ever. He couldn't have been far away and I decided to wait.

As I entered the house, I also saw blankets strewn about and dishes in the kitchen sink. I didn't want to leave without seeing my dear friends one more time, so while I waited, I began lightly cleaning the house. After all that their people had done for me, it was only natural for me to help out even if I were only a visitor. I thought back about the few days when Charles and I stayed with their family at the great lodge, regretting the passage of time as well as the distance between our lives geographically.

I walked over to the old stereo system on the wooden shelf and clicked the play button, turning the volume down to low. A soft flute music floated up into the open beams of the lodge. Then voices chimed in, all male, singing Amazing Grace—Lakota men, chanting in harmony only the music without the lyrics. A surge of emotion welled up in my throat, thinking about how Mary loved it so much during those days when we had cooked together and listened to this same music.

Dumping the contents of the hunting bucket out on the kitchen counter, I chuckled aloud a bit to myself thinking how my new uptown citified existence hadn't rendered me the least bit squeamish about bloody things inherent to a country life. I put the knife, hammer, gloves and even the hand towels in the dishwasher together and added the powdered soap along with a generous splash of bleach. I wiped down the thick wooden countertops and put on a fresh pot of Chock-Full-O'Nuts coffee to make Old Iron Eyes happy when he returned. Cooking in an open kitchen with a lively family such as theirs was something I missed and I hoped I would end up with a large family of my own someday.

When no one returned to the house, I finally gave up on waiting, sat down and penned out two thank-you notes to my old friends, adding my telephone number at the bottom before sealing the envelopes. Even as I added the telephone number I doubted they would call. They knew a phone call meant I would be inviting them to visit the big city. They simply preferred to write letters. I set the envelopes up on the countertop conspicuously so that they would be noticed.

By mid-morning I left Hot Springs in my rented car and headed for the airport at Chadron, Nebraska. The sun's rays beamed through the window and warmed me before the heater from the car could catch up. It was a forty-five minute drive and I had given myself only an hour to get there. After the short flight from Chadron to Denver, I would change planes for another three hour flight to New York City. I drove cautiously, careful not to speed on the snowy roads. At last, I reached the airport and then was seated on the plane. As the flight became airborne, I looked down at the wide open landscape as it disappeared behind us. The patchwork of farmlands and wide open stretches of woodlands was in complete contrast to the collage of my life in the city.

It had not dawned on me until exactly at that moment; the memory of our family moving to a little spot on the map which I had heard about only in Grandmother Kate's stories. I could not believe now, the degree to which I had feared my parents' decision as a child. True, many terrible things did happen, but they weren't the things that I had imagined. They were events which might have happened anyway, even if we had been living somewhere else. What glared blatantly at me now was that the events, which crept underneath my life with its previously unspoiled existence, had become the thing that caused my life to have meaning. Within these tumultuous and painful experiences, I had evolved. The strength I didn't know I needed, the gratitude simply for life itself and a significant calm had found me. My ever-present reasonable rationales had been cast out and replaced decisively with my heart's need for justice.

I vowed to never forget the peace that is offered by hills, mountains and prairies. Even a thousand miles of continent and a completely alternate culture would never separate me from my love of the natural world. It was in this world that I had tested the boundaries of my capabilities as well as my weaknesses. There was no way to know how long it might take to put my life back together once I arrived at home. Uncertainty, I knew, was the ghost lurking in even the best of plans. The only thing I knew for certain was who I was at the very core of my being. Rather than be intimidated by dark shadows and threats, I would face the complex situation in my life head-on, accepting whatever fate came with it.

* * *

Shortly after I boarded the plane in Denver, the crew announced that New York City had been hit with an unexpected snowstorm which had built up in a matter of hours. It wasn't enough to cancel the flight, but they were unsure if it would cause a delay. Anxiety gnawed at my insides as the plane departed the runway and once we were airborne, I caught up on some sleep.

At LaGuardia airport in New York City, I dragged my rolling suitcase behind me, heading toward the exit. The distinct footsteps behind me also held the sound of a shoe clicking softly on the second step each time. When I stopped, the footsteps also stopped. I turned around directly to face the sound and a startled police officer stared back at me. "You lost?" he asked.

After gathering my thoughts for a second, I said, "No. I know where I'm going," while trying to stop the panic attack that had been building up since that morning. Before I got onto the shuttle bus to my car I was nearly out of breath. Lugging my suitcase up the steps onto a full bus, I found a seat and sat down.

The radio was on with a short business report, then another reporter cut in and read the words: "Ancient Practice of Scalping Rears its Ugly Head."

"This is a joke?" one of the passengers asked, as others tuned into the report.

After a brief summary of an incident, the same passenger said aloud, "This crazy Indian still living in the dark ages. For real. Really did yesterday-- scalped somebody."

"That's just what they *think* happened," another passenger clarified loudly.

A man said loudly, "...nobody's gonna' take the scalp of another person, that's a figure of speech–you know like 'scalping' tickets..."

"Shut-up," someone else barked from the aisle pointing towards the radio. "Turn that up."

I tried follow the reporter's voice over the voices on the bus. I had heard these kinds of reactions to anything Indian-associated before. Surely, the reporter would stretch the story, proffering a sensationalized undercurrent meant to disparage a culture that I had spent much of my life immersed in.

I couldn't hear the full report because the passengers were now talking amongst themselves. "...scalp of the victim found tacked to a fence post...the meaning behind such an action was known to be historically...police say no information..."

"There'd better be justice for someone losing his scalp," a guy across the aisle said, looking around for assurances.

A middle-aged black couple wearing thick winter coats sat next to me, embracing each other. It was easy to tell that they were very much in love.

They noticed me studying them. "Strange story," the wife said to me.

"Maybe the scalping was justice for something," I offered. "Maybe the guy deserved it."

"If that's the case, I'm damned sure never going to piss off an Indian," said her husband.

His wife sitting next to him agreed. "That's a fact, for sure." She leaned into his arms and I noticed again how much they loved each other. They reminded me of Old Iron Eyes and his wife. She glanced up at me, still cozied in his arms. "The news didn't say whether it was a man or a woman got attacked. You thought it was a guy?"

"I dunno," I said, as my stop came into view. Peering out of the bus window, I readied myself to return to the life that I had built, not knowing for certain exactly where it was headed. Deep down inside I felt that I could still make a success of my new clothing line once it was produced all over again. I had planned to begin reconstructing everything I had worked on for the past three years. I stepped off of the bus and into the next chapter of my life.

I reached the last two blocks to my apartment, where I had first recognized Paul lurking in the shadows. Prior to my trip, whenever I had passed this area, I ran up the steps and inside, fear gripping me with its cold hand every second of the way. It was the section waiting just ahead, where I first thought I heard footsteps following me. An owl hooted softly somewhere in a nearby tree. Walking cautiously on, I reached the edge of the dark area where there was no longer the choice to turn back. I stepped up my pace until the wheels on my rolling carry-on luggage wouldn't run straight anymore. The luggage wobbled threatening to go off course, taking me with it. I picked the heavy suitcase up, clutching it to me as I ran nearer and nearer to the lighted end of the street.

Suddenly, I realized that I didn't need to be afraid anymore. I knew who I was. I knew my own power. I stopped running and composed myself. Ever-so-gently, I wrapped my fleece scarf closer around my neck to keep the snow from settling down in my neck. Placing my hand inside my Givenchy coat, I found the antique beaded lapel pin that Kills Enemy had given me tucked safely underneath. I walked purposefully more fluid now for the last block, then strolled up the stairs to my apartment like a cat to a waiting dish of cream.

There was a song on the wind that day which I have never forgotten. It was as if the persistent howling of the New York City snowstorm had turned magically into a melodic tune blowing through thin ponderosa pine needles. A barely audible undercurrent of a soft native flute played in such a beautiful lilt that I could hardly stand to leave it, but the rest of my life was waiting. I opened the door and stepped inside. I was home. This time I had returned strong, free and aware. This time I was truly walking wakan.